Bride of a Hustla

Ca$h Presents
Bride of a Hustla
A Novel by *Destiny Skai*

Lock Down Publications/Ca$h Presents
P.O. Box 1482
Pine Lake, Ga 30072-1482

Visit our website at **www.lockdownpublications.com**

Copyright 2016 Destiny Skai Bride of a Hustla

First Edition November 2016
Printed in the United States of America
*This is a work of fiction. Names, characters, places, and
incidents either are products of the author's imagination
or are used fictitiously. Any similarity to actual events or
locales or persons, living or dead, is entirely coincidental.*

Lock Down Publications/Ca$h Presents
Like our page on Facebook: Lock Down Publica-
tions @**www.facebook.com/lockdownpublications.ldp**
Join our group on Facebook: Ca$h Presents
https://www.face-
book.com/groups/1419253741421560/
Cover design and layout by: Dynasty's Cover Me
Book interior design by: Shawn Walker
Edited by: Lauren Burton

Acknowledgements

First and foremost, I would like to thank God for gifting me with a talent that I can share with the world. Becoming an Author was something that I thought about but I could never find the time to sit and complete the story. It took a life changing moment to realize what I was destined to be and I was finally able to complete my very first novel.

To my kids, Ethan and Torrence, I wouldn't have this strong drive and passion to succeed if you two were not in my life. You make me want to be a better mother and a stronger woman. There were so many nights the two of you wouldn't leave me alone until I took a break to have family time. Writing began to interfere with our movie nights, but you guys were persistent about the time we spent together. A quiet house was not possible with the two of you. Lol!! But I promise it will all pay off in the end. I love my KINGS more than life itself.

To my mom and dad, Robert and Denise, I wouldn't be in the position I'm in without you two and I love y'all to the moon and back. To my Thomas family in Parkway (6th Court), this journey started for me back in 2013, and you all were there for me cooking and selling dinners to raise money for printed copies of my book. ☺

There are so many to name, but my family is beyond petty, so I have to name some of them or I will never hear the end of it. Lol!!! A special thanks to my cousin, the host-ess and the one who allowed me to have the function at her house on more than one occasion, Sabrina Harris. My Aunt Sonya Thomas, for making the macaroni and cheese and collard greens. My mom for standing over the stove frying pounds of chicken wings. My sisters, Tayana and Xernora Thomas, for buying all the dinner plates ☺☺ Along with

Quontrail Warren, Genise Thomas-Bradshaw, Fannie Thomas and my Uncle Ben Thomas. Mashonda Ellison and Danielle Bender, thanks for typing my manuscripts when I was too lazy to do it. I love the both of you. And last but certainly not least, Jakara Doe, thanks for being on the cover of my original book. That was a hard task to complete, but we got the job done. Calandra Dickerson and Monic Boyd, thanks for accompanying me to functions when y'all had to be up at 5 o'clock the next morning and buying those $20.00 t-shirts. Lol.

To the rest of my family (I couldn't name you all, but you know who you are) friends and all of my supporters, thanks for believing in me as I follow my dream. I am forever grateful and I love you all. HOLD UP!!!!! Before I end this, I want to add another SPECIAL family member, Elaine Birch. There were so many days where we would be out all morning and afternoon, passing out flyers and putting up posters. It didn't matter if it was raining or just hot as hell, you were right there with me. I love you, girl.

Chapter 1

The sound of Kodak Black was bumping through the speakers as Sasha sailed through the smooth traffic. Taking a quick glance at her cellphone tucked away in her Michael Kors bag, she noticed she had an incoming call. It was her best friend, Carmen.

"Hello," she shouted into the receiver.

"Damn, girl, turn that shit down so you can hear me."

She steered with her left hand and used the other to adjust the volume and put the phone on speaker.

"What's up, fish patty?"

"Where you at?"

"Getting off on your exit."

"Stop by the store before you come here. We need some wrap."

"Bye, Felicia."

Sasha hung up the phone quickly and turned the music back up to focus on rapping to the beat and nothing else. She pulled up at the gas station, stepping out of an all-white A-8 Audi with a customized license plate that read *Mz Banks*. Glancing to her left, there was a nice piece of eye candy pumping gas and talking on his cell phone. Making eye contact, she gave him a flirtatious smile and made her entrance through the glass door. Sasha was walking up to the counter when the clerk greeted her.

"Hello, how may I help you?"

"Um, let me get two grabba leafs," she was hesitant, as if she was confused about what to get.

"Is there anything else that I can get you?"

"No, that will be it. Thanks." She paid the clerk and walked outside. Before she could make it to her car, the same dude at the pump approached her.

"Hey, beautiful, how are you doing today?" He licked his lips sexily.

Her cocoa brown skin glistened in the sun, and her beautiful brown eyes shone bright like diamonds. Her joggers fit her curvaceous hips and plump ass perfectly. She was definitely eye candy with her flawless makeup, courtesy of Mac.

"I'm fine," she smiled.

"Well, I can see that you're fine," he smiled back. "What's your name, though?"

"Sasha."

"Cool. So, fine-ass Sasha, do you have a boyfriend?"

"Does it matter? Are you trying to talk to him or me?"

He laughed. "Nah, it don't matter, not really. I just want you to keep it one hunnid with me, so I'll know what I'm dealing with. I would hate to have to fold your nigga up." He laughed to let her know he was joking. "But on the real, I wanna get to know you." He leaned to the side, admiring her body. "That ass fat, too."

He was bold, and she liked that shit.

Sasha couldn't deny she was feeling him because, truth be told, she was getting wet just by looking at him as they continued to converse.

During their conversation, she found out he went by the street name Blue and was born and raised in Miami's Dade County.

"Yawl dangerous up there. Somebody get killed every day," she said.

He shrugged his shoulders. "Hey, you live by the gun, you die by the gun. Everybody has a choice in life, and some choose to let the streets raise them instead of their parents."

"Yeah, I hear that. Anyway, I'm from Broward."

"Hold up now," he raised both arms in the air. "Broward ain't no better."

"This don't happen every day here," she sucked her teeth.

"Shit, yawl close," he chuckled.

"Nah, man, yawl Dade County niggas on First 48 every day," she answered defensively, and then the two engaged briefly in a friendly debate.

Blue saw she wouldn't concede, so he decided to let it drop. "Okay, Ma, you win. I want to get to know you; fuck the streets right now."

Never taking her eyes off of him, she noticed he had dimples, pretty brown eyes, and a set of pearly white teeth. He had a caramel complexion, shoulder length dreads, and the sexiest bowlegs she could ever imagine. He was decked out in Jordan from head to toe. Sasha was definitely intrigued by his sexiness and his smell. She had the nose of a hound dog when it came to sniffing out a baller. His 36-inch canary-yellow diamond chain and matching four-row Toni bracelet were the icing on the cake. *This nigga is definitely a boss!* she thought to herself.

Finally out of her trance, she whispered seductively in his face, "How about you give me your number and I will give you a call."

"Yeah, I can do that. But don't play games with a nigga."

She smiled. "I don't play games. Trust me, if I wasn't interested, you would've never made it this far with me."

"Alright, Ma, hit me up then."

"Okay."

Blue walked away and got inside of a tricked-out black Cadillac Escalade and pulled out into traffic. All she could think was how fine he was and what his dick game was like. He was bowlegged, so he had to be hung like a horse, and she couldn't wait to saddle up and take that ride. She was definitely going to call him, but she had to find a way to sneak around her husband of two years, Quamae, first.

Five minutes later Sasha pulled up at Carmen's place and knocked on the door.

"Who is it?" Carmen shouted.

"The baddest bitch," she yelled out confidently. She was so sure of herself, and no one could take that away from her because she was truly a dime piece.

Carmen opened the door to let her in. "Ho, you so ratchet. And what the hell took you so long? I live five minutes away from the store and it took you thirty minutes to get here," she joked.

"Uh-uh, don't do me," she waived her stiletto nail in her face. "Where da trees at and shit?" she laughed, mimicking the legendary Bernie Mac.

Carmen walked over to the entertainment center to retrieve her gold weed box. Just the sight alone made Sasha excited. She could smoke all day and all night whenever Quamae wasn't around. He didn't like her to smoke, so she did it whenever she was with her girls. Sasha grabbed the bag and sniffed the sweet contents.

"Where did you get this from? It smells good as hell."

"That's dat loud pack, bitch. I got it from Dred."

"Um," she popped her lips.

"Um, what?"

"That means you didn't pay for it."

"Hell nah. That's exactly what that means."

"Good. That means I don't owe you for it." Carmen and Sasha sat on the couch and rolled blunt after blunt. The living room was filled with smoke. The thick cloud in the air could have easily been mistaken for a small grease fire.

Sasha was in her zone as she twirled around with no beat on deck.

"Go hook your phone up. I need to hear some music."

Carmen got up to hook her cell phone up with the aux cord to play them some music.

"Bae, play my song."

"I'm sick of you," she laughed. "You just heard that on the way here."

"So? I love it, and besides, I can dance to it now."

Carmen went to YouTube and found her girl's favorite song by Kodak Black, *Skrilla.*

That skrilla, that skrilla, boy I'm 'bout my skrilla
All my niggas monkeys, we gorillas
All my niggas clutchin', we some hittas
Birds on my timeline, call it Twitter.

As the song played, Sasha was bouncing around doing the Kodak bop. Carmen was too busy laughing to join in.

A few hours later both girls were stretched out on the couch in a slight coma from the weed, and Sasha never heard her phone ringing. Quamae must have called her about twenty times to no avail. If nothing else pissed him off in life, aside from a drought, it was hearing her voicemail. That shit made him crazy. An unanswered phone to him meant one thing: she must be up to no good.

***

"Damn, this bitch really trying me," Quamae said out loud to himself as he pulled up in the driveway of their home. "I expected this motherfucker to be home sound asleep since I can't get an answer." He was still talking and cursing as he unlocked the door. "I got something for her ass," he mumbled.

The walk up the staircase to the bedroom seemed far since he was a little tipsy. He had been hanging at the trap house gambling and throwing back shots of Hennessey. Quamae was horny as fuck, and his wife was nowhere to be found. If he still had his little side chick, her ass would be in trouble that night. He was trying to do the right thing and be faithful to her, but she made that shit harder than his dick.

Before they jumped the broom, he was in a relationship with a chick named Gigi. Shorty was the total package, but her insecurities pushed him away into the arms of Sasha. He continued to sleep with her from time to time, although he tried to stop when he decided to say, "I do." Quamae wanted to call her, but decided to pass on that slip-up.

Instead, he removed all of his clothing until he was wearing nothing but a pair of Ralph Lauren boxers and a black wife beater. He stood in front of the full body mirror to admire his physique. Quamae had the body of an Egyptian God. It was like the good Lord above took his precious time in creating such a fine specimen. From his chocolate-coated skin, chiseled chest, rock-hard abs and that delicious dip that pointed in the direction of his nine-inch python, the sight of him was like a little piece of heaven. A woman could get lost in his brown, dreamy eyes, full goatee, and drown in the plethora of waves covering the top of his head.

When he was not on his grind or spending a little bit of time with Sasha, he stayed in his weight room, keeping his body intact. Stepping away from the mirror, he stretched out across their king size sleigh bed and flipped through the channels for a movie to watch. After settling on ESPN to watch the highlights from the Miami Heat game, he decided to call Sasha one more time before he lost his marbles completely.

As soon as he clicked on the phone icon to call her, it started ringing. It was Sasha. He picked up with an attitude.

"Where the fuck you at? It better be the fucking hospital."

"No. I just woke up. I'm at Carmen's house."

"Seems to me you lost your fucking mind. I called your ass twenty times and—." He paused mid-sentence. "Fuck that, you better have your ass here in the next five minutes." Then he hung up without waiting to hear a response.

Sasha made it home in fifteen minutes. She went straight to the bedroom looking for Quamae. When she walked in she saw him sitting on the edge of the bed. His hands were intertwined and resting against his mouth, and his elbows were on his thighs. His eyes were trained on her, and the frown on his face was proof that he was impatiently awaiting her arrival.

"Why the fuck you just getting home? I been calling you all night. You been fucking? Come out them muthafuckin' clothes," he demanded.

Sasha was still high, but the tone of his voice brought her down from cloud nine real quick. "I already told you where I was, and I'm not taking off shit," she defied his order and stared him down.

"Bitch, I'm not playing with you. You better get naked before I stomp a hole in your ass." He stood up and took one step toward her.

"Listen, I'm not on this shit tonight, so kill the bullshit. All I wanna do is shower and go to sleep."

Sasha let her guard down and turned her back toward him to head in the direction of the bathroom. Rapid movement could be heard behind her, but before she could turn back around, he had a fistful of her hair and slung her on the floor.

"Stop!" she screamed. "Let go of my hair!" She tried to fight him off by kicking and clawing at his hands, but she was no match for him. He released her hair from his fist and grabbed her arms while applying his weight to her small frame.

"I told you to stop fuckin' playing with me."

She continued to kick and scream. "Quamae, stop!"

"Shut the fuck up!" He freed one of his hands and slapped her repeatedly in the face.

Whap! Whap! Whap!

"I told you 'bout tryin' me."

She placed her hand over the left side of her face for protection. Tears filled her eyes and streamed down to her ears, but Quamae ignored her cries. He stood up over her, grabbed her by her pants, and pulled them off her, ripping her panties in the process. The little bit of fight she had in her had been stripped away, the same way her clothes had been.

Sasha lay there, naked from the waist down, as he ran his hand up and down her vajayjay. In the back of her mind she prayed it would be over soon. She felt violated, the same way she felt years ago as an adolescent. Pain filled her heart and exploded into a million pieces. The man who vowed to love and protect her for better or worse made her feel like a helpless woman.

"And you can stop all that crying shit. You wasn't crying when you was out in the streets. And ain't shit open this time of night but legs and 7-Eleven. You don't pay one bill in this muthafucka, so you can't do what the fuck you want to do."

This was the side of Quamae that she dreaded seeing. He rarely got out of character like that. It had been almost six months since their last episode, and she thought that was over with.

Quamae picked up her panties to examine them as if he was the lead detective. He was breathing so hard she could've sworn she felt the heat blazing from his flaring nostrils. Without further ado, he pushed her legs apart.

"Open your legs."

Without hesitation she followed his order and opened them wide. The faster she cooperated, the faster this would be over with. Sasha felt like a victim in her own home. She would've rather taken an ass whooping instead of being assaulted.

"Why are you doing this to me?" she asked, just above a whisper.

"The last time you stumbled yo ass in here, you was with another nigga. So you knew what it was before you got here."

She couldn't believe he was really going to that extreme to see if she had been having sex, but then again, she did. She cheated before, but his reaction wasn't so foul. He stepped back and headed towards the dresser where he kept his pistol. She didn't know if that was what he was getting, but it was her chance to get up off the floor.

"I wasn't doing shit," she shouted. "You so fuckin' insecure, and I'm getting sick of this shit. You probably the one that's cheating."

He turned around and ran toward her, but she took off running to the bathroom only a few feet away. Once inside, she slammed the door behind her and locked it.

"Open the fuckin' door."

"No!" she screamed.

"The longer it takes me to get in there determines the punishment."

"Quamae, just stop, please."

He kicked the door a few times, causing her to jump. He was determined to get in there. He was insecure, and he knew it, but he didn't care. She cheated on him before and he forgave her, and that was only because he had cheated on her first.

"Open the fuckin' door, and I'm not gon' say it no more."

"I'm not letting you in here. I'll sleep in here if I have to."

She laid on the floor in the fetal position and cried. She didn't know how long it would take for him to calm down, but she was not leaving the bathroom until he did.

Chapter 2

Sasha woke up and realized she was still on the bathroom floor. On the other side of the door she could hear the sound of her husband talking on the phone. Lord knows she didn't want to see his face, and most definitely not the sound of his early morning foolishness.

"Nah, nigga, we leaving at one o'clock, so have your shit ready. The early bird catches the worm, and I will leave your ass here flocking with the pigeons. Listen, make sure that nigga knows exactly what to do. We don't need any slip-ups while we gone. He better take care of shit like his life depends on it. Feel me?"

"Yeah, man, I'ma let his ass know," Chauncey, his right hand, replied.

"As soon as we get to the ATL, we picking up the family and coming right back." That was g-code for picking up dope in case the feds were listening.

"A'ight, nigga."

"One." They both hung up.

Quamae ended the call just as Sasha was coming out of the bathroom. He looked her in her eyes because the guilt was starting to weigh in. He was aware of the fact he could blow things out of proportion, but she was hard-headed and needed to be taught a lesson. "Baby, I'm sorry about last night, but I meant every word I said."

"Yeah, right, and that's exactly why you did it, so don't apologize if you don't mean that shit." She walked past him and headed toward the bed to lay down. Her body was sore from the uncomfortable sleeping arrangements she had to endure, but she stopped and turned to face him. "What you did to me was unnecessary."

"You right. I'm not sorry for snapping, but for the other shit, yeah, I am. I took that shit overboard."

He wanted to make things right before he hit the road in a few because the woman standing in front of him was his world. She was laying it on thick by poking her lip out further.

"Come here." He took her into his arms. "You know I love you, right?"

"I love you, too, but that doesn't justify what you did to me," she replied with a disgusted look on her face. Her response didn't match her true feelings, but to avoid an instant replay of last night, she was willing to match his mood.

"You know that I'm jealous and my temper is bad, so stop doing things to provoke me. I will move Heaven and Earth for you, but you can't be coming up in here late at night without permission." He let her go and reached into his pocket. "Here, it's five bands, go shopping or something."

She took the money from his hand.

Quamae knew just what to say and do to make her forget about anything he'd done to her. They shared a long, deep, passionate kiss while he caressed her. All the attention he was showing her made her hot and horny, so she didn't waste any time stripping down to her birthday suit. She lay down on the bed spread-eagle and welcomed him in with open arms. Quamae leaned down and began to lick her thumping clitoris. The friction made her shudder. He munched down on her hungrily like it was the last time he would taste her. She locked her legs and held the back of his head to keep him in that position. He was a beast in the bed, and he knew just what to do to hit the spot.

Her eyes rolled to the back of her head. "Sh. Um!"

A few minutes later her legs vibrated, alerting him she was reaching her peak. "I'm about to cum," she moaned.

Quamae stopped abruptly, interrupting her climax, so he could give his dick some action before she tapped out. He lifted her thighs and slipped into his safe haven with mad aggression, causing her to yelp.

"Ah! Beat it up, Daddy."

He long-stroked her in a quick, rough manner to make sure she would be good until he got back in town. In his mind he was making sure every time she moved, it would remind her of the punishment he was giving her.

"Throw it back," he grunted. "Damn, this pussy good."

He wanted her to be too sore to wipe. In her mind, she was thinking make-up sex was the best, and this was the only good part about fighting. She dug deep into his back and took that beating like the ho she was. She thrust her hips forward to match his rhythm. The warmth of his rod and the softness of his skin penetrating her hole was arousing. With each stroke it felt like her skin was ripping apart, but it felt so good as he hit her g-spot. The sensation built up, and she felt the urge to pee.

"Gimme that nut," he demanded.

"It's coming," she moaned as she released her fluids on the base of his stick.

His strokes were faster, yet slippery as he let off a million little soldiers into her nest. "Damn!" He laid down on her and rested his head in the crook of her neck.

A few hours later, he jumped out of his sleep from his early morning sexcapade. "Shit," he shouted after he realized he overslept. He hurried out of bed and went straight to the shower so he could get dressed for his trip. When he was finished in the bathroom, he stepped out wearing a towel around his waist. His masculine chest was glistening as the water dripped down to his biceps.

"Sasha, get up."

A sleeping Sasha rolled over. "Yeah, babe, what's up?" Her eyes were still closed because she was still half asleep.

"Get up. I need you to listen to me."

"I'm not asleep."

He sat on the bed with his back toward her and grabbed the cocoa butter sitting on the nightstand. He rubbed it all over his body. "Listen, I have to go to Atlanta, but I will be back tomorrow night. Have one of your girls come stay with you until I get back. I don't want you staying here by yourself. I'll call and check on you." He turned around to face her, "And don't be out all night, either. Just because I won't be here doesn't mean I won't know."

She rolled her eyes. "Yeah, I'm sure you will hear something."

Quamae continued to get dressed while she packed his overnight bag. "Why are you taking a bag if you going up and coming right back?"

"Do you have to ask so many questions?"

"Yeah, I do." She waited for him to respond, but when he didn't, she finished her sentence. "Well, anyway, just be careful, please, and come back home in one piece." She tilted her head to the side oddly. "And what you going up there for, anyway?"

"The less you know, the better. All you need to know is I will be back tomorrow." He hated when she asked so many damn questions. That's why he never put her in his business. That's why he took most of his calls in other rooms. The last thing he needed was her knowing about the way he ran his operation. The less she knew, the better off she was. If it ever came down to the feds getting involved, she couldn't tell them what she didn't know.

An hour later, Quamae headed out the door with Sasha on his heels. "I love you, drive careful."

"I will. I love you, too." He got into the rental car and backed out of the driveway. She watched him until he was out of sight, and then she walked back into the house and closed the door behind her. While thinking of all the shit she could do while Quamae was out of town, she picked up the phone to call Carmen.

"Hey, bae," she answered.

"What are you doing?"

"Laying in the bed watching Brotherly Love."

"Damn, is that, like, the only movie on Netflix?"

"Nope, but you know this is my favorite one on here."

"Well, anyway, Quamae is gone out of town, so you know what that means?"

"Let me guess: you're having a sleepover and you want us to come over?" she said sarcastically in her white-girl voice.

"Yeah, that's exactly what that means, so pack your bag and bring your ass on."

"You think you slick and nobody is crazy. You must be trying to do something? Please don't make him kill you. I do not want to witness that."

"Girl he is gone to Atlanta, not Palm Beach. I will have plenty of time, and besides, he hasn't been trying to spend time with me lately. So guess what? What he won't do, another man will."

"Yeah, you say that now, but that's on you. You took those vows before God, not me. I don't have a heaven or a hell to put you in."

"Man, just get your stuff and come on. We can talk about this later."

"Yeah, I'm coming."

After they hung up, Sasha walked into the closet to find something to wear. It was pretty cool outside because of the rain, so she decided to put on a sweat suit by VS Pink. On her way to the bathroom, she turned on the smart television and put it on YouTube. In order to get herself together, she needed to hear music.

After she took a shower, her phone was ringing off the hook. She ran to catch it before it went to voicemail. This time it was India. Damn near out of breath, she picked up. "Hey."

"Damn, you sound like you were running."

Sasha laughed. "I was."

"So, what were you doing?"

"I just got out of the shower. Are you back yet?" Sasha walked back into the bathroom and stood in front of the mirror.

"Yeah, I just got here."

"So, how was it?" She put the phone on speaker and sat it on the sink so she could remove the shower cap she was wearing.

"It was really nice. We had a good time. The hotel was exquisite alone, and the beaches were beautiful."

"Well, I'm glad you had a good time, because Jamaica is really beautiful. I wish me and Quamae could go back."

"You can."

Sasha sucked her teeth. "Girl, please, if it's not work related, he ain't going."

India changed the subject. She already knew where that conversation was headed. "Is Carmen with you?"

"No, but she is on her way over here. Quamae went to Atlanta, and you know he don't like me staying home alone."

"So, I guess that mean you want me to come over there, too?"

"You damn right, so hurry up and get here."

"When I leave the airport, I have to stop by the house first so Steve can pick up his car. He has to go by his office and do some work. So as soon as he leaves, I will head your way."

"Okay. I'll see you later, then."

"Alright."

As Sasha got dressed, she glanced at the security monitor and saw Carmen pulling up in the driveway. She threw on some flip-flops and went downstairs to open the door. She walked in carrying a duffle bag like she was staying the entire weekend over there.

"Damn, Carmen, did you have to bring that big-ass bag? I mean, you are going home tomorrow."

"I can really go home now, ho."

"Ya mama a ho," she stuck up her middle finger.

"No, you mean your mama, bitch."

"Fuck that, ho." Whenever the ho that birthed her was mentioned, it put a bad taste in her mouth. "Hell, a dog could have a baby, but that doesn't make it a mother. Leave that ho where she's at. Dead!" She knew Carmen didn't mean any harm, so she didn't take it to heart.

Carmen blew the bad energy out that invaded her chest and switched gears. "Damn, I'm tired," she yawned and sat down on the couch.

Sasha sat down beside her and grinned. "For what? Did you have a long night?"

Carmen sucked her teeth. "Hell no. I wish like hell I did. After you left my house last night, I couldn't go back to sleep. I sat up watching Brotherly Love again until four o'clock this morning. I tried calling you, but I got the voicemail."

Shaking her head, Sasha said, "Girl, when I got home Quamae was mad as hell. This fool had the audacity to grab me by my hair from behind and slang me on the floor. Then he made me strip naked so he can smell me. I was so pissed off with him. I should've maced his ass."

Carmen started laughing.

"Bitch, that shit ain't funny."

"I know. I'm laughing at you about the mace. You know damn well you wasn't gon' do that."

"I thought about it, though." She leaned in closer as if they weren't the only ones in the house. "Okay, so check this out, he apologized this morning. Talking about he's sorry and he loves me, but I ain't on that shit. Especially after he told me since I don't pay bills in this bitch, I can't do whatever I want to do. He got me fucked up. I'm about to show his ass."

"Yeah, right. I bet you accepted his apology and forgot about it?" she whispered back. "Hold up, why the fuck are we whispering?"

"Quamae is liable to have recording devices in here. I don't put shit past his sneaky ass, and to answer your question, I surely did. He gave me five bands this morning, and the make-up sex was everything and some."

Carmen sat back and folded her arms. "I'm glad I'm not married."

"Girl, I was joking about the recording devices, calm down." She changed the subject. "Anyway, India is back from Jamaica. She'll be here when she leaves the airport."

"Which airport?"

"Fort Lauderdale."

"So when is Quamae coming back, for real?" She was well aware he liked to sneak back into town, trying to catch her.

"He said he'll be back tomorrow night, but anyway, I met this fine-ass dude."

Carmen interrupted her. "And when was this?"

"Before I got to your house yesterday."

"Oh, so you keeping secrets now? Because clearly you failed to fill me in," she asked in a joking manner.

"No, it really slipped my mind. I haven't called him yet, but I'm gone call him since Quamae's gone."

"I hope you know what you doing."

Chapter 3

One hour had passed, and Carmen was lying on the couch when her stomach started to growl. She got up and made her way toward the kitchen. "What yawl got in here to eat?" she yelled.

Sasha didn't respond. Instead, she picked up the phone to call Blue.

He picked up on the third ring. "What's up?"

She put on her cutest voice. "Hey, Blue, this Sasha."

"Oh, what's up, sexy? How you doing?"

"I'm good. How about you?"

"Better since I'm talking to you."

Sasha blushed and played with her bonnet. "Oh, wow! I have that effect on you already?"

"Maybe," he smiled into the phone. "I know I like what I saw, and I would like to get to know you better. If that's okay with you?"

"Yeah, that can definitely be arranged. So check this out, I'm free tonight. Are you trying to see me?" she asked boldly.

"Hell yeah. That's not even a question, but I can see I'm gone like you."

She blushed. "Oh, really?"

"Yeah, you get straight to the point."

"Because I don't have time to waste."

"So, what chu wanna do tonight? Do you drink or smoke?"

"Both," she giggled like a schoolgirl. "Why are you trying to get me drunk and high?"

He laughed at her sense of humor. One thing about it, there was no pressure on his end, but he knew a chick willing to smoke and drink on the first date was down for whatever. His status alone gave him access to some of the baddest bitches, and he entertained them often.

"Nah, I'm just trying to see what you like to do."

"Oh, okay, just checking."

"I'm just joking. Let me stop before I scare you off."

"I'm not scared of you because I don't have a reason to be."

"Good, because I'm harmless."

"I hope so," she grinned.

"That's cool. So why don't you pick a place you want to go to and call me around six. I have some moves to make right now, but I will be finished by then."

"Sounds like a plan."

"'A'ight. I'll talk to you later."

"Bye." Then she hung up.

Sasha was so excited about the idea of just going on a date, period. It had been months since her and Quamae went out on a date. It felt good to be wanted by a man, and she was determined to fill her desires one way or another.

Carmen walked back into the living room. "Okay, all I found was this cold-ass Pepsi. I'm hungry, so we need to get some lunch or something."

"Yeah, we can do that. First, let me call India and see where her slow-ass at."

She called her up. "Man, where are you?"

"I'm on my way. Didn't I tell your hardheaded-ass I was going home to get some clothes? I'll be there in fifteen minutes."

"Well, hurry up."

India hung the phone up before she could complete the sentence.

Sasha and Carmen sat on the couch to watch Shottas and smoke a blunt until India showed up. At the end of the session, she finally pulled up, and Carmen was there to greet her with open arms.

"Hey, babe! I missed you. Don't ever leave me with this crazy-ass girl by myself again," Carmen said, referring to Sasha.

Sasha shot her a bird. "And you know I don't give a damn about none of that you saying. Oh yeah, and it couldn't have been that bad for you to be laying over here right now."

After hugging Carmen, she looked over at Sasha. "Well, I'm glad somebody is happy to see me."

"Yawl hos act like it's been a long time since we last saw each other," Sasha said as she walked over to give her a hug.

"You know I missed you, stop acting crazy."

"Let's get some lunch. That plane ride made me hungry."

"That's what I'm talking about. I told Sasha let's go out," Carmen replied.

Sasha walked upstairs to grab her keys, Dolce and Gabbana shades, and her MK bag. She set the alarm and they headed out.

During the drive to the rib shack in Lauderdale, Sasha brought India up to speed on what's been going on while she was away. From meeting Blue, the encounter with Quamae, all the way down to the make-up sex. There was nothing secret within the trio.

They pulled up to the spot and ordered their food. While inside, they kicked it and joked around with a few people they knew from the neighborhood. Sasha, India, and Carmen grew up in Ft. Lauderdale together. They even went to the same middle school and high school together. They knew everybody, and everybody knew when they saw one, they saw all three of them. They were like the Three Musketeers.

Carmen sat down on one of the stools and sat her purse on the counter. "Did yawl see how fine DJ got overnight?"

"Yeah, I see, but you ain't wanna give the man the time or day. Ol' funny-acting-ass. I told you, don't pass him up." India knew he would transform from the ugly duckling one day. "Now he has a wife and kids. You missed out on that, boo."

"She damn sholl did!" Sasha high-fived India.

Carmen tooted up her nose. "Nah, I'm straight. I'm just giving the man a compliment. His wife ugly, so whatever!"

Sasha peeped the hate in her voice and nudged India on the arm. "You sound a lil' jealous over there. And I just need to know, are you big mad or lil' mad?"

India and Sasha laughed at Carmen's expense.

She waved them off, giggling a little bit, realizing she did sound like she was low-key hating. "Definitely not!"

Switching up the conversation, Sasha leaned in to school her girls. "I'm going on a date with Blue tonight, so yawl have to cover for me."

India's eyebrows crept down slowly. "Why the hell you going out with somebody you just met?"

"He wants to take me out, and I'm going." She pointed her finger at the both of them. "Yawl stay at my house until I come back."

India rolled her eyes. "You think that's a good idea?"

"If it wasn't, I wouldn't be doing it."

India surrendered with her hands up in the air. "If you say so."

Carmen shifted in her seat and flipped her hair. "That's a grown-ass woman, and you can't tell her what to do."

India shook her head. "I expected you to say some shit like that. This is a married woman who shouldn't be cheating."

"Well, India, that's on her, and I for one like to mind my own business."

Sasha jumped in. "I'm simply going to dinner, so chill. No need in arguing about nothing."

India folded her arms. "I'm done. I said what I had to say."

"Good." Sasha replied.

After grabbing something to eat, the time crept by quickly, like a thief in the night, because the clock read six o'clock. It was time for Sasha to call Blue and see what was up.

"What's going on, Ma?" he answered.

"Nothing, trying to see what's up with you?"

"I'm about to head to my house and get ready. Have you decided on what you want to do?" It didn't matter what she wanted to do as long as they went out. Blue had just left his homeboy house from gambling. He cut the game short because he was anxious to meet up with her that night. Any other time he would've gambled all night, but he was trying to see what Sasha was about.

"You can surprise me," she replied.

"I can do that. Be dressed by seven thirty and we can meet up at eight."

"Okay, well, let me start putting myself together, because it's gon' take me a while to get ready."

"Be ready at seven thirty, Ma, and don't have me waiting all night."

"I won't."

After hanging up with Blue, she spent the next hour and a half getting dressed, applying her makeup, and fixing her hair. When she was finished, she stepped from the bathroom and looked to her girls for confirmation. They were engaged in their own conversation as they waited for her to finish.

"How do I look?" She was wearing a body dress with the back cut out and stiletto heels.

"Like a slut," Carmen laughed.

"Come on, bitch, I'm being serious," she pouted.

India answered, "You look cute."

"Thanks. I knew I could count on you."

"Cute and ready to fuck," India teased.

"Come on and stop playing. It's almost time for me to leave." She stood with her hands on her hips, waiting for an answer.

"Girl, you fine, so quit pouting." India stood up. "Turn around and let me see that ass." Sasha turned around in a half circle.

"Yas, bae, that ass look fat," Carmen shouted.

"Carmen, you stupid," India laughed.

"Well, I'm out, and I'll see yawl when I get back," Sasha sung as she picked up her things and headed for the door, all while dialing Blue's number. Carmen and India walked out of the bedroom behind her until they reached the bottom of the stairs.

Blue picked up on the third ring. "Are you ready?"

"Yes, I am. Where are we meeting up at?"

"Benihanas. I hope you like it."

"Yeah, that's my favorite spot."

"Okay, meet me at the one in Miramar."

"I'm on my way," then she hung up the phone. "Good choice," she mumbled to herself. "At least he's not cheap."

She turned around to look at her girls. "We all know the drill if Quamae calls the house phone?"

They knew the drill all too well. This wasn't the first time they covered for her.

Carmen sucked her teeth. "Girl, getcho ass outta here before I call him and tell him where you going."

They all laughed, and Sasha walked out the door.

It was seven thirty on the dot when she left the house, so that gave her thirty minutes to arrive. The sun had settled down due to daylight saving time, so it wasn't dark as of yet. Slow music played softly through the speakers, sending her back down memory lane when life was good with her husband. In the beginning he was very romantic, but over the course of a year the fire and desire dwindled down slowly. Sasha no longer felt sexy in his eyes. She became bored in his absence, and the sex wasn't happening as often as she would've liked. They went from having sex on a daily basis to a measly two or three times a week. If she was lucky.

After reminiscing for about twenty minutes, she was finally pulling up in front of the restaurant to valet parking. Sasha immediately noticed Blue standing out front, talking on his phone. She watched him as he ended his call and walked toward her car. The butterflies in her stomach started to rumble as she exited her vehicle with her purse in her hand.

Blue's eyes roamed her body from head to toe. "Damn, you look good."

She smiled. "Thank you."

The valet attendant stood close by and waited on them to acknowledge him.

"And you're prompt. I like that in a woman."

She smiled again and nodded her head. "I didn't want to keep you waiting."

Blue finally turned his attention to the attendant and paid him before taking Sasha's hand and escorting her up the walkway.

Once they made their way to the inside, Blue walked over to the hostess station and checked in with the reservation he made earlier that day. The hostess gave him a buzzer and said the wait wouldn't be more than fifteen minutes. He then walked away and took a seat next to his date.

He licked his lips the same way he did when they met and put his arm around her. "You wearing the hell outta that dress."

"I'm glad you like it."

"Hell yeah, I do." He rubbed his hand on her shoulder, sending chills over her body.

"You don't look too bad yourself," she joked. He looked completely different from the first time they met. He had ditched his basketball gear and replaced it with a button-up Polo shirt and some khakis. He wore the same jewelry on his neck and wrist, and he looked damn good in it.

In exactly fifteen minutes the buzzer went off and they both walked over to the hostess station. She escorted them to their table with two other couples. Blue pulled out her chair and allowed her to sit, and then he sat down beside her. She liked the fact he was a gentleman and the way he complimented her with words and affection. The waiter came out shortly after and took their drink orders as they waited on the chef to show up. During the wait they sat closely to one another and talked over drinks until their orders were taken.

"So, do you have a girlfriend?" she asked curiously, although it didn't matter since she was the married one.

"Nah," he answered smoothly.

Sasha wasn't buying that answer at all. "So you don't have anybody you talking to?"

"Nah," he rubbed his hand over his mouth. "Well, not like that. I mean, I chat with a female here and there, but I ain't in no relationship or nothin' like that. I consider myself single." He grinned. "Where yo' nigga at? Cause I know you got one."

She hesitated for a second.

"Don't lie to a nigga."

"I wasn't going to, but yes, I have one. Why, is that a problem?"

"Nah, not at all. I'm cool wit' it 'cause he ain't doing something right if you here with me." He placed his hand on her thigh and looked into her eyes. "'Cause if you was my lady, you'd never step out on me. I'd wine and dine yo' lil' sexy ass everyday and put that ass to sleep every night. You'd be too tired to even think about another nigga, let alone entertain his ass."

She blushed. "All of that sounds good."

He rubbed her thigh, causing her to wiggle in her seat. "Feels good, too. Keep fuckin' with me and I'll show you how a queen is supposed to be treated." Blue was flirting heavy, and she was enjoying every second of it.

Before they could finish conversing, the chef strolled up with his cart. Blue sat up straight in his seat and watched the chef set up his area and begin cooking the food. All eyes were on him as he sliced, diced, scrambled, chopped, and fried all of their food. He even made the Miami Heat basketball with fire flames. Blue looked over at Sasha.

"He a Dade County nigga, too, but he probably from Lil' Havana where all the Hispanics at." They both laughed.

"And how do you know that man from Lil' Havana? He look Asian to me," Sasha asked.

"Shid, they all look alike to me."

They shared a few more laughs and ate their dinner. Then Blue paid the bill and helped her out of her seat.

"After you, my lady."

Blue walked behind Sasha and admired the view. The way her ass moved in that dress made him want to head to the nearest hotel, but he decided not to rush it. Once they made it outside, they waited on valet to bring their vehicles.

Sasha stood in front of him, admiring his sexiness. "I had a good time with you tonight."

He grabbed her by the waist. "I did, too, although it ended rather quickly."

"It doesn't have to end here."

He was surprised she wasn't in a hurry to head home. "You sure about that?"

"Yep."

"A'ight, I have someplace we can go for drinks and shoot some pool. Just follow me."

"Okay."

Sasha followed Blue until they were on the outside of a billiard hall. They parked side-by-side and he got out to come and open the door for her. She couldn't remember the last time Quamae did that for her. All she knew was Blue was laying it on thick, and she could get used to that type of treatment once again. They walked inside holding hands and walked around until they found an empty pool table. A waitress walked over briskly and greeted them.

"Hi, I'm Amanda, and I'll be your server for the night. What can I get you to drink?"

"I'll have a double shot of Hennessey." He glanced over at Sasha. "Bae, tell her what you want."

"I'll have a Long Island Iced Tea."

"Okay, I'll be right back."

She was cheesing at Blue when the waitress walked off. "Oh, I'm *bae* now?"

"You could be," he winked. Blue had a way of making everything sound so damn sexy.

The waitress returned promptly with their drinks, and their fun began. Sasha didn't know how to play pool, but she was willing to learn. Blue stood close behind her, leaning against her body and guiding her fingers.

"Hold the stick like this," he instructed.

She could feel the warmth of his breath on her ear. As his hips pressed up against her round derriere, she could feel his wood pressing up against it. He was turning her on in the worst way, and it was driving her crazy. The liquor and his sexual demeanor definitely had her emotions all over the place. She was trying to contain herself, but he was making that difficult for her to do.

She cleared her throat. "Okay."

After a few rounds of playing, she was finally getting the hang of it. They were having a good time together, laughing and drinking, but the ringtone from her cell stopped her laughter. She already knew it was Quamae. She looked at Blue.

"I have to take this call. I'll be right back."

"Okay."

She grabbed her clutch, pulled out her phone, and walked away. "Hey, baby."

"What you doing?" he asked, getting straight to the point of his call.

"Hanging out at Dave and Busters with Carmen and India."

"Oh, okay."

"We decided to have a ladies night out since India came back from Jamaica today."

"Oh, okay, that's cool. Did you turn the alarm on?"

"Yes, baby, I did."

"Okay, well finish having fun and call me when you get home."

She stared down at her ring finger. She didn't inform Blue she was a married woman, so she made sure she left it home. "Okay, drive careful, be safe, and I love you."

"I love you, too."

Sasha placed her cell back into her clutch and walked back over to Blue.

"Is everything okay?" he asked.

"Yeah, I just got off the phone with my other half." She felt a little bad, but not enough to end her date.

"Do you need to leave?" he quizzed her.

"No, he's out of town."

"Are you sure?"

She smiled at him. "Of course."

They continued to drink and shoot pool until two in the morning. At this point Sasha was a little drunk and ready to go.

Blue escorted Sasha out of the building and to her car with his hand wrapped around her waist.

"Are you okay to drive?"

"Yes. I don't have far to drive." She clicked the remote to unlock her car doors.

"I can follow you home. It's not a problem," he insisted.

"Really, I'm fine."

Blue invaded her personal space, pushing her against the car, and placed his lips on hers. She kissed him back. He had waited all night to see just how soft her pretty lips were. His hand wandered freely up under her dress until he found her other set of lips. He teased her as he rubbed the outside of her thong. She could feel them become sticky. Blue broke their kiss, allowing his tongue to make a wet trail to her neck.

"Ah," she moaned with her eyes closed. His hand was in the same spot, and he was now sucking on her neck.

"The dick feels better," he assured her, but he wasn't ready to give it to her yet, so he stopped abruptly and she opened her eyes. "That shit felt good, huh?"

She was disappointed about the way he just got her aroused for nothing. "You know it did."

He smiled. "I know, but go ahead and head home and I'll talk to you later." He gave her a peck on the lips and helped her into her car. "Goodnight."

"Goodnight," she replied. Blue closed the door and walked to his truck.

Sasha drove home drunk and horny. That wasn't exactly how she had planned on ending her night, and it made her wonder what type of game was he playing with her. Whatever it was, she couldn't wait to see him again. The chemistry between them was insane and she wanted to act out on it.

It only took her ten minutes to get home. Every light she went through was green, giving her a smooth ride.

When she pulled up to her house, the porch light was on. She turned the car off and snatched off her heels, then staggered up onto the porch. She fumbled with the keys until she found the right one and unlocked the door.

Finally on the inside, she stumbled all the way up the stairs and took a peek into the guestroom. Carmen and India were sound asleep. Closing the door behind her, she walked into her bedroom and began removing her clothing and tossing them on the floor, along with her cellphone and clutch. Completely naked, she crawled into bed and fell asleep quickly.

Chapter 4

"Pass that shit, nigga." Quamae demanded.

"Damn, you impatient-ass nigga, can I hit the shit first?" Chauncey replied, agitated.

The sweet smell of loud filled the car, as well as the sound of Lil Webbie's *Just Like This*. Quamae was very cautious on his road trips. He made sure he went no faster than the speed limit, and he let the smoke circulate and go through the vents. He didn't need any encounters with the state troopers. Driving to Atlanta was the easy part. It was the trip back home that was more of a challenge. He made sure he followed every rule, giving no reason to be stopped by any LEOs, which was short for 'law enforcement officers.' Traffic was smooth. There were only a few cars riding on I-95, and the late night air was cool and dewy. Chauncey passed the blunt to Quamae, he took a deep pull, inhaled, and let the smoke fill his lungs.

"That shit smoking?" Chauncey wanted to know how he felt about the new product.

"Hell yeah."

"I got it from Dirty. He wanted me to sample the shit to make sure it's smoking."

"Sample it for what? He wanna sell weed now, too?" He took two more pulls and passed it back.

"He think we should add this to the inventory. He bought a pound from some nigga to see how the shit would move, and it moved pretty quick." Chauncey took a hit and talked in between breaths. "I told him I would run it by you first and see what you say."

"I don' know 'bout that. We got a sweet operation already."

Chauncey looked over in his direction. "Think about it before you say no. 'Cause I was thinking we should cop the shit and hand that shit off to the young niggas. That's more money for us, and you can retire a little quicker than planned."

Quamae put a little thought into it and figured it could be another power move if they could make the work disappear the same way they pushed the dope. "We'll holla at the nigga when we get back."

"That's what I'm talkin' 'bout," Chauncey laughed. "Let's get this money, baby."

Quamae grabbed his cellphone and placed a call to Sasha, but she didn't answer. He tried calling her two more times before sending her a text message. He sat the phone back in the cup holder, then put his attention back on the road so he could focus on his surroundings. He appeared to be in deep thought.

"You straight?" Chauncey asked.

"Yeah, I'm good," he nodded his head up and down.

"You sure about that, 'cause it looks like you have some heavy shit on your mind?" Chauncey knew Quamae was lying. As long as they had been friends, he knew when something was wrong.

"Nah, I'm straight. I was just calling Sasha to see if she made it in the house yet. She went out with Thelma and Louise."

Chauncey's laugh was loud. "Man, you know how they drunk-asses get when they get together."

Quamae laughed also. "Hell yeah. They get white-girl wasted."

"I know what you need, nigga," he said, making an effort to take to his boy's mind off of Sasha.

"And what's that?"

"A cup of this 1738, nigga." Chauncey fixed Quamae a cup and passed it to him. The two of them started to reminisce about their teenage years, skipping school, fighting together, and running trains on females together. They were down for each other since day one. They even shared their differences. Nothing could separate them.

They arrived in Atlanta a little after three in the morning since there was a delay at the trap house earlier, which caused them to leave much later than planned. Pulling into the first hotel he saw, Quamae got out of the car to check for any vacancies. Since it was late night, he had to be buzzed in. The desk clerk greeted him. "Welcome to Comfort Suites. How may I help you?" she asked.

"I need a room for the night."

"Okay, will that be smoking or non-smoking?"

"Smoking," Quamae answered.

"Okay, sir, your total is seventy-four dollars and fifty-two cents."

He dug inside his pocket and pulled out a wad of money, peeled off a hundred dollar bill, and handed it to the clerk.

"Twenty-five forty-eight is your change, and your room number is 303. Do you need two keys?"

"Nah, just one." There was no need for two keys since their stay would be short. It was already after three, and checkout time would be as soon as they got up.

"Okay, have a good night."

"Thanks, you do the same." Quamae exited the building and hopped back in the car to find a parking spot. Once they found it, they grabbed their bags and headed back into the building.

"Take the elevator to your left," the clerk stated while staring at them from head to toe.

"Thanks, Ma," Chauncey grinned, noticing how hard she was checking them out.

Once they were inside the room, Quamae dropped his bag and stretched out across the bed. On the other hand, Chauncey headed straight to the bathroom.

"This Remy running right through my system," he mumbled.

Quamae flipped through the television stations and stopped on *Law and Order*. Chauncey stepped from the bathroom wearing nothing but a pair of basketball shorts. He jumped onto the other bed and stretched out as well.

"Damn, I'm tired," he complained.

"For what? You ain't done shit but ride shotgun, roll blunts, fix drinks, and play music." He laughed as his partner tried to downplay his involvement.

"I stayed up with you the whole ride, though." He dug inside his pants pocket and pulled out a pack of cigarillos. He threw the pack at Quamae. "Roll up."

The two of them smoked and drank until they passed out. The next morning, Quamae was awakened by the sound of the hotel phone. "Yeah," he answered groggily.

The voice on the other end responded, "Good morning, sir. This is a courtesy call to let you know that check-out time is at noon."

"Yeah," he replied.

"Okay, have a good day, sir."

He placed the phone back down on the base. "Chauncey, getcha ass up, man, it's almost checkout time."

He rolled over and pulled the blanket from over his head. "What, man?"

"Get your ass up, that's what."

"What time is it?"

"Eleven thirty-six." Quamae walked away and headed to the shower. Chauncey followed suit and got up to iron his clothes. After he was done, he sat down to roll up again. No sooner than that, his phone started ringing. He looked at the screen before picking up, and it read Cuddy Buddy.

"Yeah," he answered dryly. Clearly he wasn't in the mood for early morning conversation, but he knew better than to ignore it, because she would call until he picked up.

The female voice on the other end was low and sexy. "Did you make it up there okay?"

That changed his whole demeanor. "Yeah, I'm at the hotel now. We're about to head out in a few. What you doing?"

"Nothing. I was thinking about you, so I decided to call. I figured you wouldn't have time to call me."

"You know I have to handle my business first. I need to be on point at all times in case some shit pops off."

Monica started laughing. "You are crazy as hell."

"I'm serious, Ma. When you in this type of business, you have to be prepared for anything. But enough of all that, what are you getting into today?"

"I'm going to get my hair done. Then later on tonight I'm going to the club, and hopefully you'll be back by the time I get home."

"Is that right?" He knew exactly what she meant, but he wanted to hear her say it.

"You know I sleep better after you lay it down."

He smiled and continued to roll his weed. "I know that's all you want from me."

"You know what I want from you, so stop trying to put it on me. I want you, but you just want to be Cuddy Buddies."

Quamae had just emerged from the bathroom. The steam from the shower followed suit as he walked out, leaving the door wide open. Grabbing his clothes from the hanger in the small closet, he began to get dressed. He wasn't fazed by doing so in the presence of his boy because they had seen each other naked before during their many training sessions.

Chauncey continued his conversation like no one was there. "You knew that from the start, so don't pull that guilt trip on me."

She whined a little to soften him up. "No, bae, it's not like that. I'm just saying," but then she paused. Like always, she had to beg and plead her case, but that wasn't happening today. If he didn't see her worthy enough to be on his arm with a title, then fuck it. "Don't worry about it, I'm good. Call me later if you feel like it," she snapped and hung up before he had the chance to respond. Chauncey threw his cell on the bed.

Quamae laughed. "Ho problems, huh? I told you it was coming sooner or later. Just when you thought shit would be sweet until you stopped playing the field." Quamae pulled his shirt over his head and listened.

"Hell yeah, that's what it's supposed to be. She better play her position and be cool with it. She'll be all right, though. I'll call her later on. You know, give her some time to cool off."

"Yeah, do that. In the meantime, get your ass in the shower so we can check out and get this work."

Chauncey walked away and headed to the bathroom while Quamae picked up the phone and called his connect. "What's up, Q?" Rell shouted into the phone.

"What da business is?" Quamae asked.

"The boat coming to the dock at six o'clock." He replied discreetly.

"Alright, I'm leaving the hotel right now."

"Slide up on me at the crib in Bankhead."

"A'ight. One."

After hanging up with Rell, he scrolled down on his call log until he saw the name Wifey. He pressed the green icon and waited for her to pick up.

"Hello." She sounded groggy, as if she had a really long night.

"What did I tell you to do last night? Why you so damn hard-headed? And I know you saw my text." His voice was calm as he spoke to her.

"You said call you, but as soon as we got here, I went to bed." She rubbed the cold from her eyes and yawned. "Did you make it up there okay?"

"I'm good, but it sounds like yo' ass was out all night. It's almost noon and you still in bed. Where is Carmen and India?"

She glanced around the room as if she was unsure of their location. "They asleep, too."

"Yeah, a'ight."

"I love you."

"Yeah." Then he ended the call and sat it on the nightstand.

Unlike most men, Quamae had no problem saying those words, especially since he meant it. It took him a while to say it when they first started dating, but when he did, he was in all the way. Right after he confessed his love for her, he asked her to marry him, and the rest was history.

Something didn't sit well with him about her going out the night before. Every since he caught her cheating with her ex-boyfriend, their marriage hadn't been the same. He had even moved out of the house for two weeks, but she kept saying if he didn't come back, she would commit suicide. She kept bringing up the fact she was dependent on him because he didn't allow her to work and she couldn't function without him. He eventually moved back because he loved her with everything in him, but he didn't trust her as far as he could see her. And that was the reason he flipped out on her at times.

Quamae got up to see what was taking Chauncey so long to get out of the shower. Beating on the door, he yelled, "Hurry up, man. It's almost time to go. You don't have time to jack off right now." He knew that would get his ass out of there.

Chauncey stepped out. "Oh, now you want to rush a nigga just 'cause you ready. You ain't shit."

"I've heard that before, but guess what? You ain't either." They laughed at their own joke and gave each other a fist pound.

Chauncey threw the towel on the bed. "I don't need to jack off; I have too many hos for that."

Quamae looked around the room. "That's funny, 'cause I don't see none of them hos in here."

On their way down MLK Drive, Chauncey popped in T.I.'s classic CD, *I'm Serious*. What better way to ride through "The A" playing the King of the South's music? Just hearing it made him crunk.

"We going to Magic City tonight, fuck going home," Chauncey yelled over the music.

"I knew that was coming next. I want to get this work and head back to the Dale."

Chauncey wasn't trying to hear that shit. Going home was the furthest thing from his mind. He told Quamae not to marry her because that would change him. He had to make his point valid and make him stay that extra day.

"Why you trying to rush home? I told you to stop trying to watch her every move, 'cause you not gon' catch it 'cause you looking for it."

He knew Chauncey was right, just a little bit. "Whatever, nigga! I run that shit, and whatever I say goes."

"Yeah, okay." Chauncey continued to bop to the music while Quamae remained silent for the rest of the ride.

About thirty minutes later they were pulling up at a cream and brown house. Quamae could spot Rell in the crowd. From the looks of things, they were engaged in a dice game. They stepped out of the car and walked up to the porch. Rell looked up. "What's up Q? What's up C?" He gave them both a fist pound. "How was the ride up?"

"It was cool," Quamae answered smoothly.

"That's what's up. So, what yawl boys getting into tonight?"

Chauncey replied eagerly, "I'm trying to hit Magic City and see some ass." He pointed at Quamae. "But this nigga trying to go home."

Rell looked Quamae up and down. "Nah, nigga, say it ain't so?" he clowned.

He knew he would never hear the end of that conversation, so he agreed to stay. "Yeah, I'm down."

"Cool," Rell replied as he shook the dice and rolled them up against the wall. "Run me my money," he shouted, then looked up at his rounds. "Instead of yawl wasting money on a room, yawl can stay at the crib."

"Nah, we cool. We can just get another room," Quamae said, declining the offer.

"Q, quit tripping. I know you got it and all, but you can just crash at the crib, on the real."

There was no more debating there, so he just gave in. "A'ight, man, we'll stay at your spot."

"That's right, you ain't got to be the big spender all the time," he joked.

Quamae shook his head. "Well, we need to hit up the mall sometime today, 'cause I ain't pack shit to go out in."

"No problem, my boy. We can hit Lennox Mall after we get this work." While Quamae and Rell continued their conversation, Chauncey walked away to make a phone call.

"Check me out, Rell. Since the work coming in at six o'clock, you know I need a stash spot until it's time for the pick up."

He patted Quamae on the shoulder. "I got you covered, bruh. Don't sweat the small stuff. We going out tonight and show these niggas how to ball."

Quamae interrupted, "Nah, you mean how the Dale ball, nigga."

They both laughed at that one. The Dale was short for Ft. Lauderdale.

As the laughter came to an end, Chauncey was walking back toward them. "So, Rell, what yawl A-Town niggas smoking on up here?"

"Oh, we smoking gas and loud up here. Come on, I got some in the house."

The trio walked into the house and Rell disappeared into one of the rooms and returned with a Ziploc bag full of weed. "Smell this. This shit right here will have you on your ass. I know the Dale don't have this," he grinned.

Of course, Chauncey grabbed the bag since he was a certified smoker. That's all he did was smoke. He put his face into the bag and inhaled the product deeply. He held his breath and released it slowly.

"What you know about that, C?"

"It's loud as fuck. It smells like it's burning, though, but you know I can't judge it if I haven't tried it first." He tossed the bag back to Rell. "Get us right."

He obliged and pulled out a grabba leaf from his pocket while he sat down to break it up. While he was busy getting them ready for a session, Chauncey and Quamae entertained themselves with the Play Station Two. During the game Quamae's cell phone alerted him of a text message. When he opened it up, he saw it was Gigi.

Gee: Wyd
Quamae: Playing a video game
Gee: R u coming over today?
Quamae: Nah
Gee: Y not?
Quamae: I'm in the A
Gee: Oh...
Quamae: I'll come see u when I get back
Gee: Ok... Be safe
Quamae: I will

No matter how hard he tried, he could not shake Gigi. He had a genuine love for her, and the feeling was mutual. It didn't matter how much time elapsed between them, he always found his way back to her. And she would always accept him back with open arms and no questions asked. He often wondered how his life would've been if he married her instead of Sasha. After all, she was there when he started from the bottom, nickeling and diming before turning to bricks.

Quamae got back into his game and waited for Rell to finish rolling up the sticky.

Chapter 5

A little after four o'clock, Rell's phone rang.

"Hello."

The male voice was loud and deep. "The birds landed early. Come on."

He jumped up, recognizing his uncle's voice immediately. "Word."

"Yeah, so go holla at the nigga."

"A'ight, we on the way." He hung up the phone and addressed his boys. "We got to go, the birds have landed."

Both of them jumped up and sat the controllers on the floor. This was the phone call they'd been waiting on, so they headed to the front door, walked outside, and jumped in the rental en route to the pickup location. Rell picked up the phone to confirm his arrival. "I'll be there in ten minutes."

"Okay, I'm already here."

"Aye, who over there with you?" Rell questioned.

"I'm solo."

"Good, you know I hate unwanted guest."

"Yeah."

"A'ight, see you in a few."

"Fo' sho."

The ride to the spot was quiet for the most part. Quamae was daydreaming, and Chauncey was stretched out in the backseat. The music from his cell phone interrupted Quamae's thoughts. He wasn't in the mood to talk to Sasha, but he picked up anyway. He was in a funk about her being out late last night. "I'm busy," then he hung up.

She called back, but he didn't answer. She called again, and this time he picked up. "Didn't I say I was busy? What do you keep calling me for?"

She snapped, "'Cause I can, that's why. What are you doing? You must be doing something?"

"Actually, I am. Now, like I said earlier, I'm busy and I will call you back when I am done. Bye." He hung up again.

They pulled up to a yellow and white house. Quamae hollered at Chauncey. "Get up, bruh, we made it."

Rell dialed the number one more time. "I'm outside."

They got out of the car and walked to the front door. The Atlanta weather was pretty decent. The cool wind was blowing even though the sun was shining bright. A heavyset dude with a Jamaican accent greeted them. "Whadap, rude boy?"

"Takin' it easy. How 'bout you?"

"I can't complain."

"Big Lou, you remember Quamae and Chauncey?"

"Yeah, I remember these boys. Whadap, homies?" he said, giving them both a fist bump.

"Coolin'," Quamae and Chauncey replied in unison.

They walked through the kitchen and went straight to the den. There was a table loaded with kilos of cocaine.

Quamae dropped the duffle bag on the floor and took a seat. "Hey, where is the money machine?" he asked, noticing there wasn't one in sight.

"Hold up," Big Lou replied. He walked over to the cabinet, opened up the door, and pulled out a cream and black money machine. "Let's count this money."

Quamae made a small hole in the package and used his pinky to scoop up a sample while Big Lou counted the money. He rubbed it on his gums to make sure it was potent. Completely satisfied with the purchase, he packed up his kilos of coke.

"Hey, Lou, you have bottled water in here?" Rell's mouth was dry from smoking.

"Check the fridge."

An hour had passed, and they were finally finished and ready to get out of dodge. Big Lou had just finished counting up the money.

"We straight?" Quamae took a seat across from Lou.

"A quarter mill, just like I knew it would be."

"Well, it was good doing business with you. I'll be back soon."

"Okay, take it easy, rude boys."

Quamae grabbed the bag and they headed out the door. They then hit the highway.

"Do you remember how to get there?"

Quamae looked at him like he asked can he fuck his bitch. "What I look like, a fool?" If he didn't remember anything else he knew exactly how to get to the trap house and Rell's house. Those two spots were important to him in case anything just so happened to go down. He cruised all the way to Rell's house to drop off the work.

***

Sasha was lying on the couch in the den thinking about her date with Blue, and it dawned on her he was like Quamae in a sense. Before they got married they went out on dates, he held doors open for her, and he catered to all of her needs. His hustle game was up to par, but he wasn't on boss status like he was now. That meant he had more time for her. Once he stepped his game up another notch and mastered his craft, he neglected her, making her fall second to the dope game.

He failed to realize all the things he did to get her were the same things he needed to do to keep her. The loneliness and her second place notch caused her to fall back into the arms of her ex-boyfriend. After her dirt was exposed, he put her back on the pedestal, but that was short-lived because now she had fallen into the arms of Blue.

Sasha picked up her cell phone sitting beside her and texted Chauncey.

Sis: What yawl doing up there?

Brother: Shit... just chillin. What up with you?

Sis: I know yawl going out

Brother: Why you say that?

Sis: No reason, but anyway when yawl coming back?

Brother: Idk y

Sis: Well me and ur bro been having issues and I wanted to surprise him when he got back.

Brother: Oh that's what's up. We'll be back Sunday morning

Sis: Okay thanks! I appreciate u

Brother: Yup

Sasha heard footsteps, and when she looked up India was coming through the door.

"How long have you been up?" India walked over and sat down on the couch beside her.

"About an hour. Are you going to the shop today?"

"No. I don't have any appointments today. I rescheduled them all."

"Is anyone running the shop for you?"

"Peaches. So, how was your date with Blue?"

She sat up erect. "O. M. Gee! I had a really good time with him. He's such a gentleman! Girl, chivalry is not dead. He opens car doors and all. He wants to see me later on tonight." The excitement in her voice was evidence she indeed had fun.

"Oh, well, I'm going home later because I have to get up early in the morning."

"I knew you were going to say that," she pouted.

"Good! Act like you know I have bills to pay and a business to run."

"Shut up!" Sasha put her hand over her mouth like she was about to throw up. "You so responsible, it's making me sick."

India shook her head and raised her hands to the ceiling. "I know, not everyone has the luxury of staying home, living lavish, and not paying a dime for it."

Already knowing what was coming next, Sasha tried to stop her before she started. She put her hand up in India's face. "Not today."

But that didn't stop India from saying what was on her mind. "You need to use some of Quamae's money and do something with it."

Sasha rolled her eyes. "I'm doing something with it. I'm spending it."

She wasn't surprised by her answer. "What I mean is what will you do if he leaves you or the money stops?"

"We're married, in case you forgot. Where the fuck is he going?" Her attitude was on high alert.

"He sells drugs, in case you forgot," India commented sarcastically.

Sasha had never considered that thought seriously, so she didn't respond. In her eyes there would always be money coming, with or without Quamae. India was the smart one in the group, and she got on everyone's nerves. She was the complete package. She had beauty and brains, not to mention she was independent and successful. Carmen and India developed the mentality that beauty and a nice body would get them far in life.

Quamae had always been her provider. She depended on him for her every want and need, so this was something she had become accustomed to. It may not seem like it to India, but there was always a price to pay, and she paid for it every time he put his hands on her or tried to control her every move.

After thinking long and hard, she responded, "I don't know, but I will cross that path when it gets here. I'm not worried about that, honestly."

Sasha turned to face India on the couch. "Well, Blue and I are chilling tonight, and I can't wait. I don't know what it is, but I'm digging him a lot."

"Maybe it's the whole idea of 'sneaking around on Quamae,'" India slickly stated, using her fingers to demonstrate quotation marks.

"I don't think it's that because this is not the first time I cheated on him."

Carmen crept into the room unannounced and interrupted a much-needed life lesson for Sasha. "Yeah, you right about that, you tramp."

"You are the fine one to talk Carmen." Sasha looked over in her direction.

"Yeah, you are absolutely right, since I am single by law; but, bitch, you are married. You don't have the right."

Sasha crossed her legs and pretended to fan herself with a hand fan like they pass out at church. "Well, the law states that if your partner isn't satisfying you, you may seek outside of the home."

Carmen burst out laughing. "The law didn't say no shit like that, a ho made that shit up."

India interjected to change the subject. "Am I the only one hungry?"

They both answered, "I am!"

"Let's order a pizza and some wings." Sasha grabbed her phone.

Carmen nodded her head. "That's cool with me, place the order."

Almost one hour later the pizza arrived, and the three of them sat on the couch eating and watching lifetime.

Thinking back on their conversation earlier, India started to talk. "Hold on. Didn't you say Quamae coming back tonight?"

"Nope, I talked to Chauncey and he said they were going to the strip club tonight."

"All I have to say is keep me on point if you plan on putting my name in it." Carmen added, "I hate to get you fucked on G.P."

India did not agree with the way Sasha gallivanted around like a single woman. "Carmen, stop encouraging her to cheat," she shook her head. "And Sasha, if you knew better, you would do better."

Waving her off, Sasha displayed much attitude toward her. "Girl, whatever! I'm grown."

"You absolutely right, grown and dependent." India stood up to leave. "I'm going home. I'll holla at yawl later."

"You must be running home to meet Steve?" She was salty about the way she had just spoken to her.

"If you must know he's meeting me at my house at seven o'clock."

Carmen paused her game of candy crush and tried to water down the tension. "Girl, when are you going to settle with Steve and stop playing with him? That man is in love with you, for real."

"Everything I do is for a reason. When I feel like going to that next level, it's going to be on my terms. Not his. He has to follow my lead."

"Keep on and he gon' leave ya ass."

"See, one thing about that is if he can't be patient and follow my lead, it wasn't real to begin with. I don't want him feeling like he running something. Feel me?"

Sasha was ready for her to go. She had worn out her welcome in less than twenty-four hours. "Girl, bye! We don't wanna hear that shit."

"I'm sure you don't." India grabbed her bag and walked out the door without another word.

Sasha looked at Carmen. "That bitch gets on my last nerve. I swear I be wanting to slap her ass."

"You know that's a saint, so stop playing." Carmen pulled herself from the couch. "I'm leaving, too. I'll talk to you later."

After India and Carmen left, she called to see what Quamae was up to, but his phone went straight to voicemail. "Damn it, Quamae." Fear flowed through her body as she dialed his number three more times. "Why you not answering your phone?"

She paced the floor several times, hoping and praying he was okay. Several minutes later her cell phone rang. Looking down at the screen, she felt a sense of relief to see his picture pop up with the word *Hubby*. "Hello."

"What's up?"

"Just sitting here worrying about you and wondering why you're not answering your phone."

"I'm good."

She exhaled a heavy gust of wind. "Are you on your way home?"

"Why?" The bass in his voice appeared out of nowhere.

"I just want to know, that's all, baby." She tried to sweeten it up to keep him from going off. "I wanted us to go out when you got back since you've been busy lately."

"Nah, we still here."

"You said tonight, so why haven't you left yet?"

Exasperation settled in and banged through the speakers. "Sound like you up to no good. Let me catch your ass doing something and it's a wrap."

"Quamae, stop tripping all the damn time."

"You think you nickel slick."

She laughed. "I don't have to wait on you to go out of town to be sneaky. If that's the case, I could do it while you here 'cause you always busy anyway."

"I see right now you gon' make me fuck you up!" he scoffed into the phone.

"I'm just being real. You make it sound like I can only fuck around on you if you out of town."

"Yeah, okay, play with me, then."

"I'm just playing, calm down."

He cut her off. "Don't try me, girl, I will kill your ass."

She sucked her teeth. "Ugh, forget it. You make me sick when you act like this."

"Well, stop saying dumb shit that will piss me off. I will be home when I get there. You just have your black ass there. Get off my line," he hung up on her.

She looked at the phone. "I got something for his ass." She called Blue.

"What's up, baby girl?"

"I'm just sitting here watching T.V. and thinking about you," she said seductively.

"Is that right?" he licked his lips because there was so much he wanted to do to her when she gave him the chance.

"Yes, it is. Is that so hard to believe?"

"No, I can believe it. I'm just messing with you."

She toyed with her wedding ring. "So, what are you doing?"

"I'm chilling at my homeboy house right now, gambling on this Madden."

"Oh, so you like playing games, huh?"

"That's the only way I play."

"How much do you play for?"

"$1,500 a game."

"What? That's crazy."

"Why is that? Based on how you dress, you could spend that on shoes or a purse."

"Yeah, that's different," she defended her spending habits.

Blue laughed, but he never took his eyes off the game. "How is that?"

"Because I'm not taking a chance, and I can see my shoes and purses."

"Ma, you are shot out. Every time I win, I see that money. Feel me?"

Sasha cut to the chase and got to the point of her call. "Well, anyway, I'm trying to see you." When she was determined to get something, she went after it no matter what the consequences were.

"Where and what time?" He was trying to see exactly what she wanted to do without him suggesting a possible sexual encounter.

"It doesn't matter to me. I just want to get out of this house."

Blue was focused on his game until she said that. "You can come by my house and chill. I will call you when I leave here. It will probably be around eight o'clock. I have some more ass to kick on the game, and then I'm out."

"Okay, I'll be waiting."

She hung up the phone, cheesing like a Cheshire cat. If only she knew Quamae's itinerary, that would make everything smooth. But in the meantime, she would go by what she knew.

Chapter 6

Chauncey, Quamae, and Rell strolled through Lenox Square Mall at a snail's pace, stopping in damn near every store until they found what they were looking for. They walked inside Macy's and made a beeline to the cologne section. Quamae purchased himself the Versace Eros gift set and walked away from the counter.

"Let's hit it."

Rell picked up his bag. "You sure about that?"

"Yeah, nigga, let's ride."

With their shopping bags in their hands, they walked out of the mall.

On the way to Rell's house, they stopped by Zaxby's to get something to eat. "When we leave here, do you need to stop by the trap?" Quamae wanted to know how much driving he had to do, because he needed some rest before going out that night.

"Nah, I'm straight. We can go straight to the crib."

After driving for thirty minutes, they pulled up at Rell's house and walked toward the door. He unlocked it and disarmed the alarm system once they were inside.

"Make yourself at home," Rell suggested. "Yawl can go ahead and fix yaself a drink. I have a stocked bar."

"Oh yeah, that's the move." Chauncey was ready to turn up. "Bring out that gas, too."

Rell came out and sat down with a few baggies. He took out a pair of scissors and started breaking the weed up on his Mary Jane plate. "So, what club yawl boys want to go to?"

"You know I want to go to Magic City, but if you want to go to Strokers, that'll work, too." Chauncey was enthused. He couldn't wait to see some ass and maybe run up in some thick shit.

"It's your call. I live here, yawl just passing through."

"Magic City it is."

Once the decision was made, Chauncey got up to fix them a cup of Grey Goose. He yelled across the room, "Bruh, you want pineapple juice or Cranberry?"

"Cranberry," he shouted back. They sat and made small talk while Chauncey was at the bar, pretending to be a bartender.

"So, how is the wife doing?" Rell asked.

"She's good."

"So, how is married life?"

Before he could respond, Chauncey walked up and handed him a cup, then sat down beside him.

"Honestly, it has its ups and downs. That shit hard work, though."

Chauncey laughed. "Man, this nigga turned into a fool since he tied the knot."

Quamae defended himself. "That's because she get out of pocket sometimes. She thinks because we're married, that's a pass to do whatever."

Chauncey couldn't wait to interrupt the conversation. "The nigga is controlling, that's what's wrong with him."

Quamae gave him the side eye. "Nigga, shut up. We have our issues, but what couple doesn't? You feel me?"

"Yeah, I do. Marriage is a beautiful thing." Rell loved to see black couples in committed relationships. He just wasn't ready to be in one.

"Aw, listen to this nigga. Let me guess, you about to get married, too, huh?" Chauncey teased.

"Hell nah, nigga. I'm not ready for that yet. The only way that's going down is if a nigga can have two or three bitches."

"Hell yeah, that's what I'm talking about," Chauncey agreed, giving Rell a fist bump.

"Yawl niggas straight foolish. I can't wait to see who gon' trap yawl asses. One of those women will change your mind," Quamae assured them.

They continued to discuss that topic while smoking and drinking. They even reminisced on the old days before any of them started hustling.

Realizing they'd been chilling for a while, Chauncey interrupted, "What time is it?"

Quamae looked at the expensive timepiece in his wrist. "Almost 10."

"Oh, well, we better get ready, then. Come on, I'll show you to the guestroom." They all stood and headed upstairs.

"Use the shower at the end of the hall," Rell explained.

Once inside the room, the duo gathered up their clothing and things to take a shower with.

"You can hop in first, I'm about to iron."

"Leave it plugged up so I can use it, too." Quamae headed for the bathroom.

"I got you."

It took all of an hour for them to get dressed. "Yawl niggas ready?" Rell asked, walking down the hall.

"Ready as we gon' be." Quamae grabbed his wallet, money, and stuffed it into his pockets.

They all walked downstairs and made their way out the front door. Rell unlocked the doors to the truck and climbed in the front seat. Quamae rode shotgun and Chauncey sat in the back seat. Rell turned on the stereo, grabbed a CD, and put it in the disc player. The system was beating like he had King Kong in the trunk. Anyone could hear them coming a mile away. The truck sat up in the air – twenty-six inches off the ground, to be exact, compliments of West Coast Customs.

After riding for about twenty minutes, they finally arrived at Magic City. He pulled into the parking lot, made sure everything was tucked away, stepped out, and set the alarm. The line was very long, but they were able to walk to the front since he knew the bouncer. He walked up to the door.

"What's up, Big D?" Rell dapped him up.

"Nothing much, homie. Taking it easy, hoping it's a good night and I don't have to slam one of these clowns tonight."

Rell laughed. "Now, you know these fools can't handle they liquor."

"They better do something, because they know how I get down," he folded his arms across his chest.

"Yeah, man, I know. But how is the crowd so far?"

"So far so good."

Rell glanced behind him. "Oh, Big D, these my homies, Quamae and Chauncey. They from the Dale."

"What up?" Big D replied, dapping them up as well.

"Coolin'," they both replied.

"How much?" Rell attempted to pull money from his pocket.

"Yawl good, homie. I know you gon' show love up in there."

"And you know this."

They walked inside the club, and it was a decent crowd. A stripper named Sexy Black, wearing an all-black two-piece bathing suit, approached them. "What's up, Rell?" She smiled while giving him a hug.

"You already know," he winked. She already knew what time it was when he said that. It was him and her later. She didn't mind because he looked out for her descent every time he came in the building.

"Well, I'm about to go on stage in a few, so I'll see you afterward."

"Yeah." He slapped her ass when she walked away. The three of them posted in a corner next to the stage and watched two females grind on each other. They danced to Future's cut *Thought it Was a Drought*.

Chauncey was very pleased with the performance he was seeing. "Now, that's what I'm talking about."

"Hell yeah." Quamae didn't blink, wink, or move a muscle. "Ain't nothing like watching two bitches fucking each other."

There was a crowd of guys standing around throwing money and watching everyone's fantasy. Two women! They slithered on each like two snakes preparing to mate. They moved seductively, then engaged in a deep lip lock just like the lyrics to the song. Quamae looked to his left and saw a female approaching. The half-naked woman walked up to Rell and said, "Hey, baby. What you drinking tonight? The usual?"

"Come on now, you know better."

She smiled at him. "Okay, I'll be right back."

Chauncey looked at Rell. "Damn, nigga, how many hos do you have in this bitch?"

"Nah it ain't like that." Rell grinned.

He gave him a look that said he was full of shit. "Well, shit, tell me what it's like. I'm trying to get on something before I leave this bitch."

"I fucked a few of these chicks in here." Rell patted him on the back. "I got you."

"Yeah, hook me up. Don't be stingy with the punanny." Chauncey wasn't taking no for an answer.

Rell looked at Quamae. "You want some A-Town pussy before you go back to the Dale?"

"Nah, I'm good."

"That's that marriage bullshit, huh? You can have that, because I don't want no parts of that."

Chauncey began searching the club for something he could snatch up right quick. "Man, it's some bad bitches in here."

"Yeah, I know. I got a bad bitch for you. She'll set you straight."

"Where she at?" he asked.

"Probably in the back. Sit tight."

The D.J. made an announcement: "And, coming to the stage, we have Magical."

This chick was bad. She stood about 5'5", weighing about a buck forty with chocolate-covered skin. She was shaped like an hourglass. She wore her hair pulled back into an *I Dream of Jeannie* ponytail with a Chinese bang. She climbed the pole, slid down slowly, legs straight up in the air, and paused. She clapped her booty cheeks together for what seemed like forever, then dropped to the floor with a split. Every man in the building started pulling out money. Just as she was finishing her routine, the waitress walked back over with a bottle of Grey Goose, cranberry juice, and cups. Chauncey turned around, went inside his pocket.

"Hey, Ma, can you bring me back some ones?"

She paused and looked Chauncey up and down in a sexual way. "How much you want?"

He pulled out a knot. "Five-hundred." He placed the bills in her hand.

"I'll be right back," she assured him and walked away.

By this time Magical has finished performing. Stuffing all her money into a trash bag, she walked off stage and bumped into Rell on her way to the dressing room. "How you doing?"

She blushed. "I'm good."

He paced his hand on her waist and whispered in her ear. "Check this out, my round want some private time. He from out of town. Can you do that?"

She glanced over to see what she was getting into and was happy to see he was a fine piece of man candy. She licked her full, luscious lips and winked at him. "Yeah, let me go and freshen up, and I'll be right back. Don't move, handsome."

Rell looked at Chauncey. "She'll be back, bruh."

"Bet that up."

They all fixed cups and waited on the waitress to return.

The club started to get thick after midnight. The waitress finally returned with Chauncey's ones, wrapped with the money bands. "Here you go, handsome."

"Thanks, Ma." Then he handed her a twenty-dollar tip. Rell and Quamae handed her a thousand dollars for some more ones as well.

When she left, they couldn't wait to clown him. "Hey, handsome," they mimicked the waitress and burst out into laughter.

"They gon' keep calling this nigga that, and he gone think handsome is his name." Rell was on a roll.

The waitress returned fairly quickly this time around, maybe because she was trying to get some play from the kid. After they were all situated, Rell gave her two bills for another bottle. Minutes later, Magical returned and was introduced to Chauncey. She took one look at him, grabbed his hand, and walked him to the V.I.P. section with no hesitation.

The next stripper to hit the stage was Mercedes. As she started to dance, Quamae's eyes were trained on her until the voice over the speaker introduced her twin, Infinity. They were identical, but their tattoos on their sides made it easy to tell them apart. Their bodies were stacked nicely, just like Serena Williams, the tennis player. He knew he had to have Infinity, and married or not, he was fucking her that night. Yeah, yeah, it was a double standard, but Sasha brought that on herself with those slick-ass comments earlier.

The twins were dancing to a slow song, but then it stopped abruptly. The D.J switched up the tempo, but not before he announced a message. "If you got a hater in the building, stick your middle finger up. You see these badass twins? They keep them some haters, so we got a song especially for yawl."

He let the beat rip and *Fuck You* by Yo Gotti dropped hard in the club. Funny thing, that's exactly how Quamae was feeling about Sasha. He rapped along with it because he felt that shit in his soul.

The club was lit up off of Gotti. Everybody in that bitch was moving and rapping out loud. Rell made a close observation of his boy watching the show, so he teased him. "Bruh, you changed your mind yet?"

He nodded his head. "I got to get at that, bruh." He kept his eyes on her. "The bitch is bad. A nigga wasn't tryin' to cheat, but fuck it. My bitch probably laid up wit' a nigga right now." He was still salty about the way Sasha talked to him earlier.

Quamae watched her every move until she walked off stage and made her way into the crowd. His eyes were glued to her every second of the minute. He watched her as she walked into the dressing room, patiently waiting on her arrival.

Ten minutes later she bounced through the crowd, looking in Quamae's direction, and they locked eyes. She walked up on him. "Did you enjoy the show?"

He looked at her ass, then back at her face, then handed her a cup. "I sure did."

She accepted the drink he offered her, and they carried on with their conversation. Fifteen minutes and an empty cup later, she was pulling up a chair so he could sit down. She straddled him so they were face-to-face and gave him a lap dance. She was grinding, gyrating, and bouncing on his lap. Quamae could feel his erection trying to bust through his pants like the Hulk.

She bent over in front of him to touch her toes and made her ass jump. He watched in excitement as he grabbed a handful of ass, slapping it to the beat of the music. That ass quaked like thunder. His hands explored her body, starting from her breasts all the way down to her pussy. He rubbed her and played with her clit right in the open until he couldn't take it anymore. The alcohol started to kick in and take over his thinking. The only thing on his mind was fucking, and the way she was teasing him made him feel she wanted it, too.

He whispered in her ear, "Let's go to somewhere a little more private."

She got up, and he followed her to the back where it was dark and empty. He sat down on the couch and she knelt down in front of him. She started to unbuckle his belt, then his pants. She stuck her hands in his boxers and massaged his thick, throbbing pole.

Lowering her head, she licked the tip of the head and then eased him into her mouth. Up and down, up and down was the only motion that could be seen in the dark room. Quamae grabbed the back of her head and rammed all nine inches of him down her throat until she pulled back. She was a pro since she didn't gag, and he liked that. She took it all in like a champ.

She sucked and sucked until he exploded, swallowing all of his babies. Quamae reached inside his pocket and pulled out a magnum. He put it on carefully, making sure everything was intact. Infinity straddled him one more time, easing all of him inside her.

Slowly riding him, she closed her eyes and moved her hips to the beat. Two minutes into it she picked up speed and bounced up and down on it. He had both hands on her hips, pumping in and out until he exploded for a second time. He snatched the rubber off and she cleaned up the leftover nut lingering on his limp friend. He stood up to buckle his pants, handed her two bills, and disappeared into the crowd without saying another word.

Quamae went back to their spot and found Chauncey fixing another drink. "Where you been at, bruh?" He recognized the change in his now-relaxed demeanor.

"A private area."

Chauncey was a little excited about his response. "With who?"

The smirk on his face was dead giveaway, not that he was hiding any info. "Infinity."

"That's my nigga. Rell went in the back with that ho we seen up front."

Quamae nodded to acknowledge what he just said. "Did you get what you was looking for?"

Chauncey was happier than a kid on Christmas morning. "Damn right I did."

Quamae fixed another drink while they waited on Rell to come back. Thirty minutes had passed and he still hadn't shown up. "Man, where this nigga at?" The irritation was clear in his voice, but he was more concerned than anything.

"He's buying up all the pussy." He turned to face Quamae. "Why, you ready to go?"

"Nah, I'm good. I just want to make sure nothing popped off."

He wasn't paranoid or nothing like that. Quamae took calculated steps with every move he made, and being cautious was his number one rule. He lived by that because at any given time unnecessary beef had a way of rearing its ugly head.

Chauncey laughed at his seriousness. "Nah, man, calm down. He's good."

"Bruh, you don't know that." He wasn't convinced everything was copasetic.

"Yes, I do." Chauncey sipped his drink.

"How do you know?"

"'Cause here he comes right now."

Sure enough, Rell walked up with his drink in hand, grinning. He had the same pleasing look on his face they had moments ago.

"What the hell in your cup?"

Rell looked down in it as if he had forgotten. "That dirty sprite."

They stayed in the club for another hour, getting dances, popping bottles, and throwing money. Finally they decided it was a wrap and headed out the door.

Chapter 7

Their brief trip to Atlanta had finally come to an end, and it was time for them to head back to the sunshine state. The sun was shining a little less through the dark clouds. The air was humid, and the earthy scent in the air indicated rain was coming. They were on their way to the repair shop Reggie owned so they could remove the bumper to hide the work. It took about two hours to get that done, and by the time they finished it was starting to drizzle.

"That's just what we need, some fucking rain," Quamae happily stated. Trafficking dope in the rain was sweet as pie. Rainy weather meant no state troopers. No state troopers meant a sweet ride home. He would still have to be aware of his surroundings.

"You going to the crib or the trap?" Quamae asked Rell.

"Nah, bruh, yawl g'on ahead and hit that highway. We don't need to be riding around with all that work. Hit me up when yawl make it, though." Rell walked up and gave Quamae and Chauncey a hug instead of a fist bump this time.

"Be easy, bruh." They got in the car and pulled off.

Chauncey yawned. "Man, I'm tired as fuck."

"Nah, nigga, you gotta shake that shit off. I need you to stay up with me."

He yawned again. "Dat part."

"Ain't no sleep, bihh." Laughter erupted in the car like a volcano.

"So, you Plies now?" Chauncey adjusted his seat.

"Nah."

"Damn, I had a good-ass time last night. I can't remember the last time we did some wild shit like that."

Quamae laughed. "Stop the bullshit, you always wild."

"I know, and I love it, but I did some shit I ain't done in a long time."

Quamae hit the interstate, and it was smooth sailing from there. He and Chauncey discussed last night's events detail-for-detail, neither one of them leaving out any small factor. Traffic was flowing, considering the rain, and there wasn't a Georgia patrol car in sight. The sound of Chauncey's cell phone stopped the conversation.

"Yo," he answered.

"What's up, baby?"

"On my way back to Florida. What's good witcha?"

"Missing you, that's all."

"Bullshit!"

"I can't wait to see you."

"Is that right?"

For the duration of their conversation he glanced out the window, observing the scenery. He explained to her when he got back, he would be busy for the first two days, but he would make time for her. They laughed and joked for about 30 minutes before they hung up.

Quamae's attention was on the highway. He was also in deep thought about his marriage, wondering if he made a terrible mistake taking those vows with her. When he was with Gigi he never had to worry about her cheating or the slick wrap from her mouth. She was submissive and he loved that about her.

The wheels in his head were spinning full circle. He picked up his phone and called Sasha. She picked up right before the voicemail caught it.

"What the fuck are you doing?"

"Here we go again," she huffed into the phone. "I'm at home, alone, doing absolutely nothing."

"Fix your fuckin' tone when you talkin' to me."

"Why do you have to keep calling with the same attitude?"

"Where were you last night?"

Sasha put the phone on speaker and sat it on the bed next to her. "I was home."

Quamae bit down on his lip and shook his head slowly. "This shit not working for us, 'cause I don't think you want to be married. And I'm not about to force it."

Sasha sat up and stared at the phone. "Did I say that?"

"Your actions showing it, though."

"You make me act like this. Why can't you just trust me?"

"You make that impossible to do."

Her blood began to boil and anger settled in. "You must have another bitch that you fuckin', and now you wanna put the blame on me."

"I just don't trust you."

"I shouldn't trust you since you're never home. You always say that it's work, but I don't know that." She was now clutching the phone in her hand.

"My pockets show it, though." He took a deep breath and they both fell silent for thirty seconds. "Listen, I'll talk to you later."

Sasha hung up without another word.

Chauncey looked over at his best friend. "Man, what's going on with yawl?"

Quamae looked straight ahead. He didn't blink, respond, or nothing. He just focused on the road. After a solid minute passed, he finally answered. "It's all good."

"Come on, man, here you go with the bull." He looked at Quamae and knew something either happened or was about to happen. He knew his brother like a book, and he knew something wasn't sitting well with him. "What's up, bruh?" He refused to give up until he got an answer.

Quamae took a deep breath and told Chauncey every-thing, starting with how she came home late the other night. About how he had flipped out on her and what he did. Chauncey didn't reply at first. He listened. Quamae contin-ued to tell him about how deep down inside he knew she was cheating, and if he caught her he would probably kill her. They had a heart-to-heart conversation.

"Bruh, on some G shit, you have to figure out what you gon' do. Truthfully, I just think you feel that way because you were always the one breaking a bitch heart. Now that you're in love, you feel like that shit gon' come back to you."

Quamae let his words seep into his head because he knew it was a true statement, and he was afraid of karma. "That might be true, but I hustle too hard to make sure she straight. She don't do shit, but that's because I didn't want her to work. As a man, my job is to provide for her, and her job is to respect me and do what I tell her to do. I don't even trust the bitch."

"If you don't trust her, then you have a serious problem on your hands. I mean, if it's like that, take a break from her and see what happens. If shit that bad, then get a di-vorce."

Quamae shook his head. "Yeah, I thought about that."

Chauncey sat up in his seat. "What? Separation or a di-vorce?"

"Divorce."

"Damn, bruh, it's that bad?"

"Man, this bitch had the audacity to tell me I don't have to be out of town to cheat because I'm not home anyway. I feel like wringing that bitch neck when I get back."

Chauncey sympathized with his thinking. "Hell nah! She ain't say no shit like that."

For the life of him he couldn't fathom why she would want to put something like that in his head. She knew damn well he was a fool at heart. He completely understood his frustration, but completely disapproved of the physical abuse he subjected her to. He tried to stay out of their business because, at the end of the day, she would still be there. If anything happened in his presence, he would leave or break it up. He never took sides. Chauncey grew up in a single parent home, and that's the one thing his mom taught him. She told him over and over, *Chauncey, never put your hands on a woman. If you have to beat her, you don't need her.*

"Man, dead that shit. Whatever she got going on will surface eventually. Don't let her get you out of character like that."

He agreed. "I know. I just don't trust her, and I wanna leave, but she rode for a nigga when I got jammed up. A nigga probably wouldn't be here if it wasn't for her."

He thought back to that dreadful night when he hustled the blocks and one of the jack boys caught him slipping. Sasha snuck up behind the dude and blew his brains out. "Sometimes I feel obligated to take care of her, and other times I'm thinkin' *fuck her*. I think I'ma just break her ass off with a moderate care package and send her on her way."

"That might not be a bad idea, bruh."

Quamae turned up the stereo and let his mind go elsewhere. Chauncey leaned back in the passenger seat and started rapping with the music. They had been traveling for about three-and-a-half hours with six or seven to go, depending on traffic. Chauncey slept for the next half hour until he was awakened by the loud, blaring sounds of sirens.

He jumped up. "What the fuck?" he panicked.

"Just lay back and chill." Quamae was very calm when he spoke. "I got this under control."

He pulled over and waited on the officer to approach the vehicle. He watched in the rearview mirror to see what was taking so long. The officer finally exited the patrol car, walked up, and tapped on the window. Quamae let it down.

"License and registration, please." He was cocky and stern with his instructions.

Quamae reached for his wallet in his back pocket. "Sure, no problem." He then reached in the glove box for the rental agreement and handed them to the trooper. He knew everything would come back straight, but he wasn't sure why he was stopped in the first place. With all the police brutality and shooting of the black population, he kept a cool head. The last thing he needed was to be shot and killed for no reason. The bricks wouldn't be found unless they were tipped off, but he wasn't worried about that.

Quamae kept the officer in the rearview mirror, watching his every move. Those bitches couldn't be trusted, point blank, period. Five minutes later, which seemed like an eternity, he finally returned.

"Sir, could you step out of the vehicle for a minute?"

"As soon as you tell me why you stopped me. I know my rights, and you have no valid reason to make me get out of my vehicle. I haven't violated any laws or regulations." He was smart thanks to his attorney, who kept him up-to-date on his rights.

"Well, your car fits the description of one that was involved in a kidnapping a few miles back."

Quamae knew the officer was lying, and he wasn't about to let him check shit. "Well, do you see a child in here?" he said sarcastically. "And that's funny, because I haven't seen an Amber alert since I've been driving.

"No, I don't. This is why I need you to pop the trunk."

Quamae was getting frustrated. "What? Are you serious?"

Chauncey responded. "Man, just let the man check the trunk so we can go. It ain't shit back there."

"Listen, sir, I'm not trying to give you a hard time. Just pop the trunk, and if there is nothing back there, you're free to go."

He looked at Chauncey. "Man, record this shit."

Quamae popped the trunk and stepped out so the officer could peek in. Once he cleared them the officer hopped back into his car and took off. Needless to say, he was pissed off.

Quamae did the same. Relieved they were in the clear, both of them sighed and thanked God. Stashing the work in the bumper and frame of the car was a golden idea. Police problems were the last thing they needed, and that's why Quamae always made sure his license, name, and face were clean. If and when push came to shove and he had to make an impromptu trip out of town, there wouldn't be any problems.

They were back on I-95, headed to the dirty south.

Chapter 8

Sasha sat on the couch with the remote control in her hand, flipping through channels. Cable was such a waste of money, she thought to herself. Finally she stumbled onto some breaking news in Broward County. They were investigating the murder of a 17-year-old boy who was gunned down at a block party. The police had not made an arrest yet. The news was so depressing she changed the station.

"I guess I can watch some videos," she whispered to herself.

She got up to and went into the kitchen to fix a drink. Relaxation was what she needed since Quamae dropped the trust bomb on her. Returning to the living room, she took a seat on the plush leather sofa. Sipping slowly from the champagne glass, the contents felt good going down her throat. This was the only time she could sit back, relax, and enjoy the peacefulness in her home.

When Quamae was there, it was everything but quiet. If he wasn't ranting and raving, he was on that damn phone giving orders. That annoyed her.

The effects of the drink were slowly kicking in, and she started to think about her future. *What if Quamae left? What would I have? Could I make it without him?* Those questions played over and over in her mind. After all, he clearly stated the marriage wasn't working, and now it had her thinking if she made a mistake. Her thoughts bounced around in her head like a Ping-Pong ball between Blue and Quamae.

Sasha knew dealing with Blue was like playing Russian roulette, but the thought of it made her want to pursue him even more. The way he complimented and touched her made her feel sexy and desired, and that was what she lacked in her marriage. His touch alone sent chills flowing through her body. She had to give it to him, though, he was fine, and that made her want him badly, so she gave him a call.

"How are you doing today?" she asked.

"I'm feeling okay, and you?"

"I'm okay, just sipping on this champagne and watching television. I was also thinking about you. I would love to see you again tonight. I enjoyed keeping you company last night."

He laughed. "That's sweet. You know you can see me, just say the word."

She sipped her drink. "Um, I got it like that?"

"Only if you want it like that."

"That's fair game. Do you want to pick me up?"

There was a pregnant pause before he responded. "Yeah. If you want me to."

"Yeah, I don't feel like driving." Creeping with a nigga's chick was one thing, but disrespecting his house was another. "Where is your dude?"

"Oh, baby, you good. He's still out of town," she assured him.

"I hope so, 'cause I'm not trying to cause any problems on another man's territory."

"Trust me, I wouldn't put you in the middle of any type of danger intentionally." She knew she was playing with fire, but just like a curious child, she needed to feel the heat to realize she shouldn't touch it.

"Danger. Is that right? So, fucking with you is dangerous, huh?" When she came over to see him, he was tempted to touch her, but decided to wait. He knew tonight was the night he would take that dive. There was no need in wasting time since her dude was out of town.

"Maybe, and that makes it more interesting, don't you think?"

"Nah, I love my life too much." He was serious.

"Me, too. So, what time are you picking me up?"

"Whenever you ready for me."

"How about nine o'clock?"

"That's a bet."

"Okay, I will call you when I'm ready and give you directions."

"A'ight, hit me up later."

A few hours later, she pulled herself from the couch and headed upstairs to the bedroom. Once she was there, she turned on the light to the walk-in closet. "What should I wear?" she asked herself.

She rummaged through clothes, clothes, and more clothes. She was so indecisive. "Come on, Sasha, get it together," she told herself.

Finally she made up her mind to keep it simple by selecting a pair of joggers and retro Jays. She laid everything out on the bed and walked into the bathroom.

The only thing on her mind was Blue. She didn't have a care in the world. She wanted to spend her last night with him before Quamae got back tomorrow.

Removing all of her clothing, she stepped into the tub with her champagne glass in her hand. She then reached for the remote to the stereo and hit the power button. The sound of Sade's *No Ordinary Love* was playing, and it was soothing to her mind and body, as she closed her eyes in relaxation.

After a 15-minute rest, she washed her body from head to toe. Stepping from the tub, she wrapped the towel around her body and went into the bedroom. Time sort of flew by, because it was almost eight. She applied lotion to her body and put on her clothes. Once the final touches were complete, she sprayed on some perfume and called Blue. "I'm ready, so you can come now."

"Where am I coming to?" He picked up his keys and walked out of his bedroom.

"I live in this community called Spring Valley Estates in Pembroke Pines. If you take I-95, you get off on—" She was cut off mid-sentence.

"You don't have to explain it. I know exactly where it is. I will call you as soon as I get in the neighborhood."

"Okay," she responded.

As she lay across the bed, she realized she hadn't spoken to Carmen since earlier that day, but not with India at all. She thought about calling India, but quickly changed her mind. India could get beside herself at times and be a little judgmental. That's the one thing Sasha hated about her. They bumped heads a lot when it came to discussions about being independent and not depending on a nigga to take care of her. India tried to put her up on getting established, but she ain't trying to hear that. As long as she had Quamae, why should she worry?

Thirty minutes had passed, and still no Blue. She decided to go down in the kitchen and fix herself another glass of champagne. She went back upstairs, picked up her phone, and realized she had a missed call. It was from Quamae. She called back.

He didn't bother saying hello. "What are you doing?"

"Nothing," she answered dryly.

"Why didn't you answer your phone?"

Irritated with his questions, she took a deep breath and exhaled into the phone. "Why do you keep asking me that? If you don't trust me that much, why are you with me?"

"Who the fuck do you think you talking to like that? Bitch, I will come through this phone and choke the life out of you. Now, let's try this shit again. Why the fuck didn't you answer your phone?"

"I was downstairs in the kitchen, sorry, damn."

"This that shit I'm talkin' 'bout, but I want you to act bad when you see me in the morning," he reiterated from their earlier conversation.

"Yeah." The phone was silent all of a sudden. She looked down and realized he had hung up.

As soon as she sat the phone down, it started ringing. She wasn't in the mood to argue with Quamae again, so she decided to send him the voicemail. When she picked the phone to hit end, it wasn't Quamae. It was Blue. She picked up the phone and gave him the house number. She had violated the number one rule of the house, and that was bringing someone to their home.

Quamae always told her to never bring anybody to where he laid his head. Chauncey, Carmen, and India were exceptions to the rule. His main focus was keeping her safe, especially when he was out of town. He would lay down the town if anyone fucked with her, trying to get him or his money.

Sasha grabbed her handbag and keys, then headed outside to wait on Blue. A set of headlights was coming up the street as she stood out by the mailbox. The truck stopped in front of the house. Blue rolled down the window. "Hey, sexy."

She blushed. Just the sound of his voice made her quiver. She climbed into the truck and they pulled off.

The night was cool and breezy, a perfect time for sex on the beach. The moon was full, and the stars lit up the heavenly sky like the Fourth of July, even though they were only in the month of May. They rode in silence. The only sound that of Jaheim playing.

"So, where are we headed?" she asked.

"I thought it would be nice if we hung out on the beach."

While he answered her question, his eyes were locked in on her thighs. He looked her up and down until their eyes met. He knew she was beautiful, but tonight she looked better than the last time. "We can go wherever you want."

She couldn't remember the last time she and Quamae, strolled the beach hand-in-hand, just talking and enjoying each other's company.

The scenery on A1A was beautiful. There were big, beautiful houses with gorgeous water views and nice yachts in the back of the houses on the docks. Shortly they pulled up into the Beach Place parking garage and grabbed a ticket from the machine. After he parked, Blue stepped out of the truck, walked to the passenger side, and opened the door for her.

She smiled. "What a gentleman." Chivalry wasn't dead after all.

"Of course. Especially when I have a beautiful woman on my arm."

They walked out of the garage and onto the strip. Ft Lauderdale Beach was very nice, and the crowd was fairly big, but not over-crowded. All walks of life were out that night: blacks, whites, Spanish, and Asians. They strolled on the beach holding hands and talking about life in general until they ended up at Fat Tuesday's. For two hours they played a few games of pool, indulged in some wings and fries and their world-famous daiquiri mixed drinks.

"Do you need a refill before we leave?"

She picked up her cup and shook it. "Yeah, I'll have another." They walked back to the bar to get two refills before returning downstairs to complete their walk.

After they conversed a little more, Sasha realized Blue was not the average drug dealer. He was an intellectual young man. He attended the University of Miami, studying medicine. He dropped out of school when his mother lost her job. He felt like it was his duty to step up and take care of his mother. She rejected his offer to move back home and help out, fearing he wouldn't return to school and finish what he started.

That was two years ago, and he was knee-deep in the drug game. He planned on going back to college in the fall so he could make an honest living. The drug game was not all it appeared to be. Fast money, flashy cars, clothes, and women were included with the game, along with beef, jail time, and looking over one's shoulders 24/7. There was always a price to pay, and sometimes it could be fatal. She also found out he was younger than her, but very mature to be 22.

They found a quiet and secluded spot where they could sit and talk without any interruptions. She was really feeling him, now more than ever. He had so much potential, and that was a bonus in her book. She took advantage of the moment and opened up about her relationship with Quamae.

She crossed her legs and got comfortable. "I need to tell you something I haven't shared with you, but I don't want to be judged."

Blue leaned his head to the side and looked into her baby browns. "Babygirl, I'm not God, therefore I can't judge you." He reached for her hand and held it. "I respect all honesty."

"Well," her heart was beating at a rapid pace while she explained. "I'm married, and I have been for two years now, but I'm not happy."

Her confession was more serious than he thought. "Why is that?"

"He's controlling because he takes care of me, and he has put his hands on me more times than I care to share." She looked away, feeling the embarrassment kick in. Explaining the pain she endured took her back to the nights when she felt helpless. The tingling sensation in her eyes alerted her that tears would soon follow. She fought back the tears so she wouldn't appear weak. "I feel trapped at times."

Blue used his free hand to tilt her chin so she could look at him. His heart went out to her because he could hear the pain in her words. "Listen to me, Ma. As long as you are dependent on him, he will never change. He will always feel like he owns you until you start taking care of yourself."

"He doesn't want me to work."

He moved his hand. "Of course not, he can tell you what to do and when to do it. Find your passion, and your strength to leave will emerge. I promise you that. If that's what you really want to do. Too many women give up their lives and independency to be housewives."

His words were soothing to her soul, and she was happy she was honest with him. Everything he said made sense to her, so she figured she should take heed of what he said. Compared to India's advice, it sounded better hearing it from a man's point of view.

Blue sat closer to her and put his arms around her.

The sound of the splashing waves was therapeutic to her heartache. She was in a happy place, cuddled up with her new boo. They glanced up at the moon that lit the night. The view was spectacular. It was like the universe swallowed them whole, and they were left in a dark, empty space.

He looked her into her eyes and could see the pain in them. "Everything is going to be okay." He leaned closer to her face and kissed her lips. He worked his way from her mouth down to her neck, igniting her body. Her hormones were running wild. She moaned softly in his ear and placed her hand in his lap. She could feel his penis harden and rise.

She rubbed up against him and whispered, "I wanna have sex with you."

"You sure about that?"

"Yes."

"Come on, let's go." Grabbing her hand he helped her off the ground then picked up their cups.

They walked across the street to the nearest hotel, the Yankee Clipper. They checked in at the front counter and took the elevator up to the sixth floor. The sexual tension between the two was amazing. They couldn't keep their hands off of each other during the ride up.

No time was wasted when they made it into the room. Sasha sat down on the bed and removed her shoes. Blue walked over to her and kissed her again.

The hotel setting made the kiss more intense than the first time. Clothing started to hit the floor as they caressed each other. He scooped her up, legs around his waist, then sat her down on the table. He pushed her legs open and French kissed her clit.

"Ooh," she moaned, gripping the edge of the table. The coolness from his mouth made her quiver. "Argh!"

He flicked his tongue across her clit and inserted two of his fingers. Her hips rocked back and forth, her breathing becoming rapid. He allowed her to come before they switched positions.

Blue put on a condom in record time, grabbed her legs, and put them up on his shoulders. Gripping her waist, he pulled her closer, digging for that G-spot.

"Blue!" she yelled, stroking his ego, making him go harder. He was focused.

The inside of her walls stretched to meet his girth. He hit places she thought were only accessible to Quamae. As the old folks would say, he was well endowed. She wrapped her legs around his waist to slow him down, but his speed never decreased. She bit down on her lip and enjoyed every thrust. Sasha squeezed her muscles together.

"Grr," he grunted, when he felt her muscles clutch around his shaft so tightly. He needed to switch positions, so he carried her to the bed and laid her down, flipping her on her stomach. He rubbed the tip of the head across her lips and slid inside, taking long, deep strokes.

"Oh yes!" she cried out while throwing it back.

"Oh shit!" Blue shouted. He slowed down and pulled out. "The rubber just popped."

Sasha wasn't fazed or paying attention. He removed the remnants of the rubber and tossed it on the floor. He looked around for the rest of the condoms, but in the moment of passion they seemed to be too far away. He re-entered her from behind and took a few more pumps. Feeling her with no barrier had him in heaven.

"Get on top," he demanded. He lay on his back and she straddled him. "My pullout game strong, but ride me with caution."

Sasha smiled and eased down on him slowly, twirled her hips. "I'll try." She placed her hands on his chest and bounced on him hard.

"Oh shit, ride that dick." He caressed her breasts and squeezed her nipples gently.

She closed her eyes and rode him to the melody of her own music orchestrated in her head. Blue gripped her cheeks and pushed his pelvis upward, meeting her thrusts.

"Damn, bae, this shit good, but you gotta slow down."

"Un-uh." It felt so good she didn't want to slow down.

"I'm about to come, get up."

She continued to grind on him. "Ooh, me too."

His muscles contracted and his semen spewed from the head. "I'm nuttin', get up." When she didn't budge, he lifted her up and used his hand to pull out. It was already dripping, so he stroked the shaft to release what was left. "Shit," he panted. "That was good."

Sasha lay down beside him and cuddled up next to him. "What does this make us? Knowing what you know about me?" she whispered.

Blue chuckled. "Probably parents."

A few hours later Sasha rolled over and noticed the time on the clock said 4:42 a.m. "Fuck!" she whispered. She knew she had to get up and go home before Quamae made it back. She made a mad dash to the bathroom, turning on the shower to wash away the stickiness Blue left behind.

She got dressed quickly and woke up Blue. He got up and used the bathroom, then got dressed. They walked out of the hotel hand-in-hand, making their way to the parking garage.

Destiny Skai

Chapter 9

On the way to her place, they drove in silence. Her mind was on her husband. She was praying to God he didn't catch her. Sasha's actions might have showed otherwise, but she was afraid of him. It just wasn't enough to make her stop since her behavior was something embedded in her since she was a child.

"What's wrong?" he asked.

"Nothing." She gave a half smile. "I'm fine," she said while touching his hand.

Soon they were pulling up in front of the house. It appeared to be dark, so she was sure she beat him home. Thank God. She breathed a sigh of relief, then leaned over, kissed him on the lips, and got out of the truck. "Go ahead, I'm okay. I'll call you as soon as I'm in the door."

"Nah, I can't do that. I'll watch you go in."

"Go ahead, I'm good."

"Call me when you get inside."

"I will."

Sasha walked up the driveway toward the door with her keys in hand. Just as she passed the bushes, she felt a blow to the back of the head, sending her into a daze.

"Who the fuck you just got out the truck with?"

The sound of Quamae's voice made her heart stop. She looked back to see if Blue was still out there, but he wasn't.

Quamae knocked her to the ground, stood over her, and squeezed her throat. She was kicking and trying to scream, but his grip was extremely tight. She attempted to pry his fingers from her neck, but was unsuccessful. Tears rolled down her face.

"Bitch, I'ma beat yo' ass. I knew you was fuckin' around. I hope that nigga paid you."

Gasping for air, she tried to speak. "Quamae I—"
He slapped her.

Whap!

"Shut up! I don't wanna hear no bullshit-ass story." He grabbed Sasha by her arms and dragged her from outside all the way to the living room. He locked the door and set the alarm behind him.

"All this shit I do for you, and this how you repay me?" He slapped her twice more.

Whap! Whap!

His eyes were watery, but they never left the sockets. His heart was aching. He was taking federal chances to provide for her, and she was creeping with the next man. She attempted to run, but he was like a raging bull chasing after his prey.

He grabbed her by the hair and dragged her upstairs. She could feel her hair popping from her scalp, so she crawled on her knees to keep him from snatching her bald.

"Stop, please," she begged in between sobs. He looked at her like she was stupid.

"Ho, I give you whatever you want, and you out here laying on your back for the next nigga."

She cried out, "It's not like that."

"Bitch, don't insult my intelligence." He hit her in the eye with a closed fist.

She screamed and covered her face with her hands. "You didn't give me a chance to explain." Her eye swelled up as soon as he made contact.

He paced the floor back and forth, rubbing his head. "Explain for what? I know what I saw." He was losing his mind, and then all of her slick comments resurfaced in his head. He walked to the closet and grabbed his leather belt.

"All you saw me do was get out of a truck. I didn't do anything, Quamae, I swear." She didn't notice the belt in his hand until she looked up. "Please don't hit me with that," she cried, scooting backward into the corner.

"You expect me to believe that shit?" He stood in front of her, prepared to discipline her like the child she was. He spoke through gritted teeth. "I'm gon' ask you one more time, who the fuck was that in the truck?" He held his hand up to keep her from talking. "Before you answer me, I want you to think before you lie to me again."

"He's nobody," she cried.

That triggered Quamae, so he grabbed her by the ankle, pulled her from the corner, and let the belt do the talking. The leather stung her skin like a swarm of killer bees. She screamed out in agony. She couldn't believe he was beating her ass, literally, like she was his child. Sweat was dripping all over his face into his eyes. He grabbed the bottom of his shirt to clean his face.

He looked down at her in pure disgust. "You ready to tell the truth? If not, we can do this all day." When he didn't get an answer from her, he unleashed the belt on her again, breaking her skin. She yelped in pain, looking at the blood dripping from her flesh.

"Ow!" she wailed. The agony in her voice was like pulling teeth with pliers. She moved around on the floor like a fish out of water, trying to grab the belt. "Please stop! I'm sorry. Please!"

"You better tell the truth, or your life will end right here."

"Please don't do this. I'm not cheating." Tears and snot bubbles covered her face.

There was nothing she could say to justify what she did. He had all the proof he needed. Quamae was about to strike her again, but she lifted her hands to block it. He paused when he got a good glimpse of her finger. He looked at her sideways. "Where is your ring?"

"I took it off when I was cleaning and forgot to put it back on."

He kicked her in her side. "You lyin'-ass bitch."

She balled up on the floor and cried. He kicked her repeatedly, then grabbed her by the leg and dragged her out of the room into the guest bedroom. He kneeled down beside her and grabbed her hair forcing her to look at him. "I suggest you find a job and a place to stay, 'cause this marriage is over." He stood up and hovered over her body, removed his wedding band, and hit her in the face with it. He then walked over to the bed and snatched the bedding off. He made sure to leave her uncomfortable and cold.

He exited the room and closed the door behind him to barricade her crying and whimpering.

***

Several hours later, Sasha was in excruciating pain. She had welts from the ass whooping, bruises, and carpet burns from being dragged and slapped around like a ragdoll. She rubbed her eyes, and the puffiness of it frightened her. She leaped from the bed without caution, and a sharp pain stung at her side.

"Ouch!" she gripped her waist and wobbled to the bathroom.

She stood in front of the bathroom mirror and didn't recognize herself. She looked hideous. Her face was covered in bruises. The ring around her eye was black and blue, with a blood clot in the corner of it. Sasha placed her hand over her mouth and cried hysterically. Quamae gave a new meaning to the glamorous word face-beat.

She grabbed her rag and ran some cold water over it before placing it on her face. "Sh!" The plain water stung her flesh while the coolness soaked through her pores. Her hands trembled with fear during the attempt to bring down the swelling from her bruised, semi-shut eye. A panic attack was creeping down on her slowly. Her chest tightened, and sweat beads formed across her forehead. Sasha reached for the medicine cabinet door and slung it open. She was in search of her medicinal fix, and she needed it right then and there. She knocked over a few pill bottles before she located the correct one. She placed two pills in her mouth and drank some faucet water to wash it down.

Sasha contemplated going downstairs, but feared a part two. But she needed to get the swelling down immediately. There was no way she could go outside in her condition.

She held onto the railing and took slow steps until she reached the bottom. She could hear him on the phone, laughing, and that made her nervous. Whenever they had fights he wore a mean mug on his face for days, but not this day.

Happiness was in his voice. "Yeah, I'll slide through in a couple of hours."

When she glanced over at him, he was smiling and rubbing his head. "I miss you, too."

He sat the phone down and glanced up at her. She looked away and proceeded to the kitchen. She looked like she had been through hell and back, but he didn't care. Her appearance didn't faze him one bit. She was lucky to be alive instead of lying on a cold-ass slab in the morgue.

Sasha stood in front of the refrigerator and opened the freezer to get some ice. She couldn't help but wonder who he was on the phone with. It hurt to know he was playing it so cool, but there was nothing she could say or do to fix it. She was just satisfied he hadn't put her out immediately. She knew it wouldn't last long, living under the same roof with him, and she needed to come up with a plan fast.

Quamae left his house in a hurry. He refused to sit around there, point blank, period. If he stayed there any longer, he would've beaten her ass again. The bruises all over her face and body had no effect on him, so he didn't feel bad for putting them there.

He was on his way to the trap in Hollywood. When he pulled up in the driveway, Dirty and Chauncey were sitting on the porch, drinking. He took long strides until he reached the porch. "What's up, my niggas?" He gave them both a fist bump and took a seat next to Dirty. "So, what yawl boys been up to?"

Dirty rubbed his hands together. "Trying to make this nigga lose some of that money on this dice game."

Chauncey laughed. "Bruh, what I told you?"

"I know you want to play Madden. I got my homeboy sliding through to play, fifteen hundred a game."

Quamae shook his head. "Yawl boys' serious about that Madden."

Dirty was hyped. "Hell yeah, you should get on it, too." He sipped from his cup.

"Nah, I'm straight. I don't play games."

"Ah, here you go with that bullshit. Quit acting like you can't blow a few dollars."

"That ain't the point, and besides, you know what I like to do."

"Yeah, yeah."

"Now, if you pull out that card table, I wouldn't mind taking some of your money." He grabbed Dirty's pockets and he swatted his hand away.

"Not today, my friend, not today."

Quamae then pulled out his cell phone to call his sister. It seemed like she answered on the first ring.

"What's up, Pops?" she joked. He laughed at her sense of humor. She would always call him Pops because he acted like her father instead of her big brother.

"I see you got jokes."

"A little bit," she giggled.

"I'm at the trap house right now, so come through and pick up the money."

"I'm on my way."

Chauncey and Dirty had a puzzled look plastered on their faces. "Who was that, bruh?" they asked in unison.

He tucked his phone away in his back pocket. "Damn, yawl nosey as fuck."

"Damn right," Dirty grinned. "Oh, I get it, one of your hos sliding through."

Quamae wiped the sweat from his forehead with the back of his hand. "Nah, man, that was Emani."

"Oh, sis coming over?"

"Yeah."

Quamae fixed a cup of Hennessey with no chaser while he waited on Emani to arrive. They sat on the porch and listened to Dirty talk about one of his wild stories.

A few minutes later a black Maxima pulled up. It was Emani. She stepped out of the car wearing an all-black business suit, burgundy silk top, and matching pumps. Her haircut was short. Her skin was like butterscotch, glistening in the sun. She had the biggest brown eyes that made her look so innocent.

"Hey," she said in a baby-like tone.

"Damn, sis, where you headed?" Chauncey asked.

"I had a job fair at school today."

"A'ight nah, don't make us come out there and hurt one of them young niggas."

"I won't." She turned her attention to her brother.

"So, how is school?" he asked.

"It's fine. I just hate living on campus." She exhaled heavily to show her aggravation with her current living conditions.

"And why is that?"

"I don't get any privacy, and it irritates me," she whined, making sure to lay it on thick to ensure he said yes. She knew he was a sucker for her and would do anything to make her happy. "And all my roommate wanna do is smoke weed and turn up all day. I'm sick of it."

"I guess you trying to tell me you want an apartment?"

She smiled. "Yes, that would be nice."

"I guess I can do that for you as long as your grades stay up, but we can talk about that later."

She gave him a hug. "I love you."

"I love you, too. Come on so I can walk you to the car."

She took a step off the porch, then looked over her shoulder. "See yawl later."

"A'ight, sis," they both replied.

Quamae handed her some money once she was in the car.

"Thank you."

"Anything for you."

"I'll call you when I get back to the campus."

"Okay."

He stepped back and headed to the porch to get his cup. "I'm about to head out." Just as he was about to step down, a black Cadillac Escalade pulled up in the yard.

Dirty looked up. "Game on."

"Who is that?" Quamae asked.

"My lil' dawg who I gamble with on that Madden. Young nigga got some bread, too."

"That's the move. He a hustler, huh?"

"Natural born hustler. Young nigga jumped in the game two years ago and came up quick."

Two dudes hopped out of the truck and approached them. The first one said, "What up, Dirty? You ready to lose that money?" The other one acknowledged them with a head nod and a handshake..

Dirty chuckled. "Nah, are you ready?"

"I stay ready."

"This is my dawg Blue and his homeboy Quint."

"What's up?" Blue acknowledged the new faces. Chauncey and Quamae dapped him up.

Dirty interrupted. "Okay, enough with the introductions and shit, let's get on this game."

They all walked into the house and sat on the couch while Dirty turned on the television. He made small talk with Blue while Chauncey lit up a blunt to put in rotation.

"I hope you came to play, 'cause last night you bailed on a nigga for some ass."

Blue laughed. "Yeah, man, that was that baby last night. I had to shake life on yawl niggas when she called."

"Damn, bihh, she must've put that good shit on ya ass."

"Yeah, man, I fucks with shorty the long way. I'ma rock wit' her and see where it leads."

Dirty walked over and handed him a controller. "Listen to yo' lovesick young ass," he teased. "She got you sprung already with that cougar puss, and yawl just met two hours ago."

"Man, g'on wit' all that." He sat up on the couch. "Come on so I can beat yo' old ass, take yo' money, and take that baby out on yo' dime, nigga."

"Lets run it, then."

They passed several blunts around and watched Dirty and Blue square off on a tie-breaker game. Quamae stood up and looked at Chauncey. "I'm out. Be ready in the morning so we can handle that business."

They slapped hands. "I'll be there bright and early."

He nodded his head, looked over at Dirty, and said the same thing.

"I'll catch yawl boys later."

He walked out the door, locking it behind him, and called Gigi.

"Hello," she answered.

"Whe'e ya at?" He got in the car and pulled off.

"Home."

"I'm on my way."

"Okay."

Chapter 10

Monday morning was a busy day for Quamae: he had to distribute all the work he picked up from his trip. Dealing with Sasha and her infidelities put a delay on the deliveries. She was lucky his buyers were consistent, otherwise he would've had to whoop her ass again for making him lose money.

He was up long before sunrise, even after his long night with Gigi. After he shaved, shit, and showered, he got dressed and waited on Chauncey and Dirty to arrive. He walked over to the guestroom to see if Sasha was still in there. He hadn't seen her since he left Sunday morning. When he opened the door and peeked in, she was still asleep. He closed the door and went downstairs into the den.

Quamae walked behind the bar and poured a shot of Hennessey. It was too early in the morning for him to be drinking, but from the way he was feeling, he needed it. Sasha had really fucked him up, and he hated her for that.

The chime from the doorbell put him back on hustle mode and dismissed all thoughts that would get in his way. Making his way to the front door, he opened it and let Chauncey and Dirty in.

"What's up, my boy?" Dirty walked in first and gave Quamae dap.

"This werk."

Chauncey stepped in next and G-hugged his nigga. "What up, baby? You good today?"

"Nah, man, but we'll chop it up later." He said it low enough for only Chauncey to hear.

In the den they separated the bricks and handed a few to Dirty to deliver. Quamae placed them in a backpack for him. "Bring back sixty bands."

"I gotchu," he sat the bag by his foot. "So, what's up on the weed tip? I'm telling you, bruh, the shit bumping. I can off that shit by myself, but I got a few hungry lil' niggas that's trying to eat, too."

Quamae wasn't really feeling the idea of selling weed, but he knew Chauncey wanted to go through with it. "I don't think it's necessary since we pushing enough of that white girl. But this nigga," he pointed at Chauncey, "is down for it."

Chauncey was on board with making more money. That's what he hustled for. "Damn right! We need to get money all across the board. The weed game sweet right now. All these niggas and bitches wanna do is smoke loud and pop pills."

"Well, we ain't selling no pills," Quamae put a stop to any thought he had about that product. "That's where I draw the line."

"Slow ya roll, fam, we ain't on that." Chauncey wasn't trying to sell pills either; weed and coke were all he needed. His next move was to get a house, and with the way business was booming, he would have that in no time.

"Good." Quamae placed a few bricks in his backpack. "We can start off with a few pounds and see how that shit moves, and if that's where it's at, then we can add it to the inventory." He pointed a finger at Dirty, "And you responsible for the niggas you talking about. Don't bring them niggas around me, and they are to buy from you. If some sneaky shit going on, you responsible for sending them to meet their maker."

"I got this, my G, I won't let you down." Dirty grabbed the bag from the floor and threw it over his shoulder. "I'ma go handle this business, and then I'll go holla at the nigga for the trees."

"Yeah, do that." Quamae walked him to the door and secured the locks after he left.

Now it was only him and his partner left, and he could finally vent about what went down between him and his wife.

When he was back in the den, Chauncey was packing his keys up in a duffle bag. He looked up and made brief eye contact. "You ready to chop it up?"

"As ready as I'm gon' be." Quamae took a seat on the bar stool and dropped the dime on his girl. "I was right all along, bruh. I caught Sasha cheating last night. She pulled up in a truck with some nigga, five in the morning."

He held a fist over his mouth. "Nah! She ain't do no shit like that?" Chauncey was thinking that was a bold move on her behalf.

"Yeah, she tried it. The bitch had a nigga pick her up from my crib, dawg."

"Damn, that's fucked up. What you did?"

"I beat her muthafuckin' ass! I wanted to kill that ho." The tone of his voice displayed the anger in his heart. "The nigga lucky he pulled off, 'cause I would've wet that shit up for disrespecting me."

"Bruh, don't jeopardize your freedom like that, 'cause she ain't worth it." His brown eyes were filled with sincerity. "You have too much to lose."

"She lucky I didn't put a bullet in her head. That's what I really wanted to do."

"And what would that solve? She'll be dead and you'll be in prison for life. While I'm out here running a solo operation." He shook his head because it was going to be a task within itself to change his mind frame. "Just talk to her and see what's up with your girl.

"That shit dead, my nigga! She gotta go. I told her she has to find a job and a place, because I want a divorce."

"Well, just don't put the girl out and she don't have a place to go."

Quamae looked at him sideways. "So, you Captain Save-A-Ho?"

"Nah, bruh, but yawl done been through a lot of shit together. Just give it some time and see what happens. I know you love her." Chauncey's phone rang. He looked down at the screen and sent the caller to voicemail. The situation in front of him was way more important. "I'm not justifying what she did. All I'm saying is just think this through before you do something you may regret later. Maybe yawl need a break or something. But if it's that bad, then leave her. File for divorce and go yawl separate ways."

Quamae didn't respond, just looked at him and folded his arms. Deep down inside he knew Chauncey was right, but that was something he wasn't ready to admit.

Silence fell over the two of them for about ten minutes until Chauncey got up to leave. "I'm out, but think about what I said."

They G-hugged once more before Chauncey left. "I love you, man."

"Love you, too, bruh!"

Quamae left shortly after to go and make his deliveries. He didn't like to ride with dope, but he wasn't bringing any of those niggas to his house.

***

Sasha had just awakened from a much-needed nap. She was finally able to sleep underneath a warm blanket. Her body ached and her side felt tender. She hoped her ribs weren't broken. She walked into the master bedroom and gathered some items to pack an overnight bag. Before she left she stopped in the bathroom to clean her face and brush her teeth. Looking in the mirror made her emotional all over again, and the tears welled up in her eyes. Out of all the altercations they've been through, this was the worst. She finally made it outside, jumped in her car, and left. She picked up her cell phone and called Carmen.

"Hey, bae," Carmen sung into the phone.

"Where you at?" she cried.

"Home. What's wrong?"

She was hysterical. "I'm on my way over there."

Carmen panicked. "What's wrong?"

She wiped her tears with her shirt. "Me and Quamae had a fight. It was bad, real bad," she sobbed.

"Okay, come on."

Twenty minutes later Sasha pulled up. She used her key to gain entrance and walked straight through the door. She sat down on the couch with her face in her hands. Carmen walked into the living room.

"So," she flopped down on the couch. "Tell me what happened."

Sasha looked up. Carmen's heart sank to the pit of her stomach when she saw all the bruises. "Damn, Sasha, look at your face. What the fuck did he do to you? Tell me what happened." Her questions were coming non-stop. She wanted answers, and she wanted them now.

Sasha started with the root of the problem, which started when he was in Atlanta, then ending it with her getting caught getting out of the truck with Blue.

"Carmen, he came home and just flipped. He was outside waiting on me by the bushes. He dragged me in the house and up the stairs by my hair." She wiped her tears. "He was hitting me in my face and kicking me."

"Oh my god, that's horrible. I'm sorry you had to go through that." She scooted closer to her and noticed the welts on her skin. She pointed at them, "How did you get those?"

Sasha cried harder. "He beat me with a belt."

"Hold up! Where was Blue when all of this went down?"

"He wasn't there. I told him he didn't have to wait." Sasha remembered she hadn't spoken to him since he dropped her off. She sent him a quick text recapping minimal details about what happened to her and asked him to get her a room. When he texted her back, he agreed and said he would text her the details.

Carmen shook her head. "You need to press charges and go to the hospital."

"No, I don't want to."

"Why not?"

"They gon' ask too many questions, and I don't want to press charges."

Carmen was baffled by the dumbass remarks she just made. "You kidding me, right?"

"You know I can't do that to him. He's still my husband."

"Husbands can get restraining orders, too. Besides, look what he did to you. That man almost beat your ass to sleep." She got up to go get her keys and purse.

"Come on, I'm taking you to the hospital." She wasn't taking no for an answer, and she didn't care what the outcome would be. He needed to go to jail.

***

Blue sat patiently in the suite at the Hollywood Beach Hotel, awaiting Sasha's arrival. She said she would be there in 30 minutes. So, while he waited, he rolled a blunt to take the edge off. He put the perfectly-rolled blunt to his lips and put fire to it. He pulled the weed too hard and it made him choke. "Shit," he coughed. "That's that pressure."

He walked out on the balcony to check out the ocean view and to finish smoking. His thoughts were on Sasha, and he wondered how bad she could possibly look. The thought alone had him feeling some type of way about how things panned out that morning. If he would've stayed out there longer, none of that would've happened to her, and he put that on his dead grandmother. Granted, their relationship was early in the game, but he had a soft spot for her every since she opened up to him at the beach.

Knock, knock, knock!

Blue stepped from the balcony and closed the curtains. He already knew it was that baby. He eased it open, and in front of him stood a battered woman. She removed her shades to give him a better look. Nothing could've prepared him for what he was staring at. Her beautiful face was covered in bruises, and one of those big, brown eyes he loved so much had a black and blue ring around it. He felt crushed and guilty at the same time.

Sasha felt uncomfortable and dropped her head. She suddenly felt like allowing him to see her in that condition was a mistake.

"Don't be embarrassed around me, Ma. You don't have a reason to be. I'm here for you." He grabbed her by the hand and walked her over to the king size bed. It was still early in the day, but the burnt orange curtains made the room dark.

Sasha sat down and tried to speak, but she couldn't find the words to say. Her appearance had her feeling self-conscious, and he could sense her struggle.

He sat down beside her and wrapped his arms around her. "Damn, Ma, I'm sorry you had to go through that shit." He rubbed her back. "You don't have to say anything. You can talk when you're ready, and when you do, I'll be right here."

She placed her head on his chest and cried him a river. "I don't know what to do. Look at me." Her voice cracked as she sobbed.

"What do you want to do?" He was genuinely concerned about her well-being, and he needed her to know that. "Just tell me what you want to do, because this shit ain't healthy."

"I don't know where to start."

"Do you want to leave?"

"I want to leave, but I don't know how."

"Just take some time and think on it, 'cause I know you're in a tough place." He wasn't pushing the envelope on her dipping out on her husband because he knew she was willing to stay for all the wrong reasons. "I know what you facing, but sometimes holding on hurts more than letting go. Whateva you need, I gotchu."

"Can you just hold me?"

"I got you, Ma."

He got up and pulled the blanket back far enough for her to climb in, then he slid in behind her. Sasha flipped on her side and nestled her head in the crook of his arm and closed her eyes. For the first time in a long time, she felt safe and secure, but that didn't stop the tears from falling.

Blue hummed while he rubbed her head and planted a kiss on her forehead, then he started to sing. "You don't have to hurt no more, baby he's over. I'll be what you're looking for, let me take over. You don't have to hurt no more."

The sound of his baritone voice was angelic enough to stop her tears from falling. He could really sing, and that surprised her. Sasha wiped away the remaining water from her face and smiled. "I didn't know you could sing."

"I can do a lot of things you don't know about."

Blue continued to hold her until she fell asleep. He looked at his sleeping beauty and knew he had to do something to help her escape the hell she was living in. He closed his eyes and a wicked smile spread across his lips. He was about to take the law into his own hands, and he couldn't wait for the day he stood toe-to-toe with his arch-enemy.

Chapter 11

Three weeks later

Quamae was at home contemplating his next move. He loved Sasha, but their marriage was over. For the life of him he couldn't understand what her problem was and why she felt the need to cheat and mess up what they established together. There were plenty of females that wanted to take her place, but he didn't let that happen because the majority of them knew her. He wouldn't dare give those hos the satisfaction of throwing it up in her face.

Sasha didn't think that way, though. Hell, she didn't think at all. She reacted on impulse and hormones, something he should've peeped from the jump.

Quamae headed to the den to get a workout in and blow off some steam at the same time. He was still heated about his wife's indiscretions.

Thirty minutes into his workout, there was loud banging on his front door. He looked around at first to see if his mind was playing tricks on him, but the banging got louder. *Who the fuck banging on my shit like they're the police?* He placed the weights back on the bar and grabbed his fie. He didn't know what to expect since Sasha's late night rendezvous. For all he knew it could've been the police or the nigga she was creeping with.

Quamae looked through the peephole first and saw a rugged woman standing there with cornrows in her hair. Her attire consisted of khaki pants, a white t-shirt, and a pair of blue canvas sneakers, compliments of the department of corrections. They gave that same outfit to everyone upon their release if their family didn't send out that exit attire. She didn't pose as a threat, so he figured he would open the door and tell her she had the wrong address.

Quamae swung the door open with his gun in hand. "Why the fuck you bangin' on my door like you live here?"

The woman looked him up, down, and up again, locking her eyes on his sweaty chest and six-pack. "Well, ain't you a sexy, rude devil."

He wasn't in the mood for the bullshit, but she managed to make him crack a half smile. There was something familiar about the older woman's face, but it wasn't registering at the moment.

"Well, are you gon' say something?"

"How can I help you?" He lowered his tone.

"Well, we can start off by you telling me where my whore of a daughter is?"

Now she made him more confused. "What? I don't know your daughter. You got the wrong house."

She reached into her pocket and pulled out an old photo, then handed it to him. "That's my daughter, Sasha. Do you know her now?"

Quamae could not believe his eyes or ears. The picture she gave him was definitely the younger version of Sasha. The resemblance was uncanny, and all he could do was stare.

"I just got out of prison. Fifteen long years to the door because of that bitch, and she owes me."

"She said her mother was dead. What's your name?" He couldn't believe what he was hearing, but he was anxious to know all about it. "What happened?"

She stepped closer to him. "Carol, and if you let me in, I'll tell you all about her."

He stepped aside and closed the door behind them. He escorted her to the kitchen. "Would you like a drink?"

"Hell yeah. You got some alcohol?"

"Henny." Quamae pulled the cold bottle from the fridge and poured them both a cup. "I'm listening." He was ready for her to start talking.

She looked at him and grinned wickedly. "You might want to sit down for this." Quamae took her advice and sat on one of the stools that surrounded the Lanai and prepared himself to hear the worst.

"When Sasha was fifteen, she was sneaking around with this drug dealer named Nate, who was twenty-one at the time. I found out about it and I confronted them. Both of them denied the accusations, but I knew they were lying because they were the talk of the projects." Quamae nodded his head to let her know he was listening. "I won't lie, I used to get high and do some shit I'm not proud of, but I was human and I made mistakes." She took a sip of the Hennessey. "I used to disappear for a few days at a time when I was binging. So one day I returned home after being gone for three days. I could hear loud moaning, hollering, and screaming, so I go to Sasha's room door, and that's where the noise was coming from. I picked the lock, and when I opened the door, Nate was on top of Sasha, fucking the shit out of her. We got into a scuffle and he ran out the apartment."

Quamae sipped from his cup and kept on listening.

"A few weeks later she kept throwing up, and come to find out the bitch was pregnant. So I did the best thing I could do to terminate her pregnancy. I took her to a friend of mine that did abortions in her home, and we got rid of the baby. Sasha hated me after that because she thought that baby was gon' make her life better with Nate."

Quamae shifted in his seat. He was unaware of her past. He was angry at himself, the bitch sitting across from him, and Sasha for not being honest with him. He wondered if that was the reason they didn't have any kids. All he wanted was to be a father, and those chances were probably over for her. The things Carol just told him made it that much easier to file for divorce.

"After the abortion, they were still sneaking around, so I tried keeping her on a tight leash. That didn't work, so I started beating her ass on the regular. I was still using drugs, so one day Nate gave me an eight-ball and that sent me on a heavy binge. When I returned home the police, along with Child Protective Services, were waiting on me because I left her in the home for days. They searched the house and found drugs and a crack pipe, so they slapped the cuffs on. I was hauled off to jail without a bond. They charged me with child abuse, child neglect, child endangerment, possession of cocaine and possession of paraphernalia."

Tears fell from Carol's eyes as she continued with the heartbreaking story. "She told them crackas I was an unfit mother who did drugs and traded her off for sex in exchange for drugs. She even told them about the abortion. I was a repeat offender with previous drug charges, so they hit me with the Recidivism Act. I did 15 years to the door."

"Damn." Quamae shook his head. His mind was racing trying to digest the accusations against his wife and wondering if she was capable of doing such a thing.

"That girl been fucking since she was twelve. The neighborhood boys used to run trains on her and all."

She could tell he was disturbed by the bomb she just dropped on him. Quamae downed his cup because now he understood why she had a hard time being in a committed relationship. If that wasn't the straw that broke the camel's back, he didn't know what did.

"You alright? I take it she didn't tell you."

She knew damn well she just fucked his world up. He shook his head yeah. He wasn't about to tell her how he was really feeling.

She looked around, admiring their beautiful home. "You have a nice home." She put the emphasis on him. "'Cause I know she ain't help pay for shit." She smiled.

"Thanks." He poured himself another drink and let her comment roll off his back.

"It's real quiet and clean in here. Yawl don't have no kids?"

He gave her the meanest mug. "Nah."

She defended herself. "That ain't the only abortion she had. She's had quite a few, so I didn't ruin her."

"I don't doubt it."

"How long you and her been together?" She was trying to see if her daughter was still up to the same old tricks.

"Three years together, married for two."

Carol was shocked. "Damn, she snatched you right on up." She stood up to stretch. "I got to give it to her, she sho' know how to pick them, because you fine as hell."

He didn't understand why and how she was there telling him about her past. Something didn't seem right about her impromptu visit. "I'm confused about why you're here and how you knew where we lived."

"I told you, that bitch owes me 15 years of my life, and I have my sources. The streets talk, you know." She pulled out a pack of Newport cigarettes. "Can I smoke this in here?"

He wanted to say no and show her to the door, but he needed more answers, so he gave her permission to do so. "Knock yourself out."

She lit the cigarette and took a long pull. "Where she at, anyway?"

"She ain't here."

"Yeah, I figured that much."

"Can you answer my questions now?" He was getting impatient.

She sensed the annoyance in his voice, so she spoke. "She owes me, and I'm not leaving until I get it."

***

Checkout time approached quickly, and Sasha dreaded every minute of it. Over the past few weeks she spent a great deal of time with Blue at the hotel and away from home. He didn't force her out of the home, but she figured some time apart would do them some justice. Lord knows she didn't want to go home, but it was time to face the beast better known as her husband.

As she emerged from the double doors of the hotel, she was greeted by dark, cloudy skies. This was a friendly reminder that hurricane season was finally here.

She clicked the panic button on her key ring because she could not remember where she parked her car. The faint sound of the alarm was coming from the far right corner of the parking lot. She approached a similar Audi, but quickly recognized it wasn't hers because the license plate on the back didn't say *Mz Banks*. She hit the panic button one more time, and that's when she realized her car was a few spots down.

The meds had her a little high, but she was okay for the most part. Sasha threw her overnight bag into the backseat and prepared for the short drive home. She needed to get her thoughts together, and Rihanna had become her voice of reason. She hooked the aux cord to her phone and made her selection. The music started, and she sang along. Fresh tears took over her eyesight as the words attacked her soul.

And I hate how much I love you boy (yeah)
I can't stand how much I need you (I need you)
And I hate how much I love you boy (oh whoa)
But I just can't let you go
And I hate that I love you so (oh)

Every single word she sang applied to her marriage with Quamae, which caused her to cry uncontrollably. She was stuck, and she hated that feeling. She loved him to the moon and back, but her brain hated him with a passion because of what he did to her. Their relationship wasn't always bad. She shared a lot of good memories with him, which made it difficult for her to walk away. And that was the reason they had to hash things out once and for all.

Sasha pulled up into the driveway alongside Quamae's truck and said a quick prayer. *Lord please don't let this man kill me today, or me kill him for that matter, Amen.* She stepped from the car and left everything in God's hands.

Chapter 12

When Sasha walked into the bedroom, it reeked of marijuana. Quamae was lying across the bed, smoking a blunt and watching *All About the Benjamins*. The volume was extremely loud, so she wasn't sure if he didn't know she was standing there or if he was just flat-out ignoring her presence.

Quamae was laughing hysterically. Sasha stood there a good five minutes staring at him, waiting for him to acknowledge her. Not once did he take his eyes off of the flat screen television.

She walked a little closer and dropped her duffle bag on the floor, trying to get his attention. "Can we talk please?"

He put the blunt to his lips and took a long pull. He was trying to get high and enjoy his movie, not entertain her whorish ways.

She asked him again when he didn't answer. "Quamae, can we please talk?" This time she walked closer to the bed just in case he really didn't hear her.

"I don't have shit to say to you."

His tone was stern, but she ignored it. She really wanted to squash the beef between them, but he was making it very difficult to do. At the very least she wanted to apologize to him. "Can you at least look at me, please?"

"Nah, I'm looking at something already." He was so calm all of a sudden, and she was determined to have that much-needed conversation.

"Quamae, we really need to talk."

"That's what you came here for?"

"That's one of the reasons." She stood there with her hands folded in front of her, waiting for him to at least look in her direction.

"Oh, you found a job and a place?"

"Not yet."

He finally looked over at her, but he had a sullen look on his face. "I suggest you speed up the process, because time is ticking." He considered taking Chauncey's advice, but Carol showed up and erased any possibility of him being cordial with her. She was a stranger in his eyes.

Quamae's attitude was so cold to her, she felt like hauling off and fucking him up on general principle. But she knew she couldn't beat him physically, so it was useless to start a fight she wouldn't win.

"Do you have to be so cold to me?" She didn't bother waiting on a response, nine times out of ten he would probably remain silent. "I've put up with a lot of shit from you. I have forgiven you several times for cheating, fucking with this ho and that ho. I fuck up one time," she held up one finger. "And it's the end of the world. That's bullshit, and you know it."

Quamae rolled out of their king sized bed and took one giant step to stand face to face with her. She knew she pushed a button because his nostrils were flaring. A sudden wave of fear took over her body and pumped through her veins like kryptonite. Her heart was racing and her hands begin to shake. She watched his every move with wide frightened eyes. He intimidated her and he knew it. The display was plastered permanently on her face.

"Let's get one thing straight." He pointed a finger in her direction. "You and me are not equal, so get that shit out your head. You can't do what I do because I take care of you, and I have paid for my mistakes." He held both of his arms out. "Look around you in case you forgot that. When you married me, you knew what it was."

"You can't buy forgiveness," she cried.

"Since when? I bought it from you."

"Wow," she gasped. "That was hurtful."

The space between them was too close for comfort, so she took a few steps backward. In case he decided he wanted to fight, she had plans on making a mad dash to the bathroom and locking herself in there.

"My wife can't fuck niggas and get away with it," he yelled.

"You right and it's okay. I'm sorry for what I did. I never meant to hurt you, and that's the truth. I still love you, no matter what." Tears started to fall from her eyes. "I'm not perfect, and you knew that before you married me."

"Nah, there's a lot of shit about you I should've known before I married your ass."

From the time Carol graced him with her presence, vivid images of her childhood kept flashing in his mind. All he could imagine were the unthinkable acts she performed on different types of boys and men. The woman he loved had turned into a woman he now despised.

"Like what?" He peaked her interest. "You know everything about me."

"Nah, I really don't."

He walked toward the dresser, causing her to flinch.

When he turned around he was holding what appeared to be a picture. He handed it to her. The shocked expression on her face gave the impression she knew exactly where the photo came from. "Familiar, huh?"

She gripped the photo tight in her hand. "Where did you get this from?"

"Your mother."

"My mother?" She held her hand over her mouth.

"Yeah the mother you said was dead. The one you sent to prison for 15 years 'cause you wanted to be a ho at a young age. She was here yesterday." He held no punches, nor did he care about her feelings. "Damn," he sighed. "I'ma give it to you, that pussy still tight for somebody that's been fucking since 12," he gave her a round of applause. "Now I finally understand why my seeds ain't running around this bitch making noise." He titled his head to the side. "So, you can't have kids?" he pointed in her direction. "Ho, you knew I wanted kids, and you can't give them to me."

She dropped her hand to her side and began to take long, deep breaths. She could feel a panic attack coming on. "I. Can. Explain."

"You better tell me something." He waited to hear what lies she would come up with.

"Wait. How did she find me?"

"That's not important."

As Quamae sat patiently for her performance, Sasha knelt to the floor and searched her bag for her Zoloft. Her hands were trembling as she fumbled through papers and everything else that consumed a woman's purse. With her pill bottle in her clutches, she dumped two pills in her hand and tossed them in her mouth. There was a half empty bottle of water close by, so she used that to wash it down.

Sasha sat all the way down on the floor, no longer afraid of what he would do to her. He could kill her right now and she wouldn't care. She was at a point in her life where nothing else mattered, because after she explained everything, she knew he would leave her for good. Sasha braced herself and went back to where it all started.

***

Eighteen years ago.

"Sasha, get your ass up and clean up this mess," Carol yelled, referring to the dirty dishes scattered all over the kitchen. "You don't want to do shit but play with baby dolls all fuckin' day."

Sasha sat her cabbage patch doll down and did as she was told. Her mother stood there with her hair flying, looking a slap-ass mess. She walked into the kitchen and clicked on the lights. A few roaches could be seen scattering across the counter to take cover. Sasha filled the sink with water and washing powder and began to bust the suds.

There was a knock on the door. "I'll get it," Carol yelled.

When she opened the door, Frank walked in. He was an older cat that ran drugs throughout the neighborhood. He never talked when he came in; he always walked straight into the bedroom with Carol on his heels, closing the door behind them. This was one of many days when all Sasha would hear was the sound of her mother moaning and the constant squeaking of the raggedy bed she slept on.

Lying across the bed, she could hear her mother and Frank arguing. The walls were so hollow she could hear every word they were saying. She might not have understood the content of their conversation, but she heard it.

"Bitch, your credit days are over!"

"How about some pussy?" her mother begged.

"I want some pussy that's nice and tight," he paused. "Like your daughter."

"You can have me, she's too young."

"Bitch, what did I just say? If I can't have her, then you gets nothing, and I will make sure none of my boys serve you again."

"Okay, okay! Just don't cut me off, please. I'm begging you." Her mother's bedroom door creaked, alerting her they were finish. Fear took over Sasha as they walked into her bedroom.

Carol looked at her daughter with her eyes beaming wide. "Um, sweetie, just do what he says, okay?"

Sasha was confused about the proposition. "What do you mean, Mama?" she whispered in a childlike voice.

"Just lay on the bed and be quiet, okay?"

Frank pushed Carol out of the room and closed the door. Sasha backed up against the wall in fear. Her heart was beating fast. He grabbed her by the arm and pulled her close to remove her clothing. Once she was naked, he pushed her on the bed and unzipped his pants, letting them fall to the floor. He climbed on top of her and pushed inside her virgin walls.

"No!" she cried. Frank put his hand over her mouth to muffle her cries. She swung her arms, kicked and screamed, but he continued to rip her insides apart. The smell of fresh blood filled the room. She bit his hand to stop her attacker, but he backhanded her in the face. "Ow," she screamed.

He pinned her arms behind her head and lay on top of her to keep her still. She lay there, paralyzed under his weight, as she choked out weak cries, praying it would soon be over.

For the next 15 minutes he continued to pound on her savagely, and the only sounds that could be heard from Sasha's bedroom were painful cries. Carol sat on the dirty *carpet in the living room holding a glass pipe to her lips as the sounds of her daughter's cries went unanswered.*

When the torture came to an end, Frank left Sasha's room and headed out the front door into the afternoon sun.

Sasha stumbled from her bedroom to the bathroom and ran some water in the tub. Her thighs were sticky from the blood that gushed out when Frank forced his way into her vagina, breaking her hymen. Tears streamed down her face as she sat down in the scalding hot water, changing its color from clear to light pink.

The abuse she was subjected to would continue off and on for years, and her baby figure started to fade. Her body began to develop rather quickly, spreading her hips and ass at the age of 15. This transformation brought attention from the neighborhood boys, but there was one in particular who caught her attention, and his name was Nate.

"What's up, Sasha," he asked. He took a seat next to her.

"Nothing," she sighed. She pretended she wasn't interested, but deep down inside she was happy to see his face. Nate was one of the many boys that served for Frank, and he was 21 at the time. He had a baby face with small dreads that were starting to develop, smooth brown skin, and a full set of gold teeth. Nevertheless, he was a cutie. She could tell he was making some money by the way he dressed. He matched from head to toe on a daily basis, and he always wore a gold necklace with a cross on it.

"Why are you sitting out here so late? Shouldn't you be in the house at this hour?" he asked.

"Just getting some fresh air," she replied. She didn't lie, but she wasn't telling the absolute truth, either. She wasn't about to tell him she was outside because she didn't want to hear the moans of her mother's sexual encounter

or smell the dreadful scent of crack in the air, although she was certain he knew what was going on in her home. Hell, that wasn't a secret, everybody knew.

Nate sat on the steps with her until his pager went off. He removed it from his hip to see if it was a lick. He slid it back in his pocket and grabbed her hand. "Come on, come ride with me somewhere." He rode Sasha around with him as he busted his licks, and over a course of time this would become their normal routine. Nate was well aware what went on in her home, or at least he thought he did, and wanted to protect her as much as he could. He had an apartment not too far from the projects, and that had become her safe haven.

Nate was giving Sasha the attention and validation she desperately wished her mother would have given her. He took his time with her, and when it came down to their first time having sex, he was gentle with her. He was disappointed when he realized she wasn't a virgin, but angry when he found out why.

Nate had grown to love Sasha for various reasons, and the feeling became mutual. He began to plot the demise of Frank and a way to wipe Sasha's mother off the map without killing her. Death was too easy for her. He wanted that bitch to suffer.

After careful planning, Nate had two of his boys kidnap Frank and tie him up in an abandoned house. He didn't give Sasha the full details, but he did tell her Frank was going to suffer for what he did to her. He drove her over to the abandoned house and escorted her inside. Once inside, Sasha couldn't believe her eyes. Nate had gone through extreme measures to protect her, to show her he loved her, and that was something her own mother never did. However, it was weird staring in the eyes of the predator that constantly forced her to do despicable acts. She didn't fear him anymore because Nate was by her side, and he made her feel safe and secure. Nate reached up under his shirt and pulled out a semi-automatic pistol. He handed it to Sasha.

"Take this nigga out of his misery," he instructed. "Shoot him right between the eyes."

Sasha held the pistol in her hands and walked up closer to him. She could see the sweat pouring from his forehead. The house was hot thanks to the scorching sun. She aimed between his legs, the thing that destroyed her, and pulled the trigger. Frank rocked in the chair, unable to scream because of the duct tape. She knew he was in pain, and she laughed about it. She never thought shooting someone could feel so good.

She caught Nate by surprise. He didn't expect her to perform the way she did. She leaned forward and met his stare.

"That's how I felt when you took my virginity, you sick bastard, and now you're going to hell for it."

She spit in his face, put the gun to his forehead, and pulled the trigger. BOOM! Brain matter and blood covered the walls. Sasha turned around and ran to Nate with open arms. He rubbed the small of her back.

"It's okay, baby. Now it's your mother's turn."

Two months had passed since Sasha killed Frank, the nightmares had finally subsided, and everything was back to normal. Well, almost. Sasha soon discovered she was pregnant with Nate's baby. She wasn't sure how he would react, but when she told him he was ecstatic. He suggested she move out of her mother's apartment so they could raise their baby together, but Carol wasn't having that. She had to figure out a way to get rid of the baby since Sasha refused to have an abortion.

Sasha was asleep in her bedroom when she was awakened by sudden movement. When she opened her eyes, two shadows were standing over her. One was her mother, and the other was some lady she recognized from the complex. She tried to move, but her arms and legs were in restraints.

"What are you doing?" she whined.

"Getting rid of this baby, you whore."

Sasha squirmed, but there was nothing she could do to stop them. "Mommy, please don't kill my baby. Nate loves me, and he wants to be a family."

"That boy doesn't love you, all you are is a piece of pussy."

All she could feel was a cold hanger digging inside of her. Dizziness took over as she screamed and begged for her mother to stop, but she didn't listen. Sasha soon passed out.

After hearing what Carol did to Sasha, Nate knew it was time to put his plan into motion. The next day he approached her and gave her an eight ball. Upon acceptance, it sent her on a six-day binge. When she arrived, the police were there to arrest her for numerous charges. Sasha testified in court, and the jury deemed her unfit and guilty of the charges filed. Carol was sentenced to 15 years mandatory with no gain time.

With her mother in jail, Sasha thought things would be better. She moved in with Nate, and they were making plans on starting over with a family of their own until one dreadful day. This day would change Sasha's life forever.

Early morning, 3:00 a.m. to be precise, Sasha and Nate were sound asleep in their cozy apartment until they were awakened by the Ft. Lauderdale SWAT team. Word on the street was one of Nate's boys got caught with a brick and they hauled him in. He was offered immunity in exchange for his testimony.

Nate was booked for the murder of Frank Smith and sentenced to 15 years in the penitentiary. The trial ended quickly, and Sasha received more devastating news: she was pregnant once again with his baby.

Unable to provide her baby with a caring home, she made the one decision her mother wouldn't allow her, and that was to carry the baby full-term. Sasha gave birth to a beautiful baby boy and gave him to a loving family that would provide him with his every want and need. Sasha couldn't fathom the idea of getting rid of a child by a man who loved her unconditionally. To this day she had no idea where her baby boy resided, and Nate never knew his baby boy existed. She named him Nate Jr.

***

Sasha was crying hysterically after explaining every detail of her sordid past. Revealing her loss and traumatic events made her want to end her own life. She didn't ask to come into this wicked world, and at times she wished her mother had just swallowed the nut that fertilized her nasty-ass egg so she wouldn't be in the situation she was in.

Quamae was speechless and didn't know what to do or believe. He allowed a stranger into his home and she told him things about his wife's past he should've known about. The only thing he could do was get up and walk away.

Chapter 13

After receiving the most gut-wrenching, devastating news, Quamae found himself at the one place he didn't need to be: Gigi's apartment. He needed somewhere to go and he could've easily stayed in a hotel, but he didn't want to be alone. He could've called Chauncey, but the subject was too sensitive and he really wasn't in the mood to talk about it. For some reason he wanted female companionship, and he knew she would give him that.

Quamae walked up to her apartment door and knocked three times. She answered wearing a pair of booty shorts and a halter top. Gigi was easy on the eyes with her honey-colored skin and hazel eyes. She smiled as her one true love graced the threshold of her door. She hadn't seen him in a week, and she missed him.

"I'm surprised to see you here. Trouble in paradise?" she teased.

"Something like that," he replied.

"You want to talk about it?" she asked.

"Nah, I'm straight." He brushed past her and went in the direction of her bedroom.

"Come on, let's go to the kitchen."

Quamae followed her, took a seat at the table, and watched Gigi as she reached up under the cabinet and pulled out a bottle of Hennessey. "I know exactly what you need." Gigi stood on her tippy toes to get two glasses from the cabinet.

"I could've got that down for you, 'cause I can see the struggle is real."

Looking over her shoulder, she grinned. "That's okay, you just enjoy the view."

Gigi knew exactly what she was doing, and she did a great job at enticing him. Quamae stared at her ass and he could feel his Johnson wiggle just a little. She still had that effect on him, although he didn't show it. Quamae rolled a blunt as she fixed them a drink, then she quickly joined him at the table.

"It must be pretty bad," she stated.

"Why you say that?"

She pointed at his bare ring finger. "You're still not wearing your ring."

"You can say that." Quamae licked the wrap, sealed it tight, lit it, and took a long pull.

Quamae had Gigi mesmerized. She couldn't take her eyes off of him. She couldn't help but wonder what he saw in Sasha that he didn't see in her. It hurt her even more because the day before he proposed he was snuggled between her legs.

"You wanna hit this?" he asked, referring to the blunt.

"I want a shotgun, and I want it the way you used to give it to me."

He smiled. "Come on."

Quamae scooted his seat back from the table, giving her room to straddle his lap. He took another pull and she placed her mouth over his, cupping her hands at both sides of her cheeks. She inhaled the smoke and blew it from her mouth slowly. They continued those same steps until the blunt was gone.

Gigi was lightheaded from the loud and buzzed from the Henny. Their eyes were studying each other for what felt like a lifetime, and then it happened. Just like hypnosis, they leaned in slowly and their lips touched. Their kiss was passionate, yet electric. Gigi could feel his erection pressing up against her. Quamae placed both hands on her ass as she ground down on him. Anxious to take that dive, he rose to his feet and carried her into the bedroom.

With Gigi still in his arms, he sat down on the bed and lay backward. As they continued to kiss, he slowly removed her halter top, giving him full access to her breasts. He took one in his mouth and latched on like a newborn baby.

"I want to feel you," she moaned.

"Take your shorts off." He helped her pull them off and tossed them to the floor.

Once they were completely naked, they climbed back into bed. Quamae lay on his back and Gigi straddled him once again, but this time she was getting all of him.

"Do we need a condom?" She was hoping he said no, but she figured it was only right she ask.

"Nah, we good."

Happy with the response she was given, Gigi slid down slowly on his shaft and rode him. "Damn, I missed you," she hissed. "It's been too long since I felt this."

"Show me how much you missed me," Quamae responded with his eyes closed.

Gigi took those words as an opportunity to win him back. Her sex was like a weapon, but she knew it would take more than that to steal his heart away from Sasha. Tonight was her night to put something on him that he wouldn't forget. She wanted him to think of her day and night, and even as he lay in bed next to his estranged wife.

Gigi rode Quamae hard and long, forcing him to throw-up an enormous amount of semen into her uterine walls. Her orgasm came shortly after.

Deciding not to go home, Quamae spent the rest of the night and early morning laying pipe.

***

Quamae strolled into the house later on that afternoon with little regard for his wife's feelings. After the long night with Gigi, all he wanted to do was take a shower and get some sleep. He wasn't in the mood for arguing or fighting, so when he walked into the house he headed straight for the shower.

Sasha was trying to fight the tears, because she knew why he was just getting home. She wasn't stupid. *Why else would he come home and jump straight in the shower?* She was willing to bet her last dollar he spent the night with Gigi. Ever since Sasha and Quamae got together, she had always been a problem. She was that one ex-girlfriend that wouldn't go away. Quamae had even cheated a few times on Sasha with her during the beginning of their relationship and marriage.

The shower stopped running, and Sasha prepared herself for what was about to happen. There wasn't a snowball's chance in hell he could stay out all night without her saying anything. She didn't care that they were having problems, he needed to respect the fact she was still in the home. As soon as he came out of the bathroom, she questioned him.

"Where were you all night?" She sat twiddling her fingers, waiting for his response.

"Out," he replied, never making eye contact.

"Oh, so you can stay out all night and not explain anything to me?"

He rubbed his hand over his face irritably. "Listen, man, I'm tired and I'm not in the mood to argue about my whereabouts. We are not together."

Quamae walked over to the bed, but Sasha stood in the way to prevent him from lying down. She put her finger in his face.

"We're still married, so you're going to answer me. I've been up all night crying and waiting on you. I know you was with that bitch Gigi." She looked into his eyes to search for the truth. The look in his eyes spoke volumes, and when he didn't deny it she lost her marbles.

Sasha cocked back and slapped him across the face as hard as she could. She wasn't afraid of the repercussions because there wasn't anything else he could do to hurt her besides what he had already done. Sasha was swinging her arms wildly, catching him a few times in the face. Quamae was too exhausted to fight back, and besides, he knew he was wrong. He grabbed her by the arms and shook her.

"Stop hitting me, man," he shouted.

"No, fuck you," she spat angrily. "I'm sick of this shit with you."

"Calm the fuck down, because I don't want to hit you back."

After making several attempts to calm her down, he realized he wasn't making any progress. He needed to put her in a position where she didn't have a choice. Quamae managed to put her in the full nelson. His arms were under her armpits, and his fingers were interlocked behind her neck. She breathed heavily and cried. "Let me go," she pleaded.

"No. Not until you calm down, 'cause you tripping."

"You fucked that girl and I'm the one tripping?"

"If you say so."

"Nah, I know so. Why else would you come in here and go straight to the shower?" She wiggled her body in an attempt to break free from his strong grip. "I'm not stupid.

That's the same shit you used to do when you were cheating with her before."

Quamae didn't bother to defend himself because her assumptions were absolutely correct. "I'ma let you go, but I'm telling you now, don't put your hands on me."

Sasha relaxed her body and exhaled slowly to decrease her heart rate. All she wanted was for him to let her go. Her shoulders had become numb, and the tingling sensation caused her body to go limp.

"Let me go, please," she begged.

Quamae released her and took a step back in case she tried to hit him again. He was relieved when she walked away without a fight. He didn't trust her enough to sleep with the door open, so when she went into the guest room he locked the door behind her. There was no telling what she would do to him while he was sleeping.

Quamae decided that the both of them needed to have a serious talk in order to figure out what they were going to do. True enough he loved her, but the deception was too much to bear. The trust between them was out the window along with the loyalty. Once the trust was gone, what did they have left? *Absolutely nothing.*

***

Sasha stood in front of the bedroom window in a daze, feeling defeated. True enough he was a hustler, but since he acquired a new position that never kept him out until the next day. Anything that required late night action, Chauncey always handled it. It didn't feel right, and she could see it in his eyes. He didn't have to say he was with her because she already knew he was. Back when they had problems before, his behavior was the same way, and the pattern was the same.

She walked away from the window to look for her cell. She needed someone to talk to, and she knew just who to call in her time of need. She thought about calling Blue, but she didn't want to burden him with her problems. It was bad enough he witnessed the aftermath of the abuse, which was embarrassing. But to shed light on her past was something she wasn't ready to do. So she reached out to someone who knew her a little bit better.

Sis: I need to talk to you. Can we meet up?"
Brother: Yeah I'm at my place come thru
Sis: K... I'm omw

Sasha grabbed her car keys and left the house in a rush. On her way to Chauncey's place, she thought about what she was going to say and how much she was going to tell him. He didn't know about her past, so she would make that information limited.

She drove through the smooth traffic for twenty minutes before she pulled up to the gate. She used the gate card he had given her and let herself in. Once she parked the car, she took the elevator to the fifth floor and knocked on the door. He opened the door with a smile.

"What's going on wit'cha?"

She walked past him and went to have a seat. "Everything," she pouted. "My life is a mess."

Chauncey closed the door, then walked over to where she was sitting and sat down beside her. "What happened now?" He knew it wasn't a physical altercation because there were no bruises present.

"Well, my mother showed up and started some shit." She took a deep breath. "I don't even know how in the hell she found me. Then Quamae is just getting home from last night."

Chauncey was confused by what she just said. "What'chu mean, yo' mama? I thought she was dead?"

She stared down at the black-tiled floor. "In my eyes she is, but I'll get to that in a minute."

Sasha sat back and got comfortable on the soft leather sofa to tell the story. She started off with everything Quamae told her. Then she gave him the watered down version of her childhood, purposely leaving out the horrid details of her rape and the murder of Frank. Everything else she shared with no hesitation, including her son.

"Damn! So, you have a teenage son."

She nodded her head. "Yes."

This time around when she spoke about it she didn't feel the urge to cry. She had shed so many tears over the past few weeks that she was tired. It was time she accepted what she did and moved on with her life, with or without Quamae. Nevertheless, she was still sad about the situation.

He stood up. "Damn, I need a drink and a blunt after hearing all of that. You want one?"

"Yes."

Chauncey went into the kitchen and fixed them both a drink. Moments later he returned with two cups and a blunt dangling from his lips. He sat back on the couch and handed her a cup.

"Here."

"Thanks. I appreciate you listening to me and not judging me." She took a gulp from the cup. "Shit has been really crazy for me lately."

"Everybody got a past, so it's cool."

For the next hour they drank and smoked while engaging in friendly conversation. All of her problems were temporarily washed away by the liquor and weed. She knew she could count on him to make the pain she was feeling go away. From day one he had always been a voice of reason. Silence fell into the room, and they gazed at one another for what seemed like an eternity. Chauncey leaned toward her, she leaned toward him, and their lips interlocked with one another. He placed a hand on her thigh and caressed it.

The sudden ring of his phone broke their kiss. He reached over and picked it up. It was Monica. He silenced it, then picked up where he left off. His phone continued to ring back-to-back, so he powered it off.

Sasha didn't see who the caller was, but she assumed it was Quamae. "Who was that?"

"Monica."

"Oh, you still messing with her?"

"Something like that, but don't worry about her." He pulled his shorts down, freeing his semi-stiff joystick and pulled her closer to him so she could sit on his lap.

She lifted her dress, then straddled him. "Oh, I'm not worried at all."

"Good, 'cause I've been waiting on you for weeks to get over here and give me another dose."

She used her hand to guide him inside, easing down on it. "Ooh, I missed you, too." She ground on top of him and rolled her hips.

He squeezed her booty and pushed up inside of her repeatedly. "I can't tell, 'cause – Umph – I heard you got another side nigga."

"That's not true. He's just a friend."

"I'm supposed to be your only friend. This shit been going on for months now."

"I know."

She placed her finger over his lips to silence him, then leaned forward and kissed him. She didn't want to discuss Blue. All she wanted was for him to take her to ecstasy. She placed her hands on the back of the sofa and bounced up and down on it, throwing her head back.

"Grr! Damn, I missed yo' ass."

"Ah, me, ah, too!" She thought back to where their romance started.

***

Eight months ago Sasha, Quamae, and Chauncey took a trip to Orlando for the Florida Classic. Due to short notice with hotel bookings, they only had one two-bedroom suite left, and they all ended up staying together. After the game, they returned to the room drunk and high. Sasha and Quamae went into their bedroom, leaving Chauncey in the living room watching television.

Thirty minutes later she returned to the living room because Quamae had too much to drink and passed out on her. Chauncey was sitting on the floor smoking, so she sat down in front of him Indian-style and joined in. After the blunt was gone, he observed her rocking her leg, and he knew she had nothing on underneath her nightdress. He felt like she was doing it on purpose, but he used his better judgment and gave her the benefit of the doubt.

Sasha glanced up at him and saw he was looking between her legs. She smiled, but he pretended not to notice. She then stood up and walked closer to him until she was directly in his face. He didn't look away. Instead, he reached up and rubbed her clit with his thumb. The bed-room door was closed and Quamae was out until morning, so she wasn't worried about being caught. That was the first time of many more to come she would sleep with him.

***

"Ooh, Chauncey, I'm coming," she cried.

"Come for me, baby," he moaned.

She rode him faster and he played with her clit until she released her fluids all over his wood. Then he gripped her waist tight, applying pressure, and took deep thrusts inside of her until he got his nut five minutes later.

"That's what I missed right there."

He stood up with her and carried her to his bedroom. "Let's go take a shower."

Chapter 14

A few days later Sasha and Quamae were finally about to have that much-needed conversation. She was supposed to meet up with Blue, but she had to cancel at the last minute. The constant silence in their home had finally driven them to talk to one another. Sasha suggested they have the discussion at J. Mark's restaurant to level the playing field and eliminate a physical confrontation. Truth be told, she picked that restaurant because that was where they had their first date. She needed him to remember where it all began.

Quamae sat across the table and took a sip of his drink. "It's time we both came clean about our infidelities. In order for us to move past this, we have to be honest with each other. Consider this as confirmation to what we already know," he baited her.

"Okay, I'll go first," she insisted. This was her chance to come clean if she wanted to save her marriage. "The night you caught me getting out the truck, I went on a date with this guy. But the only reason I went was because we haven't been on a date in a long time."

"So you cheated because I've been busy?" He was searching for a solid answer. A real reason behind her cheating.

"Yes."

"Have you ever heard the saying, 'If you don't want a sorry man, you have to deal with a busy man?' Everything I do, I do it for us. I'm out here takin' federal chances and you round here committing adultery."

She leaned back in her seat and looked at him in astonishment. "Yes, I have, but you changed on me completely. You stopped telling me how beautiful I am, how much you love me, and you abandoned my needs. The only time I get that is after we fight, and it shouldn't be that way. It took another man to tell me those things when I have a husband at home." Her voice trembled as she pleaded her case.

"So that nigga told you all of that?" She nodded her head up and down. "And you fell for that shit?" He wanted her to feel stupid for the choices she made. "A nigga would say anything just so he can fuck. I thought you were smarter than that. Who the fuck is this nigga?"

She thought the purpose of their heartfelt talk was to listen without judgment, but he was using this as a chance to add insult to injury. His words were painful, and they cut her like a steak knife. "Quamae, don't do that. Can you just hear me out for once?" Tears pricked the back of her eyes as she became emotional.

"Did you fuck him?"

And there was the moment of truth. For some reason his bluntness caught her by surprise when it shouldn't have. She knew that question was going to come up, whether she wanted it to or not. Her heart rate increased out of fear of what he would say or do. She rocked her leg rapidly under the table. She was slowly, but surely losing her nerve to come clean with him. She looked down at her uneaten plate of food, wishing she wasn't there.

Quamae was getting impatient by the millisecond. "Come on, spill it, don't stop talking now. Did you let the man fuck?"

Sasha counted to ten in her head before she answered his question. "Yes."

He bit down on his bottom lip and closed his eyes. "How many times? And did you use a condom?"

"Six, and yes, we used a condom."

"Was it the night I caught you?"

She nodded her head. "The other times were after you said you wanted a divorce."

"So you kept fuckin' the nigga?"

"Only because—"

He held his hand up to stop her from talking. He finally opened his eyes. "Don't even explain." He leaned forward. "I guess it's my turn," he folded his hands and placed them on the table. "Well, I've been fucking Gigi lately. The morning I came in and took a shower I had just left her house, and no, we didn't use a condom. And when I was in Atlanta I fucked this chick I met, and yes, we used a condom."

Sasha couldn't contain her anger and the tears streamed down her face like a running faucet. "I knew you was still fucking that bitch."

He stood up in a hurry. He was heated, and it was time to go before he ended up in jail for assault and battery. He dropped a buck fifty on the table. "Let's go, this shit over."

Sasha scrambled to grab her purse and run out behind him. She couldn't risk taking her time and being left behind.

Quamae found it hard to forgive her for all of the lies, especially the fact she had a teenage son out there. God Almighty would have to come down from his thrown and look him square in the eyes and say forgive her before he agreed to do such a thing. However, he gave her a pass on her childhood issues since that was beyond her control. Carol hadn't returned since she showed up and blew up the spot. He thanked God for that, because he wouldn't blink at the thought of killing her.

The ride home was completely silent. Nothing could be heard except the wind against the window. The tension in the truck was as thick as the lump in Quamae's throat. He gripped the steering wheel tightly to keep his hands from squeezing the life out of Sasha. To hear she slept with the next man was one thing, but to learn she had a mental connection was another.

His thoughts were brought to a halt when his phone rang. The screen lit up and he saw Chauncey's name, but he let it go to voicemail since he wasn't in the mood to talk. His round called him two more times, and that was out of the ordinary, so he answered.

"What's going on, bruh?"

"About time you pick up, nigga, we got an emergency."

"And what's that?"

"It was a shakedown in The East."

"A'ight, I'll meet you in a few. I'm headed home now."

"I'm on standby at yo' house, so hurry up."

"Be there in five."

Quamae put the pedal to the metal and got there in record time. When he pulled up, Chauncey was standing outside his car smoking a black n mild. He got out of the car and went to unlock the front door so Sasha could go inside. Then he walked up on Chauncey to get the full details on the robbery.

"What da fuck happened in The East?" The East was a drug-infested neighborhood in Ft. Lauderdale, better known as a hustler's dream spot. A lot of Haitian niggas lived in that area, and they got money on the regular. Quamae had linked up with Dred and set up shop. The money was good until this incident happened.

"Dred hit me up and said he needed two bricks. I told the nigga I would have Dirty drop the shit off and to give him the money. Long story short, D dropped the shit off, and while they were inside the house, two masked men came in and shook shit down."

"Masked men, huh?"

"That's what he said."

Quamae stood in a defensive stance with his hands in his pockets. "What you told the nigga when he said that?"

"I told him it was cool and don't worry about the bricks or the money. We would just take the shit as a loss, so that way when we slide on the nigga, he won't suspect shit. And I told Dirty to just chill, 'cause we gon' handle the shit."

Quamae didn't believe that bogus-ass story for a second. "Good, good," he agreed with his tactics. "'Cause that shit foo, my nigga," which meant foogazy. "How the fuck these niggaz knew when to hit shit? That shit was a setup, but that nigga gotta see me 'bout my cash."

"You goddam right."

"It's time to suit up and go pay this shank-ass nigga a visit."

***

It was two in the morning when they pulled up to Dred's house. The streets were dark and quiet. Quamae and Chauncey sat inside an older model Impala with dark tints, dressed in all black, peeping the scene.

"This nigga thought he was safe, but he a fool if he thinks I don't know where he lay his head at."

"How you found out?" Chauncey was puzzled.

"I had Freeman look the nigga up." Freeman was a dirty cop Quamae had on the payroll.

"How we going in?" He looked over at Quamae. "Back door?"

"Front door." Quamae held up a key. "The nigga slipped and left his keys in my truck, and I made a copy."

"Damn, nigga, that was a good move."

"I had a feeling I couldn't trust the nigga after he questioned me about the connect. From there I knew I had to watch his ass closely."

"Well, let's go up in that bitch, 'cause ain't nobody out here. I'm ready to do his ass in."

They pulled their hoodies over their heads and stepped out of the car into the hot, humid air. Their disguises were genius: the hoodies had dreads stitched on the inside to throw off any witnesses.

Quamae slid the key into the door and unlocked it without making a sound. They walked in one-by-one, taking light steps to the hallway with the burners in hand. Halfway there they heard noises coming from the bedroom.

As they got closer, they recognized a female voice and knocking from the headboard. They crept slowly to the door and saw some chick bucking on top of him. The light in the room was dim, but they could see his eyes were closed.

"Ah. Sh. Oh!" she cried out.

They walked into the room unnoticed. Quamae pointed his banger on Dred. "Open your eyes, fuck nigga!" The chick screamed, and Chauncey hit her in the head with the butt of the gun, sending her crashing down while holding her head.

Dred's heart was beating out of his chest. He grabbed the blanket and covered himself "What the fuck!" he shouted in his thick Jamaican accent. When he saw the gun, he panicked. "Take what you want, just don't kill me and my girl, please," he begged.

"Nigga, shut the fuck up!" Quamae spat.

Dred squinted his eyes. He'd recognize that voice from anywhere. "Q?"

They both removed the hoodie from their heads.

154

"Turn the light on, nigga."

Dred leaned over and clicked the light switch on. He was taken aback by the view. Quamae and Chauncey had their bangers pointed at him with silencers on the tips. His eyes grew wide like flying saucers. "Wha-wha-what yawl doing?" he stuttered.

"Where the fuck is my dope and my money?"

Sweat seeped from his pores, making his forehead glisten. "We got robbed. I told Chauncey."

Chauncey inched a little closer toward him. "Nigga, you thought I believed that shit?"

"Bu-bu-but you said everything was cool."

"Nigga, I lied, so where the fuck is our product and money?"

"I don't have it."

Quamae aimed his gun at the chick and shot her in the head. "You still don't have it?"

Dred hollered as he watched the blood ooze from her head and splash on the covers. "Come on, Q, you didn't have to do that. Me not steal nuttin' from you."

He kept his focus on Dred in case he tried something. "Tear this motherfucker up until you find it, C." Chauncey tucked his banger away and went to check the closet. "You never bite the hand that feeds you. Didn't your mother teach you that?" Dred was too afraid to answer Quamae. "Hold out your hands."

He did as he was told, and Quamae shot a hole in both of his hands.

"Argh," he squealed, rocking back and forth, screeching in pain."

Chauncey yelled from the closet. "It ain't shit in here."

"Keep looking."

Chauncey walked away from the closet and looked underneath the bed. He pulled out a duffle bag and unzipped it. "Jackpot, nigga!"

"That's our shit?"

"You fuckin' right it is."

Quamae shot out both of his kneecaps. "Argh!" he screamed.

"I know it's more money in this bitch." Chauncey stood to his feet. "Where is the rest of it, nigga?"

"It's in the hall closet in the safe. The code is 77542."

Chauncey got up and went to check it out. One minute later he returned. "It checked out, and this nigga loaded with weed and cash. Smoke this nigga and let's go." Chauncey walked out of the room to clean out the safe.

Quamae turned his attention back to his victim. "You should've never crossed me, nigga." He fired one round into Dred's forehead and walked out of the room.

After Chauncey finished loading up the duffle bag, they pulled their hoodies back over their heads and left just as quietly as they came.

Chapter 15

"Hey, bae," Carmen shouted.

"What's up?" Sasha laughed.

"We have you on a conference call. Say something, India."

"Hey, girl," India added.

"Hey." Sasha's reply was as phony as a three dollar bill. "Tuh, somebody feeling better these days? 'Cause I haven't heard from you in weeks." She hadn't spoken to India since the blow-up at her house.

"You know I can be petty at times." It took Carmen to call and tell her she needed to reach out to Sasha.

Sasha was driving down Pines Blvd, trying to get home. She used her free time to get a pedicure and her nails done, along with some shopping. After the week she had, she deserved to do something therapeutic for the soul. "So, what's up?"

Carmen replied, "Girl, I had to call you and give you the tea and see if you wanted to go out on Saturday."

With no hesitation in her voice, Sasha responded, "No, I'm going to pass on this one. I'm trying to work things out with my husband, but I will love a sip of tea."

"What?" India chimed in.

"Yeah, we're trying to figure things out." There was no need to go into details about it because it really wasn't their business. She learned her lesson weeks ago when India became judgmental and Carmen suggested she send him to jail. From there on out she was going to keep their issues up under their roof. Because at the end of the day, she could forgive him for his wrongdoings, but her friends wouldn't be so quick to do so.

Carmen was hesitant. "Oh, I guess that's a good thing." She wasn't a fan of Quamae since he beat the brakes off her ass and she wouldn't press charges. "Well, anyway, remember Dred who I was getting the weed from?"

"Yeah."

"Girl, he got killed last night."

That threw her for a loop. "Damn, for real?"

"Girl, yes. It's all over Facebook. Somebody ran up in his shit and killed him and his girl. I heard they was naked when they found them."

"Damn, that's fucked up."

"I know, and I bet it was some hating-ass, broke-ass niggas that did the shit. These some petty-ass niggas. They love to rob and kill a bitch instead of getting they own money."

"Damn, I'm thrown right now. I don't know what to say about that. You have to be careful out here. The hate is real, and the love is so fake. I bet it was one of his homeboys."

"Girl, you know it was." India added.

Sasha pulled into the driveway and spotted Chauncey's car immediately. "Well, I'm home, so I will talk to yawl later," then ended the call. Sasha peeped Carmen's little snide remark, but didn't feel the need to call her out on it. She just left it alone so she could get the dirt. She didn't expect her friends to understand her reasons for wanting to stay, and she didn't care to elaborate on it, either. If it meant she had to keep them at a distance, then that's what she would have to do.

When she walked through the front door, she could hear laughter and music coming from the den. She followed the sound and observed Quamae and Chauncey sitting on the couch playing Madden.

"What's up, sis?" Chauncey smirked.

"Nothing much, just taking it easy."

"Did you enjoy your day out?" Quamae asked. They were being more civilized, although their heart-to-heart didn't go as well as she hoped.

"Yeah, I did."

"On Friday I need you to go with Emani and help her find an apartment by the school."

"What time?"

He shrugged his shoulders. "I don't know, call her and find out."

"Okay." She stood there and watched the next play. They were joking and talking cash shit to each other.

"Bruh, I'm about to kick your ass," Quamae shouted.

"Nigga, please, you already down seven points."

"I'm 'bout to get this touchdown on that ass in a minute."

Sasha left them alone to continue their game and headed upstairs. She walked into their bedroom, but suddenly stopped to remind herself she no longer slept there. She made her way to her living quarters and sat her shopping bag on the floor to prepare for her shower. Once she had everything together, she went into the bathroom, turned on the water, and stepped in. The water from the showerhead was steaming hot, yet relaxing to her body. She closed her eyes and reminisced back to her childhood days when she was young and innocent, without a care in the world.

She often dreamed about Prince Charming picking her up on his white horse and rescuing her. And then all of that changed when her innocence was abruptly taken away by that evil whore. Nate was her Prince Charming for a brief moment, and she often wondered how her life would be if he wasn't taken away from her and thrown into prison. She thought about him often, but never picked up a pen to write him. That's the least she could've done since he took her murder charge. Sasha couldn't face the fact she gave his son up instead of taking responsibility for their child.

Stepping from the shower, she dried the remaining drops of water from her body. Then she slipped into a cotton pajama set before heading back to the room and climbing into bed. Just as she reached for the remote control, her cell phone beeped, alerting her she had a text message.

Brother: Don't yawl look happy

Sis: Grow up cuz we're hardly happy (frowning face emoji)

Brother: Well cum in here and tell him u leaving him (winking emoji) bring ur shit and cum on (luggage emoji's)

Sis: U think everything funny. I'm glad u find this amusing

Brother: (peace sign emoji)

***

The next day Sasha rolled out of bed and rubbed the sleep from her eyes. She grabbed her cellphone. She had no missed calls or messages from anyone. Her last point of contact was Chauncey. She figured she had fallen asleep because she didn't reply to his last message. Sasha stood up and walked through the house because it was so quiet. She peeked out the window and saw Chauncey's car was still there. Walking into the den, she found both of them sound asleep, stretched out on the couch. She grabbed two blankets from the linen closet and covered them up.

It was still early, so two more hours of sleep would be good for her, then she would get up and cook breakfast.

Two hours came and went. She finally got up, went into the kitchen, and started cooking. They were still asleep. She made a buffet-style breakfast that consisted of sausage, bacon, eggs, hash browns, French toast and orange juice. The aroma from the kitchen lingered through the house, and a few minutes later Quamae staggered in.

"Damn, it smell good in here." He rubbed his stomach.

"No doubt," Chauncey added, as he walked in behind Quamae.

"I knew it wouldn't be long before yawl got up." She fixed two plates for them and some orange juice. "I see yawl had a long night."

"Yeah, I smacked his ass around all night long." Chauncey was smiling while taking a sip of his orange juice. Sasha peeped his subliminal comment, but ignored it. She knew he was talking about their recent sexual encounter.

"Give me a few more days and I'ma kick your ass, then we can put that cash on the table."

"Bruh, you ain't saying shit, I'm ready now." Chauncey pulled out a wad of money and slammed it down on the table. "What you want to do?"

Quamae was hard-down laughing at his competitiveness. "Come on, bruh, you know I can't beat you right now. But I guarantee in two weeks I'll stomp that ass. Then I want you to throw that money on that table just like that."

"Are yawl serious?" Sasha was staring at them like they lost the little bit of sense they had left.

"As a heart attack." Quamae picked up his fork and started to eat.

"Damn, my nigga, how you jump from a few days to two weeks? It's cool, though. I want you to get all the practice you need, because I don't want to just take your money so easily. I want to work for that cash, so don't give it to me without a fight."

"Yeah, bruh, talk that shit now, because in two weeks I won't be able to buy a vowel from your ass."

"We gon' see."

After breakfast Quamae and Chauncey left to go and handle some business at the trap. When they pulled up, Dirty was sitting on the porch.

"What's up, fool?" Quamae said as he dapped up Dirty.

"I'm outchea." Dirty held his arms out. "Bitch-ass Officer Freeman been on the scene today."

Chauncey arched his eyebrows. "Man, I was telling him I don't trust that nigga."

Dirty sat up in his chair. "I'll murk that nigga if he get outta line."

Quamae picked up a cup to fix himself a drink. "He ain't shit but a dirty-ass cop, but we need him to be our eyes and ears. Trust and believe I got enough dirt on that nigga to make him serve a life sentence without a jury."

Dirty pointed his trigger finger and reiterated what he just said. "If the nigga get out of line, I'ma twist his cap back."

Quamae didn't argue with him because he knew Dirty wouldn't hesitate to take him out. "I know you will, bruh. So, what's up with weed? Is that shit bumping?"

"Hell yeah. We gon' need to cop some mo'." Dirty already knew it was gonna bump. He just had to prove it to Quamae.

Chauncey was satisfied with the answer. "I told you that shit was a good move," he looked over at Quamae. "And you was worried the shit wasn't gon' shake."

"Nah, it ain't that. I just don't want to be greedy with my hands in all the pots, but if that's what yawl wanna continue doing, then we can add it to the inventory. I might as well go out with a bang." He was ready to get out of the dope game before it was too late. There were only two places guaranteed with that lifestyle: dead or in jail. And he didn't want either one.

Dirty thought back to the robbery. "I like how yawl boys handled that business and sent that message loud and clear. That nigga tried it and thought shit was sweet."

"You already knew how we was coming. This nigga was waiting on me in the driveway when I got to the crib. We got suited and booted and made shit shake."

Chauncey was sitting back, shaking his head, and smiling while he sent Monica a text. "That nigga was scared as fuck. You should've seen that nigga face when we hit the fuckin' lights." He laughed and kept his focus on his phone.

Quamae was ready to get back to business, so he turned his attention back to Dirty. "So, how much weed you got left?"

"I have a few more QPs to get off and it's done. But the young boys already called and said they'll be through later to pick up what's left."

"A'ight, so give me the money you made, 'cause that cash can't be over here like that. And when you done, hit the nigga up and we'll re-up."

"It's already bagged up and ready to go. You know I know what time it is out here."

"Good, good. So, go grab that, 'cause we 'bout to head out. I got a couple niggas that owe me bread for that work, and it's time to pay the piper."

"I feel you on that shit." He stood up and went inside the house to get the bag. He returned a few minutes later and handed it to him. "That's a little over a hundred grand."

"A'ight, bruh, we out." They slapped hands and G-hugged. It was time for Quamae to pick up his money or paint the city red.

Chapter 16

Sasha sat on the phone, giggling like a teenage girl speaking with her high school crush. Blue was much younger than her, so he had a way of making her feel young all over again. The eight-year difference was nothing but a number.

"All jokes aside, a nigga miss you. I let you stand me up for your lil' dinner date the other day, but it ain't goin' down today. So, you might as well g'on ahead and leave now before he come home."

He gave her butterflies through the phone. "Okay, bae, I'm on my way."

"Good, 'cause I got something for you when you get here."

Her body ached to feel his tender touch again. "I bet you do."

Blue smiled hard through the phone. "Nah, it ain't that. Although you gon' get that, too."

"Hmm, I can't wait to see what it is."

"Well, hurry up and come see."

"Okay, I'm leaving now."

"I'll be waiting."

"Okay, bye."

Sasha got out of bed quickly and grabbed her things so she could leave before her husband made it home. The way Blue made her feel desired was something she lacked for a while now. She ran downstairs quickly and out the front door.

As she backed up out of the driveway, she slammed on her brakes suddenly to keep from hitting some woman behind her car. She rolled down the window to apologize for frightening the woman, but became speechless when she recognized her as her mother.

Carol walked up to the window. "First you send me to prison, now you want to run me over with your car. What's wrong with you, girl?"

Sasha couldn't believe her eyes. She hadn't seen Carol in fifteen years, and truth be told, she looked better than she remembered. True enough she looked like a butch, but she looked much better to say the least. Every piece of hatred resurfaced, and her blood boiled at an all-time high.

"What the fuck are you doing here?" Her tone was bitter and nasty. She hated Carol with a passion, and all of those images from her past started to play in her mind. "Did you come to ruin my life again? Take away another man that loves me?"

"I didn't take Nate away from you. He went where he belonged. Prison!"

"And where did you belong? Because I think that place was designed especially for you."

"I'll take that."

Sasha gripped the steering wheel tight. "You don't have a choice."

Carol held her hands up in front her. "Oh, aren't we jazzy?"

Sasha completely ignored her last comment. "Why are you here? You shouldn't be here."

She wiped the smile from her face and got serious. "Just like I told your fine-ass husband, you owe me, and I'm not leaving until I get it. So get used to seeing my face until I get my money."

Sasha rolled her neck and looked her birth mother up and down. "Ha ha ha," she thought Carol was a joke. "It takes a special kind of bitch to show up here and demand money. But let's make one thing clear, I'm not giving you shit! So get the fuck out my yard."

Carol laughed as if she had just heard some sort of joke. "Oh, is that right?"

"That's a fact. So again, get the fuck off my property before I call the police, and don't you ever dot my doorstep again. This my first and last time telling you this."

"You gon' regret talking to me like that, bitch."

Sasha rolled the window up on her while she was talking and hit the gas with much force, sending her car zooming out of the driveway in reverse. She drove at a high rate of speed on I-95, cutting her forty-minute drive to Blue's Coconut Grove house down to twenty-five. Carol had her hotter than Florida's summer weather. She pulled up in the driveway next to his truck and got out to ring the doorbell.

He answered the door wearing a pair of joggers that complimented his bowlegs and a tank top that exposed his cut frame. He greeted her with a kiss. "This is the fastest you ever got here."

She slapped his arm playfully. "Be quiet."

They walked through the house and Sasha scoped out every room. The first time she came it was dark, so she was unable to peep the scenery. So, she took her time and noticed the house was immaculate. Nothing was out of place. The white leather sofa set indicated there were no children in the residence. They continued walking until they reached his room, closing the door behind them.

"Sit on the bed and close your eyes," he instructed.

Sasha removed her shoes, sat down on his Platform bed, and closed her eyes. She was nervous and anxious at the same time, because she didn't know what he was about to give her. She could hear him open and close the drawer. Her heart beat rapidly in anticipation until she felt him place a box on her lap.

"Open your eyes."

When she opened them she looked down and saw a gift box. She removed the top from the box and pulled out a Louis Vuitton handbag. "Oh my gosh, I love it." She looked up at Blue with teary eyes.

"I knew you would."

No matter what she went through or how she felt, he always found a way to brighten her day. "I love it!" she screeched. "Thank you."

"You're welcome."

Sasha sat the box on the bed and reached her arms out. "Come let me show you how much I appreciate you." She had never given him oral pleasure before, but today he deserved it.

Blue smiled and took a few steps toward her. He knew the gift was a good idea after all she'd been through. She needed someone to make her feel good, and he was the man for the job.

Sasha pulled his joggers down far enough to gain access to his wood. Freeing it, she placed her hand on it and stroked him gently before placing her warm mouth on it. Blue placed one hand on top of her head and closed his eyes.

"Mm, that's what I'm talkin' 'bout."

***

On the other side of town, Gigi sat patiently on her toilet seat, waiting on God to decide her fate. She shook her legs uncontrollably, as the results surfaced slowly. *Positive*. She was happy because her plan had finally worked. Her only problem was she didn't know how he was going to react to the news. Getting rid of the baby wasn't something she wanted to do, so she hoped he would take it well.

If it all boiled down to it and he was adamant about an abortion, then he was out of luck and stuck. There was no way she was terminating her pregnancy. Money wasn't an issue because she worked at the hospital as a Registered Nurse and had been on her job for two years. To keep herself from going crazy, she sent him a text.

Gigi: I really need you to come over it's an emergency please come over now

Quamae: What's wrong? Are you okay?

Gigi: Please hurry

Quamae: Omw

Gigi: K

Gigi sat on the couch, unsure of the way Quamae might react. She was with him for four years, so she was well aware of how bad his temper could get. It wasn't like she was trying to trap him. They had spent hours having unprotected sex, and not once did he think to pull out. She needed to calm her nerves, but there was nothing she could take, and a shot of liquor was out of the question.

Forty-five minutes later those three special knocks on the door let her know Quamae had arrived. She took a deep breath, put the pregnancy test in her pocket, and answered the door. He walked in with a concerned look on his face. "What's wrong?"

"I need to show you something." Quamae followed Gigi to the couch and sat down. Gigi reached into her sweatpants pocket, pulled out the pregnancy test, and handed it to him. "Here."

Before he grabbed it, he questioned her. "What's that?" He didn't even look at it.

"Just read it."

Quamae took the test from her hand and stared at it. "What's this supposed to mean?"

"I'm pregnant."

"And what does that mean to me?" He spoke to her in a calm manner. He knew how sensitive she could be at times.

"It's your baby."

Quamae sat there rubbing his head because he couldn't believe half of what he was seeing and none of what she was saying. Gigi had never given him a reason to ever doubt her word, but all that shit she just said sounded foreign. "Are you sure about that?"

She had to look at him to make sure she heard him correctly. "You just asked me was I sure?" She pointed at herself.

"No disrespect," he held both hands in the air to declare peace.

"I've only been with you, and you know it, but tell me this: how can you question me when you always fucking me with no condom?" She was pissed. "How many times have you popped up over here unannounced and caught anybody in here? None. I don't have to lie to you because you're a married man and you don't belong to me." Gigi started to breakdown. "I let you in here whenever it's convenient for you and you don't give a fuck about me. I haven't moved on because my dumb ass still fucking you."

She stood up to leave before she said something she might regret. "You can let yourself out." She walked away without another word.

Gigi lay in her bed, balled up. Her fresh tears soaked the pillow. Things had gone exactly the way she thought they would. Quamae had completely dismissed the fact he got her pregnant. Then she thought maybe this was the wrong thing for her to do.

Gigi felt a strong presence close to her. She opened her eyes to find Quamae standing over her. He crawled into bed and kissed the side of her face.

"I'm sorry, Gia." That's what he would always call her whenever he messed up. "I didn't mean any of that shit I just said. You caught me off guard."

She shook her head up and down. "Yes, you did."

Quamae rolled her over so they could see eye-to-eye. "I'm sorry."

He leaned in and kissed her softly on the lips. She fought the urge to kiss him back. She turned her head slightly. "Stop! Just leave me alone."

He turned her face toward his, so she could look into his eyes. "I should've never said any of that to you. I'm sorry." He kissed her again, but this time she didn't fight it. She was weak when it came to him, and that's why she couldn't move on without him. "I love you."

Gigi's heart stopped the moment those words pierced her ears. A lot of time had passed since he last said those words to her, and she was happy to hear them again. "I never stopped loving you," she cried.

He smoothly removed her sweatpants and panties without breaking their kiss. He spread her legs apart with his thighs. Using his left hand, he rubbed his throbbing dick and down her slit, making it wetter. "I should've married you instead. I fucked up." Quamae eased himself into her opening and stroked her slowly in and out. He kissed away the tears on her face and apologized to her again.

Gigi put her arms around him and held him tight. "It's not too late to fix it." As Quamae thrust down into her slippery tunnel, she tilted her hips forward and matched his pace, a soft moan escaping her lips. "Mm," she bit down on his neck and sucked on his skin.

There was something different about the way he handled her body. There was no rough sex that day. He was gentle with her, and that was something he hadn't done to her in a long time. Quamae made sweet, passionate love to the woman under him. She was different now, and he would never disrespect her again. Gigi was about to be the mother of his child, and because of that, she would always hold special strings to his heart.

Quamae was on the verge of reaching an orgasm. His speed increased, and Gigi wrapped her legs around his waist. "Ah, ah, ah," she screamed softly. She wanted to make sure he hit the right spot, so they could cum together. And just like that, they did.

Quamae lay on his side and held Gigi in his arms. The moment of truth had presented itself again, and she wanted a straight answer. She didn't need sex clouding her judgment whenever he was around. A lump in her throat formed as she began to talk, but she swallowed hard so he could hear her loud and clear. "What are we going to do?"

"It's your decision. I'll be there for you no matter what you choose."

"But I'm scared."

He was curious. "For what?"

"Raising a baby alone."

He already knew where she was going with that statement. "I'll never make you do that." Quamae rubbed his hand over her flat belly. "Do you want to keep the baby?"

She shook her head, then said yes. Quamae smiled because the moment was bittersweet. Just a few weeks ago he found out his wife was probably barren, and now he had a chance at being a father.

"What about your wife?"

"Don't worry about her, that's my problem. Hell, we might be divorced by the time the baby get here anyway." He grabbed her by her cheeks and kissed her once again on those soft lips. "You just worry about you and my baby in there, okay?"

She nodded. "Okay.

Chapter 17

Friday rolled around quicker than Sasha expected, and she was tired from apartment hunting with Emani. They searched complex after complex, and she still hadn't found an apartment that met her standards or Quamae's requirements. The next stop was Milagro Coral Gables, and Sasha prayed the apartment would be satisfactory for her picky-ass sister-in-law. Sasha put the car in park and looked at Emani.

"Girl, you picky as hell. What was wrong with the last three apartments?"

"I didn't like them. Did you see what I saw?"

"Yeah, and they were all nice and in your brother's price range."

Emani folded her arms and pouted. "No, they wasn't. He need to let me at least find something for twelve hundred. The cost of living is high anyway. He just being cheap."

Sasha looked at her spoiled-ass and laughed. "That's a shame how he got you. Stop being selfish, because he still has to give you allowance, and he refuses to make you work."

Emani cut her eyes and pointed her finger in her direction. "I know you didn't just say that. Where you work at again? And look at that Celine bag you carrying, that costs more than my rent." She frowned and hit Sasha with the puppy dog eyes. "Call him, Sasha, please, and tell him to give me a higher budget. I don't wanna live in the ghetto."

Sasha laughed hysterically. "You need to cut it out. Get out this car so we can get this over with. We have been searching for hours, and you still haven't found anything."

She sucked her teeth. "Alright, but if something happens to me, it's yawl fault." She opened the car and got out. Sasha did the same.

When they made it on the inside, they were greeted by Javier, and he took them on a tour of the property. He escorted them into a one-bedroom model unit. "Step inside and take a look at our marvelous apartment. It's to die for."

Emani smiled. "Ooh, I like the sound of that."

They walked inside the apartment and Emani's eyes lit up. "Oh my gosh, I'm in heaven right now." She immediately fell in love with the layout and stainless steel appliances. "Granite countertops in the kitchen and the bathroom." She walked over to the closet. "And a stackable washer and dryer. How much? I love it."

"Well, this unit is fifteen seventy five, but the electric bill is included in the rent."

A sad expression appeared immediately on her face. "I know I can forget about this, 'cause El Cheapo ain't going for it."

Javier laughed. "Who is El Cheapo, your boyfriend?"

"No it's my brother, better known as my daddy." She poked out her lip.

Sasha put her hands on her hips. "The one that has to pay the rent."

"Well what's your budget?" Javier asked out of curiosity.

"Eleven hundred."

He placed his hand over his chest and exhaled. "Oh my, we don't have anything in that price range." He was truly a queen.

"See, Sasha, what did I tell you? Can you please, please call him and make him pay more? I'm begging you. He'll do it if you tell him to."

"Is this your mother?"

Sasha cut her eyes at him. "Hell no! I'm not old."

"This is my sister-in-law. She's married to El Cheapo, and she can make him pay more, but they want me to live in the ghetto so I can be robbed, raped, and killed."

"Emani, stop, 'cause that's not true."

"Don't come to my funeral either, you or him."

Javier cracked up off of her expense. She was a true character. "Okay, I can see how serious you are about this. I'm going to call my manager, who is also my uncle, and see if there is anything we can do for students that attend the University of Miami."

A little hope was all she needed. "You'll do that for me?"

"Yes, darling, 'cause you are too funny." Javier was obviously gay, but Emani liked him to say the least. She didn't care what he was as long as he could find her a discount from somewhere. "I'm going to step away and call him. I'll be right back."

"Okay, thank you so much."

"You're welcome, honey." He walked away and made his call.

Sasha and Emani sat on the barstools in the kitchen and waited on Javier to return. In the meantime, she texted Blue since she was in the area.

Sasha: Hey are you home? Cause I'm in your area.

Blue: Yea I'm here. What u doing up here?

Sasha: Apartment hunting with my bratty sis in law

Blue: Oh

Sasha: I'll be there after I drop her off

Blue: Cool

Javier returned with a smile on his face. "Okay, Miss Emani, I have some good news for you. With the student discount, we can get you in for thirteen hundred a month."

She immediately looked at Sasha. "Look at God, won't he do it!"

"Well, call your brother and see what he says."

"I already know what he gon' say."

"Just say everything that you said to me. I'm sure he doesn't want a hair harmed on that pretty little head of yours."

Emani picked up the phone and called him, but he didn't answer. She pressed send again, but he was returning her call.

"What's up, E?" Quamae asked.

"I found an apartment that's going to give me a student discount."

"Where and how much?"

"Milagro Coral Gables. They're not far from the school and it's only thirteen hundred."

"And that's two hundred over your budget."

"But they have twenty-four security, washer, dryer, exercise room, granite everything and a balcony. Please Quamae," she rambled.

"You killing me, E. I said eleven hundred, and that's it."

Emani was so mad, her eyes watered. "If I get robbed, raped, or killed in the hood, don't come to my funeral because you're not concerned about my safety," she screamed.

Quamae was silent for a minute before he spoke again. "Put Sasha on the phone."

She handed her the phone and the two of them talked about the apartment. After speaking for five minutes, Sasha hung up the phone. "You're brother said he loves you."

Emani swatted Sasha away with her hand. "Yeah, right. I'm ready to go now."

Sasha looked at Javier. "Yes, we can leave now, and I would like the paperwork for the apartment."

Emani looked up. "He said yes?"

"Yeah, crybaby, now come on."

Emani was so happy she didn't know what to do. She was finally getting her own place, and it felt good, too. Good riddance to bad roommates. "It worked, though."

On their way back to the car, Sasha felt sick all of a sudden. She stopped in her tracks and vomit poured from her mouth. She bent over and coughed violently as the fluid continued to splash on the concrete.

"Ew! You okay?" Emani was disgusted by the scene. "What's wrong with you?"

"I don't feel too good."

"Well, I can see that. Let me find out you prego," Emani joked.

"I'm not."

She walked over and grabbed her bag. "Give me this purse so you don't get throw-up on it."

***

Sasha lay across Blue's bed with a terrible stomach ache. The cramps in her stomach were kicking her ass. "I feel like shit."

"Well, what did you eat?" He sat down beside her and rubbed her head.

"Chick-fil-a."

"And that shit got you feeling like that?"

"That's all it could be."

"Hold on, I'll be right back."

He walked out of the room and closed the door. While he was out, she decided to send Quamae a text so he wouldn't be looking for her. She told him she stopped by Carmen's and she wasn't feeling good, so she was going to lay down for a few. She was surprised when he texted her back with the single word response: *okay*. She put her phone on silent and laid it face down under the pillow.

Blue returned with a BC powder and ginger ale. "Here, take this, it should settle your stomach."

"You sure about that?"

"I use it when I have a hangover, so it should work."

Sasha sat up in bed. "We'll see."

He watched her dump the powdery substance in her mouth, followed by the drink. His hands were folded in his lap. "My mama asked me if you are pregnant."

Sasha spit ginger ale from her mouth. "What? Why would she think that?"

"She's a Obstetrician, in case you forgot, and she said you look different from the first time she met you. She said you look motherly," he grinned.

"I'm so embarrassed."

"For what? She know we fucking. She said she heard you one night and she thought I was killing you in here," his laughter echoed in the room. "She was gon' knock on the door, but she changed her mind."

"That is not funny. Now I'm really embarrassed. What did you tell her?"

"I told her I didn't know."

The knock on the door stopped their talking. "It's open, Ma."

Blue's mother walked in. She was a petite woman, standing at four-foot-eleven, with long dark hair and brown skin. He resembled her a lot. "What's up, baby?" Sasha loved his relationship with her. She wished she had a good relationship with her mother growing up. "I came to see what's wrong with Sasha."

Sasha's eyes fell to the floor. "I'm okay."

"That's not what Darian just told me."

Blue looked at his mother, "Lady, what I told you about using my government name?"

"I am not one of your friends, so I will not be calling you Blue."

He surrendered. "A'ight, Mommy, you got that."

She turned her attention back to Sasha. "You don't look okay to me. I have been a nurse for years, and I know a pregnant woman like the back of my hand. So get up and let's take this pregnancy test." She helped Sasha out of bed and pointed a finger at Blue. "What I told you about using condoms. Boy, you just don't listen."

"Ma, she ain't pregnant, though."

"We're about to see."

They walked out of his room and down the hall to the bathroom. Darlene handed Sasha a plastic cup and closed the door. Sasha sat on the toilet and emptied her bladder. She wiped herself, then flushed the toilet and washed her hands. When she opened the door, Darlene came in with a test they use at the hospital, and she was thrown because she wondered how many girls she tested on her son's be-half. She put on a pair of latex gloves and stuck the stick inside the cup and waited for two minutes. She picked up the stick, looked at the coloring, and handed it to Sasha.

Darlene was calm. "Here are your results. You can go show this to Darian."

Chapter 18

The following day Sasha was assigned to errands by Quamae. Her job was to make sure Emani got the money for the deposit to hold the apartment, pay the remaining balance on Emani's car loan, and pick up his clothes from the cleaners. That meant she had to go by the bank and deposit the money into her sister-in-law's account before noon. It took all of thirty minutes to get the deposit done, and then she was on to the next task.

By the time she was finished it was one in the afternoon. She was sweaty and smelled like the outdoors. The sun wasn't playing that day. The hot beams from the sun burnt the back of her neck, so she ran to her car.

After running for cover, she put the air on blast so she could cool off quicker. "Damn, it's hot as hell out here." She adjusted the vents until they were on her directly. She took out her phone to call Quamae.

His phone rang for a long time before he finally picked up. "Yeah."

"I just called to let you know everything is done. I sent the money, paid off her car, and picked up your clothes. I'm on my way home now to drop it off."

"A'ight, thanks."

"You're welcome."

Sasha then placed a call to her girls to let them know she was headed home to take a shower, and then she would be on her way to meet them for lunch. There was no way she was going out smelling like that.

The light changed fairly quickly, and she slammed on the brakes. The car behind her was just inches away from taking off her bumper. It startled her. "Shit, let me put this phone down." She looked over her shoulder and shouted, "Don't hit my car with that old-ass car."

When the light changed, she pulled off, then switched lanes, and the car behind her did the same. She turned the music up and kept her eyes on the road. It didn't take her too long to get home since everything was in the same vicinity. When she pulled up into the driveway she saw the same car ride past her and go up the street.

She rushed upstairs to find a change of clothes and took a five-minute ho bath. In less than thirty minutes she was completely dressed and ready to go. On her way out of the subdivision, she saw the same car coming out after her. She got nervous. "Are they following me?" she asked herself.

When Sasha arrived at T.G.I Friday's, India and Carmen were standing outside, waiting on her. She walked up and greeted them. "Hey!"

Carmen had her hands on her hips. "Hey my ass, you late."

"And I'm hungry," India added. "I haven't eaten all day, waiting for lunch."

"Keep calm! I'm here now, and I told yawl I was gonna be late." She looked over her shoulder to see if she could see the car, but she didn't.

"Who you looking for?" Carmen peeped her paranoia.

"This old car been following me for the longest, but when I turned in here they kept going."

"You sure you not just being paranoid?"

"No, they followed me to my neighborhood and then here. I don't know what's going on, but that shit got me nervous."

"Did you call Quamae and tell him?" India looked worried.

"No."

"You don't think you should?"

"I'll tell him later."

"Make sure you do."

They walked into the establishment and avoided all wait time since it wasn't crowded. They were seated at a booth and the waiter didn't hesitate at taking their orders. They were in the middle of listening to Sasha's drama-filled life when the waiter returned with the appetizer and their drinks. Sasha waited until he walked away to continue with the conversation.

"I'm pregnant," she blurted out.

"You're what?" Carmen shouted while shoving a mozzarella stick into her mouth.

"Sounds like she said she pregnant," India replied as she sipped on her margarita.

"That's exactly what I said."

"Ooh, I'm gonna be a godmama," Carmen said, clapping her hands.

India rolled her eyes. "No, bitch, she needs a responsible adult."

Carmen stuck up her middle finger. "Is that responsible enough for you, ho?"

"Just remember that behind every bird is a pile of shit," India laughed.

Sasha shook her head. "Yawl know the baby is going to have both of you bitches as godparents."

"Why, 'cause you don't want to pick one?" India fussed.

"No, because she doesn't want to hurt your feelings. You know how you get, all sentimental and shit." Carmen threw a piece of ice at India, and she threw it back.

"Stop it, dumbass girl."

Sasha interrupted the kiddie fight. "Yawl need to grow up, so childish. And this is why I'm not choosing neither one of you crazy bitches."

"So, what did Quamae say? Is he happy?" India bounced around in her seat. Sasha looked sad all of a sudden, and the look on her face made India answer her own question. "He's not happy, is it?"

"I haven't told him yet."

India did the digging while Carmen sat and listened. "Why not?"

Sasha remained quiet for a minute, thinking of a way to answer the question. India and Carmen were unaware Quamae wanted a divorce and the fact the two of them had been sleeping in separate rooms. As a woman, it was embarrassing to not know who fathered your baby, but these were her sisters, so she figured they would understand.

Before Sasha could open her mouth to respond, Carmen jumped right on it. "Ooh, you don't know who the daddy is, do you?"

The waiter walked right into the middle of their conversation. "Do you ladies need a refill on anything?"

Carmen smiled. "No, just our lunch." He walked away and headed in the direction of the kitchen.

"He needs to hurry up with the food, damn. I don't want shit else to drink." India was tired of waiting.

Sasha had this blank stare glued on her face. "Are you in a rush or something, India?"

"Hell yeah, I'm hungry as a hostage, but don't try to change the subject, 'cause we waiting on the answer."

"I don't know."

India frowned when she confirmed Carmen was right. "So wait, you let Blue hit it raw?"

***

Dirty slammed down his last domino. "Dominoes, muthafucka!"

There was a lot of noise coming from the playing table. "Shut up, you lucky-ass nigga," one of the guys yelled.

"Nigga, pay up or get the fuck up." Everybody threw their bills on the table and he snatched them up quickly. "Come on, Chauncey, I want some of your money."

Chauncey sealed the blunt he was rolling. "I bet you do."

"Sit your ass down, then."

"As soon as I roll up, I'm gon' sit down, beat your ass, and take your money."

Dirty sat up in the chair and fixed another cup. "I want to see dis shit."

"Yeah, nigga, drink up so this ass-whooping will be painless."

As soon as he was done, he sat at the table with Dirty. "Come on, nigga, don't procrastinate now. Hurry your ass up."

Dirty was ready. "Put that money up."

"I got mine, nigga, let's play."

Everyone stood around, waiting to see who was taking whose money. Six games and six hundred dollars later, Chauncey got up from the table. "It was fun taking your money, but I'm done."

Dirty stood up. "You got lucky this time. It's cool, though."

He smiled at him. "I know it's cool. You lost, nigga, fair and square. I told you to quit while you was ahead."

Chauncey sat across the table and observed Quamae playing with his phone. He wasn't paying attention to Chauncey because he was too busy texting Gigi.

Quamae: How are my babies doing over there?

Gigi: We're good. R u coming over?

Quamae: Not tonight

Gigi: (crying face emoji)

Quamae: I promise I'll be there tomorrow (winking emoji)

Gigi: K... I have my first doctor's appointment next week to find out how far along I am. Do you want to come?

Quamae: Yea... didn't I tell you I'll be there every step of the way. Just let me know the day and time.

Gigi: I will

Quamae: GN... Cu 2maro

Gigi: GN (kissing face emoji)

On the way home, Quamae thought about his unborn child. He promised he was going to be the best father he could be. There was no way in hell he would force Gigi to become a single mother. He was raised in a single parent home, but his child wasn't going to go through that. All he had to do now was figure out when and how to tell Sasha. Regardless of what happened between them, she was still his wife, and she deserved to know. He decided tonight would be the night he came clean about the baby. There was no point in holding off any longer because it wasn't like they were together. And maybe this news would make her speed up the process with her transition in moving on. He hoped for the best.

Chapter 19

After returning home from her lunch date with the girls, Sasha decided she might as well tell Quamae and Chauncey about the baby. Blue already knew thanks to his inquisitive mother, and she made it clear she wasn't happy about the baby. Her only concern was that he go back and finish his degree in medicine to become a doctor. Her voice kept playing in her head: *Darian, a baby will only hinder your plans to finish school. You wanna sell dope for the rest of your life?* She had no idea Sasha was married, so Blue kept his mouth closed, because he knew there was a chance the baby wasn't his. He wasn't mad about the situation, but he wasn't sure what the outcome of their relationship would be if he wasn't.

She had no idea who she was pregnant from. There was a possibility it could be from any one of them. She had slept with them all within a short period of time, so even if she knew how far along she was, it was still too close to tell. *How in the hell did I end up with three possibilities?*

One of the potential fathers was walking through the door. She suddenly became nervous about telling him, even after she had rehearsed what she would say in the mirror over and over again.

Quamae walked into the room and stood against the wall. "We need to talk."

The expression on his face let her know whatever was on his mind was heavy as a cement block. She had a feeling it was about her moving out quicker, since time was flying and she still hadn't found a job or a place, although she wasn't looking.

Sasha looked at him with sunken eyes. "Yeah, we do need to talk, but let me go first before I lose the nerve to tell you."

He agreed with a head nod.

There was no point in beating around the bush, so she just came out and said it. "I'm pregnant."

Quamae felt like the wind was just knocked out of him. He needed to make sure he heard her correctly. "What?"

"I'm pregnant."

He looked her up and down. "How?"

She wasn't all that surprised by his comment. "What do you mean, how?"

"I thought you couldn't have kids."

"I never said that. You assumed I couldn't."

He powered off his cellphone in his hand and placed it in his pocket. "Well, who you pregnant from?" He folded his arms across his chest.

"Who do you think?" she snapped.

"I don't know, that's why I'm asking you."

She was frustrated with his nonchalant attitude. "You." She assumed he would be somewhat happy about the news since he wanted kids so bad.

"Okay, let me help you out a little bit, because I can see you having a hard time remembering. I'm not the only one you slept with. Do you remember the nigga that dropped you off at five in the morning?"

"We used condoms."

"I don't know that for a fact, and you not gon' sit here and tell me you made the nigga strap up every time."

"I'm telling you we did."

"I don't believe you, simple as that." He was going to get to the bottom of it, and he was doing it now. He looked over on the dresser and saw her cell phone sitting on it. He walked over and picked it up.

"Quamae, what are you doing?" She tried to snatch the phone from him, but he pushed her back on the bed.

"Sit the fuck down before I beat yo' ass and make you lose that muthafuckin' baby."

He opened the phone and went to her messages. He read text after text message between her and Blue. With each passing minute his eyes grew darker and darker, his breathing was heavy and his chest moved up and down rapidly. Out of nowhere he slung the phone against the wall, shattering it to pieces.

Quamae moved closer to her. "You lying-ass ho." He reached out to punch her in the face, but she moved her head and he caught her in the mouth. Blood oozed from her lip.

She cried out in agony. "Ow!"

"You fucking this young-ass nigga, Blue?"

She was astonished. *How does he know that?* she thought to herself. He caught her expression, but she wasn't about to press the issue because it was clear he indeed knew him.

"Bitch, don't look surprised. Yeah, I know the lil' nigga. He got dreads and he drive a black Cadillac Escalade with rims on it. Bitch, you better be lucky you pregnant, because I'll beat you to sleep in this bitch, and I'm telling you now I ain't doing shit until I get a DNA test. Call that nigga and tell him you need somewhere to stay. You gettin' the fuck up outta here. Go stay with that nigga and his mama."

He walked away and slammed the door behind him. She must have thought he was a damn fool to believe there was a chance he was *her* baby's daddy. *The trust is out the window, and there is no coming back from this shit.*

***

The time had come for Quamae to go to the doctor with Gigi. He started off their morning with breakfast at the Original Pancake House before heading to her first doctor's appointment. Upon arriving at Dr. Joyner's office, there were four other expectant mothers sitting in the waiting area. One of the women looked like she was due three months ago. She was huge! The thought of being fat and getting stretch marks made Gigi cringe, but she was willing to look like a tiger for the man she loved. She stepped to the window and grabbed the clipboard so she could sign in. Quamae was sitting down, flipping through a parenting magazine as he waited for her to sit down.

"You know you suppose to read to the baby so he will be smart?"

He still made her blush after all this time. "Yes, and we can do that together." He promised to be there, so he agreed. Quamae leaned closer to her and whispered so no one could hear him. "I can't wait for you to get big like that lady over there."

"Why?" she laughed.

"So I can see how you look fat."

Gigi slapped his arm playfully. "Hush."

The receptionist opened the window. "Gianni Gaddis."

Gigi stood up and walked to the window. "Fill these out, and when you're done, bring them back to me along with your driver's license."

"Okay." The packet was thick as hell.

Once she completed the paperwork, she handed it back to the receptionist. "The doctor will see you shortly," she smiled.

Dr. Joyner was a short, petite black lady with long, dark hair. "Okay, my name is Darlene Joyner. Nice to meet you both." She extended her arm for a handshake to them both.

"Nice to meet you, too," they replied on one accord.

She looked down at the chart in her hand. "Okay we have mister and misses Gaddis?"

Gigi raised her hand. "I'm Gaddis."

"Oh, I apologize, I assumed you two were married."

Gigi cut her eyes at Quamae and smirked. "No, I'm not married."

"Okay, so let's start off by asking you a few questions. When was your last period?"

She hesitated. "Um, May 10th, I think."

Dr. Joyner pulled out a small, circular hand-held calendar, "So you are six weeks and three days. Your due date will be February 14th."

Quamae smiled. "On Valentine's Day!"

"Yes. Now these next questions are very important, so make sure you answer them truthfully. If you want to answer them in private, we can have Daddy step outside."

Gigi didn't resist because she had nothing to hide. She wasn't sleeping with anyone else, so it didn't matter. "He can stay."

Dr. Joyner nodded her head and read off a list of questions. "Have you ever had any STDs?"

"No."

"Have you ever been pregnant before?"

"No."

Gigi answered each question honestly. Dr. Joyner continued to ask a million questions. They ranged from sexual history down to family history. She was comfortable answering them because they had been in a relationship before that lasted four years, and there was nothing he didn't know about her. The questions finally came to an end, and she instructed her to undress from the waist down and lay on the table. The doctor handed her a paper cloth and walked out. Gigi removed her clothes and sat them on the counter.

"Quickie?" Quamae joked.

"You are so nasty."

"But you about to let the doctor play with it. That's okay, I'll feed my junior later." He winked.

Quamae was playing poker on his cellphone when the doctor walked into the room. "Okay, first I'm going to do a Pap smear to make sure everything is normal. Then we are going to see if we can listen to the baby's heartbeat, and lastly, draw some blood."

Quamae put his phone away and took his place next to Gigi. The blue gel she squeezed on her belly was cold. She placed the Doppler on her tummy and rubbed it around in a circular motion. At first the only sound coming from the speaker was a bunch of static. She moved it to the opposite side and there it was: the faint sound of the baby's heartbeat. *Thump, thump, thump, thump, thump, thump.*

"That's my lil' soldier right there. It has to be a boy." He held Gigi's hand. "I can't wait to meet him."

The look on Quamae's face was priceless, and the sound alone filled his heart with so much joy. He had never experienced something so beautiful. He couldn't wait to hold his little one. "I am going to give him the world, you better believe that."

"Bae, it's going to be a girl." She was extremely happy her plan was falling into place. He was crazy in love with their unborn child already. She had been tracking her menstrual cycle for weeks before she got pregnant. She bought a few ovulation kits to assist with the conception, and it worked. Quamae was about to be back home where he belonged, and she couldn't wait for the day Sasha found out about the baby.

"Nah, it has to be a boy to carry my name for decades. All girls wanna do is get married and change their last name."

Gigi looked into his eyes with a faint smile. "I wish you would change mine."

He patted her hand. "One day."

Just the idea of a human life growing inside of her made him realize he needed to make some changes in his life. And that included Sasha.

After the visit, they went back to Gigi's place and the two of them had passionate sex for the rest of the afternoon.

Quamae was laying on his back, dozing off and on, when his phone vibrated loud on the nightstand. He stared up at the ceiling. "See who that is."

Gigi leaned over and looked at it. "Your sister."

"Put it on speaker." She answered it and did as she was told. "What's up, E?"

"Javier just called me and said I can move in on August 1st."

"What's the move-in?"

"Well, with your credit, sir, it's only five hundred. See, you getting a discount, El Cheapo, and you was doing all that crying about nothing."

Gigi laughed.

"Tell Sasha to shut up, 'cause I can hear her laughing."

"That ain't Sasha."

"Um, excuse me?" She was quiet for a second. "So, who is that in the background? Let me find out you cheating."

He didn't want to go into details in front of Gigi, so he would address that later. "When do you need the money for the deposit?"

"Soon. I need to hold my place."

"I put the money in your account already, so you can go pay it. I see you haven't checked your account."

"No, I didn't check it."

"Is there anything else you need?"

"Duh, furniture and a bedroom suite."

"E, you need a job. You killing me."

"No, I have to focus on school. Do you remember saying that?"

"Just use your credit card, and do not spend over three thousand dollars, and I'm serious. Do not call me and tell me you went over on the price. Not even a dollar. "

"Yes, master, I won't go over my budget," she giggled.

"E, I'm serious, don't play with me or yo' ass will be flipping burgers.

"Ew, God no. I promise I won't."

"Good. Is that it?"

"Yes," she hummed into the phone. "Oh, quick question. Is Sasha pregnant?"

Her question threw him for a loop, and Gigi was now looking him dead in the face, waiting on him to answer. "No, why you asking me that?" Now he wished he had picked up the phone.

"'Cause when we went apartment hunting she was throwing up all over the place."

"Nah, she ain't."

"Oh, okay. I thought I was about to be an auntie."

He needed to get her off the phone quick. "A'ight, E, I'll talk to you later. Be safe, and I love you."

"I love you, too."

Gigi rolled on her side with her back facing him. He sensed she was bothered by what his sister said. "I know you don't have an attitude?"

"No, I'm good."

"Quit lying, 'cause you was fine until she said that." She ignored him. "Man, that girl ain't pregnant, so stop all that. You gettin' mad for nothing."

He put his hand on her stomach and rubbed her belly until he fell asleep. She didn't know what to believe, so she cried silently until she fell asleep as well. Maybe her plan didn't work after all.

Chapter 20

One week later

Chauncey and Dirty knocked on the door and waited for Quamae to answer. When he opened the door, Dirty looked him up and down.

"Wake your tired ass up, nigga. It's money day."

He locked the door behind them and they headed to the den. Chauncey sat the duffle bag down on the pool table and pulled out several pounds of marijuana. He used a knife to tear open one of the packages. The scent was highly potent. He pinched off a piece and rolled up a blunt. The sample was smoking hard, just like the first batch.

"Hit up ya homies and let them know trees on deck," Chauncey said as he looked at Dirty.

Quamae was sluggish, and that brought attention from Chauncey. Apparently it was true a man could carry at least one pregnancy symptom, and he was experiencing fatigue.

"Man, what's wrong with you? You sick or something?"

"I ain't been feeling right lately," he yawned.

"What's going on?" Chauncey asked.

Quamae hadn't been forth-coming on what had been going on lately, so he decided to bring them up to speed. "Gigi pregnant."

Chauncey and Dirty were surprised. "From who?"

Quamae sat down on the barstool. "Me. Man, I took her to the doctor and she's two months pregnant with my seed."

"Damn, man, I ain't know you was still hitting ol' girl." Chauncey thought their fling had ended a long time ago. In his head he was thinking Sasha was getting what she deserved because he told her to leave him, but she didn't listen. He couldn't wait until she found out, and he wasn't going to be the one to tell her, either.

"I wasn't. This happened after I caught her that night. I was mad, so I went to Gigi house and took my frustration out on her and ended up getting her pregnant."

Chauncey was curious. "You told Sasha?"

"Nah, not yet. I have to figure out how I'm gon' tell her."

"She gon' snap when she find out."

"Yeah, I know, but that ain't even the fucked up part."

Dirty walked over to where Quamae was sitting and handed him the blunt. "What's worse than the shit you just said?"

He put the blunt to his lips, took a hit, and released it slow. "After Gigi tell me she pregnant, Sasha turn around and say the same shit."

Quamae wasn't paying attention to Chauncey, because if he had he would've peeped his facial expression, and that alone would have raised a red flag.

"So, you got two babies on the way?" Dirty asked.

"Nah, I don' know about Sasha. That's what she say, but that could be your homeboy baby. I have to get a DNA test first. I'm not taking care of the next man baby."

Dirty was confused. He tilted his head to the side. "Who homeboy?"

Quamae nodded his head toward him. "Yours."

"What homeboy?"

"Blue."

"Bullshit."

"I shit you not. I saw the text messages in her phone. She been fucking that nigga. That's who dropped her off that morning."

"Damn, bruh, that's fucked up. I swear I didn't know."

"I know you didn't."

"So, she must be the older chick he was tal'n 'bout."

"Guess so."

Chauncey just sat back and listened to everything that was being said before he picked up his keys from the table. "I'm going to the car. I'll be right back."

After Quamae dropped that bombshell on him, he had to straighten Sasha. He wanted to know why she didn't tell him. He dialed her number as soon as his Ferragamo sneakers hit the pavement outside. He unleashed a brutal tongue lashing on her as soon as she picked up the phone.

"Why da fuck you didn't tell me you was pregnant?"

She stumbled over her words because he caught her off guard. "You. I. I mean, I don't know. I wanted to tell you in person."

He walked toward the sidewalk in case Quamae decided to come outside. "That's bullshit. You got me over here looking stupid in the face when this nigga tells me you pregnant. You pregnant from him?" He waited for her to respond.

"Yes."

"Well, that's not what I heard. I heard you might be pregnant from Blue," he sighed heavily. "You been fuckin' that young-ass nigga?" The phone went silent, so he looked at the screen to see if she hung up on him. He saw she hadn't. "Answer me, and stop fucking around. That's the nigga you been fuckin'?"

"It sounds like you have the answer already."

"I tell you what, don't worry about leaving the nigga, because I'm done with this shit. From this day forward you do you and I'ma do me."

"But you might be—"

Chauncey chomped her off quick. "I might be what? The daddy. Nah, I don' think so. I'm done, so don't call me or text me no more. I'm good on you."

Chauncey hung the phone up in her face.

*****

Sasha sat in her car and cried in the parking lot. She had just left the Apple store from purchasing a new phone since Quamae broke the other one. Chauncey was the first person to call, and it was anything but pleasant. Her life was unraveling right before her eyes, and there was nothing she could do to stop it.

Traffic was horrible on the way to the shop, so it took her longer than usual to get there. She parked her car next to India's silver Mercedes and did a look-over in the mirror. She had to make sure her eyes weren't too red from the crying. The shop wasn't as busy because it was a weekday.

As she made her way through the shop, Peaches greeted her. "Hey, Miss Thang. Where you been?"

Now, Peaches was the only guy that worked in the shop, but according to him he was a *woman!* He was a full-figured tranny and could pass easily as a female.

"Hey, girl. I've been home."

"Uh-huh."

She stopped in front of her workstation. "What's that supposed to mean?"

"Honey, nothing, but your skin just glowing."

Sasha tooted up her nose and looked at India as she started to speak. "Is that right?"

"Why you looking at me like that? I didn't say anything," India replied.

"You know why, you big-mouth heffa."

Peaches was twirling her curling rod in her hand. "Honey, nobody had to tell Ms. Peaches nothing 'cause it's written all over your face. I know all about that motherly look."

India smiled. "You better tell her, girl."

Peaches popped her lips together. "'Cause, honey, let me tell you, when I was pregnant I was lit up like a glow worm."

Sasha and India were tripping out on that comment. Ms. Peaches was too much to handle. You couldn't tell fish she didn't have a uterus, fallopian tubes, or eggs.

Sasha sat down with the strangest look on her face while she rubbed her stomach. Peaches asked, "Why you looking like you just lost your best friend?"

"My stomach is killing me. It's that damn morning sickness driving me crazy." She got up and went to use the restroom. The truth was she was hurt about Chauncey breaking things off with her. When she returned, her face was flushed.

India looked at her with great concern. "Are you okay?"

"Yeah."

"Did you throw-up?" India was doing the finishing touches on her last client of the day.

"I feel so much better."

"Yes, baby, you remind me of myself when I was pregnant," Peaches added.

"So how come I never saw the baby?" Sasha laughed because she knew better than to think Peaches had a baby.

"Yes, you did. I know you saw Cavali."

"Who?" Sasha didn't know whom she was talking about.

"Cavali is my Yorkie."

She laughed and shook her head. "I'm not playing with you."

By the time they finished gossiping, the shop was cleared out, and Sasha sat down in India's chair so she could do her hair.

"My feet are killing me. I've been up and working since eight o'clock this morning, and I am beat."

"Well, I took a nap after I left the doctor's office, and I'm still tired. I see right now this baby is going to wear me out, but after you re-curl my hair you can rest."

"Oh yeah, how was your appointment?" India picked up the comb and parted Sasha's hair.

"Fine until she asked all of these personal questions about my past."

"Uh-oh, what happened?"

"Nothing, you know I hate talking about it, that's all. But I'm almost two months, and my due date is February 27th."

"Did Quamae go with you?"

"Girl, no. He said he ain't doing nothing until he gets a DNA test."

Peaches couldn't wait to jump in. "Well, why he need a test?"

"'Cause she cheated on him," India shouted with no hesitation.

Peaches shook her head. "Girl, no, you didn't cheat on that fine-ass husband of yours."

She gave Peaches and India a brief run down on some of the things that had been going on while India wand-curled her hair. She also told them how she had a change of heart about becoming a mother. Hearing the baby's heartbeat was amazing and something she would never forget, but now she was questioning if she should go through with the pregnancy or not.

"I'm just tired of being in the house with him. I want to leave, but I don't know how. Where in the hell am I supposed to find a job at?"

"Well, you are the one that put yourself in this predicament." India didn't mean to be insensitive, but it needed to be said. Sasha needed to take responsibility for her actions, because it was her fault she was going through hell.

"Yeah, I did, but he doesn't have to be so disrespectful."

"Well, you can't tell him how to act. All I can say is do what you feel is right and make sure you have a backup plan so you can take care of yourself if it's not his baby." India was so self-righteous, and it irritated the hell out of Sasha.

"Oh, I'm not leaving empty-handed."

Peaches was clearing off her work station and jerked her head back at Sasha's comment. "Yes, honey, don't leave like a mad black woman, leave like a mad white woman."

Sasha laughed and flipped her hair. "I heard that."

When India finished her hair, Sasha stood in the mirror admiring her curls. India sat down to check her appointment book to see what time her first appointment was going to show up. She needed to know what time to come in the next day. There was no point in showing up too early when she could sleep a little bit longer.

"How are you getting home?" India asked Peaches.

"My dude picking me up today."

"Well, alright," Sasha replied.

"Sasha, do you feel like going to the store with me?"

"What store?" Sasha was still standing in the mirror admiring her hair. She felt like shit on the inside, but on the outside she looked good.

"Saks, and I wish you would sit down somewhere."

"Yeah, I'll go with you."

"I have to get a dress for Steve's banquet."

India locked up the shop and they stepped outside into the cool evening air, which was a result of a few minutes of rain. Florida weather was funny like that. Sasha rubbed her arms as she shivered from the breeze. She stared as she watched Peaches get into the car with an attractive older man.

"Serve the base, bae," she yelled, letting Peaches know to give the girls hell.

Peaches snapped her fingers in a Z formation. "'Cause I slay."

Sasha and India walked to where their cars were parked. India hit the button on her keypad to unlock the doors.

"What about my car?" Sasha asked.

"You can leave it here until we come back."

Sasha looked at India like she had just smoked some crack. "Hell no." She didn't like the idea of leaving her in a plaza for a few hours unattended.

"I do it all the time, the security guard doesn't leave until nine o'clock."

Sasha stood on the passenger side and pointed her finger at India. "Bitch, if something happens to my shit, I'm holding you responsible."

She brushed her off and opened the driver's door, but then she paused. "You know what, just follow me to my house, because I have to get something anyway."

Sasha was relieved. "Okay."

When she got into her car, she immediately called Blue. The way he picked up so quickly let her know he had been waiting to hear from her.

"Where have you been?" he asked.

"I haven't had a phone in a week. I just got one today." She pulled out and followed behind India.

Blue muted the television in order to hear her clearly. "What happened to your phone?"

"Quamae broke it when we got into a fight." She lowered her voice. "I told him I'm pregnant and he lost it. He snatched my phone and read all of our text messages."

The name alone made him think. He knew he heard that name before, but he wasn't sure where he heard it. "He put his hands on you?"

"He bust my lip."

"So, why didn't you call me?"

"I don't know your number by hand."

"Why the fuck you keep letting him do that to you? I don't fuckin' understand you." He was enraged, because he never raised his voice at her before.

"It's complicated."

"Well, un-complicate it for me, shit, 'cause I'm more lost than a muthafucka. You like that shit or something?"

Sasha couldn't handle another man cursing her out. She was already pregnant, and that made her more emotional than she already was. "I can't explain it," she sobbed.

The crying on the other end of the phone softened his heart, and he stopped yelling at her. "I'm sorry for yelling. Just come over so we can talk and figure things out."

"Okay. I'm on my way."

She ended the call with him and called India to tell her she wasn't able to go. She knew something was wrong with her friend because she could hear her crying on the phone.

India tried to convince her to come over, but she refused. She needed to be with Blue. She turned off the main road that led her to India's house and made her way to the interstate.

It wasn't long before she got to his house, and he greeted her at the door with something she needed more than anything: a hug. He held her in his arms tight and rubbed her back. "Everything gon' be okay. I'ma fix it. I promise."

His heartfelt words alone started the river back to flowing, but it was because she knew he really cared about her. Their tight embrace came to an end. He then grabbed her hands and looked into those beautiful eyes he loved so much without the bruises. "Despite the things my ol' girl said, she'll be there if it's my baby, and so will I. She's just afraid I will lose focus and never get my degree in medicine."

She nodded her head. "You promise?" Tears soaked her face, and he wiped them all away.

"I do."

Sasha fell asleep during the massage he gave her. Blue sat back and watched her, wondering what she was dreaming about. He knew it wasn't a good one because she looked sad, and her body flinched constantly. It made him wonder how many ass-whoopings had she suffered, and how bad were they? He already witnessed what Quamae could do after he beat her ass the first time.

When she finally stopped moving, he picked up her cell phone and scrolled through her gallery. He stopped when he saw her pictured with a familiar face. A wicked grin spread across his lips as he bobbed his head back and forth. He finally had a face to the name, and all he needed was the phone number.

Chapter 21

Sasha walked into the house carrying a shopping bag after spending the night with Blue. She was less of an emotional mess than she was the day before thanks to him. He was everything she needed in her life: sweet, charming, thoughtful, and understanding. He took her to the mall earlier that morning to get her something to wear so he could take her out to eat on South Beach.

Her thoughts were interrupted by laughter coming from the kitchen, and she was well aware of who was there, so she proceeded up the stairs and into her bedroom. After the confrontation she had with both of the men in the kitchen, she did not want to see or hear either one of them.

Sasha's body was tired and out of whack. "Morning sickness my ass," she mumbled. "More like all-day sickness to me." In between stress and the throwing-up, she knew this was going to be a long and miserable pregnancy. She was at two months and had seven more to go. It was bad enough she didn't plan on getting pregnant in the first place, but now she had a feeling she would be facing it alone. If Blue was her baby's father, the nightmare she was in would finally come to an end. She needed something to take her mind off of things to give her some comfort, and a hot bubble bath is what she chose.

She put a silk black bonnet on her head, filled the tub with hot water and added bath beads. Then she selected Musiq Soulchild's *Don't Change* from her playlist, her and Quamae's wedding song, and put it on repeat. The candles were burning to set the mood. She sat down in the tub, causing all of the water to drift up to her collarbone. Positioning a pillow behind her head, she leaned back, closed her eyes, and enjoyed the sweet sound. Tears streamed down her face as she reminisced on the happiest day of her life. It hurt to know he no longer felt that way about her.

As she slept peacefully in the bathtub, Quamae emerged from the hallway and stood at the door. It was cracked, and he could hear music playing when he reached the top of the stairs. He walked in to check on her since she had been in there a while. His attention went to her cellphone when he recognized she was playing their wedding song, but he wasn't affected by it. That was a time when he was so in love with her and couldn't imagine life without her. Now, with the turn of events, he couldn't imagine his life with her. He walked over and sat on the edge of the tub to wake her up. He shook her gently on the shoulder. "Wake up."

She stirred in her sleep. "Huh?" she blinked.

"You fell asleep in the tub."

She looked around and realized she was indeed in the tub and the water had turned cold. Quamae stood to leave the bathroom when she grabbed his hand. He wanted to pull away, but he didn't.

"Remember when we danced to this on our wedding day?"

Of course he remembered. It was the happiest day of his life, but now happiness with her no longer existed. "Yeah, that was a long time ago, when we were in love."

"Quamae, don't talk like that." Sasha interlocked her fingers with his. "I don't want to lose you."

"I didn't want to lose you, either, but." he paused.

She frowned. "But what?"

"We can never make this work. We can't trust each other."

Her heart dropped to the pit of her stomach. That was not the answer she was looking for. "We can work on it."

"Trust takes years to build and seconds to lose. Once you lose that, it's hard to get that back. We've done so much damage it's beyond repair."

Tears crept slowly from her eyes and slid down her face. "So you don't even want to give us a chance?"

Quamae fought with his own tears. He still loved her, but he was far too damaged to let her slide. "Sasha, there is so much about you I didn't know. You hid the most crucial details of your life from me, and I don't know if I could ever trust you again. If your mother never showed up on our porch, I would still be in the dark about you."

Sasha looked deep into his soul through his eyes. She could feel the hatred he had toward her. She wrapped her wet arms around him and cried harder. "I'm sorry. I didn't want you to judge me or push me away because of my past. Bad things happened to me, and I just wanted to forget about it."

"But you took away my decision to choose you over your past. Your past wouldn't have determined our future."

"So don't let it."

"I don't know if I can."

"Please try," she cried. "Don't give up on us. I'll do whatever it takes. I'll even go to counseling."

"I can't be sure you won't cheat again."

"You cheated, too. This is our chance to get it right, and now I'm about to have your baby. Can't you see we were meant to be?"

Quamae lifted her head and kissed her forehead. "It could never be me and you again. You shared an emotional connection with him. It wasn't just sex between y'all. I heard this man talk about you at the trap house, and if you feel the way he do, he has your heart already." She opened her mouth to speak, but he stopped her. "You said it yourself, he validated you when I didn't." He got up and walked away.

Quamae knew for a fact men could cheat and not become emotionally attached, but when women cheated their feelings always came into play. He felt deep down in his heart the chances of him getting her pregnant were slim to none, and he had a better chance at winning the Powerball.

Sasha got out of the tub without bathing and dried off. She was too sleepy and hurt to do anything else.

***

Quamae struggled with sleep that night after having that talk with Sasha. He wished he would've just walked straight to the room and went to bed. The room was pitch black until his phone lit it up. Gigi was calling.

"Hello." His voice was groggy.

"Were you asleep?"

"Nah, what's up?"

"I'm sick, I can't stop throwing up, and I'm weak," she gagged hard. "Ugh, this baby is killing me."

"What do you need?"

"Can you bring me some crackers, orange juice, and pickles?"

He knew that meant he had to make a late night run to Walmart. He thought that was the nastiest request, but since that's what she wanted, he jumped up to go get it. "Yes, I'll be there in an hour."

"Please hurry."

He arrived at her place in exactly one hour since Walmart wasn't crowded. He unlocked the door and walked in. He figured since he would be paying her bills, he was entitled to have a key and show up anytime, night or day. She was okay with that because she was willing to do whatever it took to get him back. Gigi knew Sasha was skating on thin ice, and she wanted to take advantage of that fact. Quamae walked through the apartment and found Gigi on her knees with her head damn near in the toilet. He dropped the bags and rushed to her aide.

"Baby, you okay?" he asked.

She shook her head no, and a large amount of fluids poured from her mouth. Quamae held her hair and rubbed her back until she was finished.

"I feel like I'm about to die." Tears filled her eyes, although she wasn't crying, and she could see red dots moving around the room.

"Baby, you need some mouthwash," he joked.

"Shut up."

He stood up and looked in the cabinet up under the sink for it. He poured some in the cap and handed it to her. "Here swish that around in your mouth for a little bit." Gigi did as she was told, then handed him the cup back. Quamae washed her face and then carried her to the bed so she could get comfortable. He tucked her in under the covers and sat down on the bed beside her. Her stare matched his stare.

"Why you looking at me like that?" she asked.

"I can't believe you about to have my baby." He rubbed her hair.

"Are you happy about that?"

"Yeah, I am." He leaned down and kissed her forehead. "That's why I'm here to make sure yawl okay. I promise to be here until my casket drops." And he meant every word he said.

Quamae stood up to get the bags off the floor and take them to the kitchen. He returned to the room with his keys in one hand and a glass of orange juice in the other. He handed her the cup.

"Drink this."

Gigi downed the cup quickly and gave him the glass. "Are you leaving?"

"Nah, I'm spending the night."

He kicked off his Jordan slides, pulled his shirt over his head, and sat it neatly on her dresser along with his IPhone. He was about to take off his basketball shorts, but then he paused. "Since you sick, does that mean I'm not getting any tonight?" She shook her head no. "Well, I guess I'll keep these on."

Just as he was about to crawl into bed, his cellphone vibrated loudly and lit up with Sasha's picture and the word *Wifey*. Gigi glanced in its direction and frowned when she saw it.

"I guess you leaving now." Yeah, she knew they were still married, but that didn't dismiss the fact she was bothered by her existence. She hated the bitch on that screen with a passion.

"Nah, I ain't going nowhere." He turned the phone face-down on the nightstand, turned off the lights, and slid under the covers with his baby's mother. His hands roamed underneath the sheets until they found her stomach. He rubbed her tiny baby bump until they both were knocked out.

Sleep didn't come so easy for Quamae through the night. The constant vibration from his phone pierced his ears, and he knew it was Sasha calling back-to-back, but he wasn't about to answer. Gigi was a hard sleeper, so she didn't hear a thing. He wished he would've just put it on silent from the jump.

Quamae got up to go to the bathroom and drain the main vein. Upon his return, he silenced the phone and climbed back into bed. Gigi's derriere was tooted in his direction, and that made it hard for him to resist her. While lying on his back, his growth was starting to rise, pitching the covers like a teepee.

Fuck it. He rolled over on his side and lifted up her nightdress. He used one hand to guide himself in from the back and took long, slow strokes. The warmth of her vagina made him nut prematurely in less than ten minutes, and he was finally able to go to sleep.

Quamae didn't return home until late that afternoon. The level of disrespect was at an all-time high, and he didn't give a fuck what she had to say about it. He didn't care how she felt because it was her fault he was treating her that way. She broke their vows in the worst way, and he was going to make her suffer the same way.

"I've been calling you all night. Why didn't you answer your phone?"

"I was working."

"You a lying-ass bastard. You know damn well you wasn't working dressed like that. You act as if you don't have a wife at home."

"Do I? 'Cause last time I checked, we wasn't together. Don't get confused behind that conversation last night. Because I never said we would fix this."

"You a disrespectful-ass nigga." She put her hand in his face, purposely invading his personal space.

He backed up. "Don't put your hand in my face, and I'm not gon' say it again. We are separated, and you need to understand that." All of that shit she said went in one ear and out the other. She'd better be glad she was pregnant, because he would've kicked her ass for talking to him crazy like she didn't know why she was suffering.

"Why didn't you come home last night?"

"Because I didn't want to. Are you happy now?" He walked away to get his bedroom shoes from the closet. "You should've went to spend the night with Blue and his mama, so you could stay out of my business."

"Are you serious right now?"

"As a heart attack."

He stepped from the closet with his shoes in hands and she blocked his path. "Can you please move, so I can take a shower? I'm dirty, and I need to hit this water before I go."

"You should've took a shower at the bitch house you just left."

"I can shower wherever I want to. I pay all the bills here, in case you forgot."

Sasha was heartbroken behind the way he was treating her, and he was enjoying every minute of it. "Why are you doing this?" she cried.

"Man, you trippin' hard right now. You already know what the deal is between us. I'll be a fool if I take you back."

"How many times have I forgiven you?"

Now he was pissed and slowly reaching his violent peak. "I keep tellin' yo' ass my wife cannot cheat on me and think it's okay. I'm a man, that's different, and you can't do what I do. Do you know how that shit looks in the streets?"

"Fuck the streets."

"I'm done with this. I'm not about to keep arguing with you about this. Just go, find you a place, and I'll pay for it.

I'll even give you ten bands to start over." He walked away and went into the bathroom. Sasha dropped to her knees and screamed as loud as the volume in her lungs would allow her. He never looked back.

Quamae took a quick shower so he could hurry up and pick up the money from his workers and a few niggas he gave work to on consignment. When he walked back into the room, Sasha was gone. He dressed quickly in a pair of Robin jeans, a black V-neck, and black retro 11s. He placed a 30-inch Cuban link on his neck with a medallion and grabbed his Glock in case he had to lay a nigga out over his money. A lot of niggas wondered what he did to stay free all those years, but that wasn't their business. But his rules were simple: he knew when to slow down, kept his ears to the street, and the law on his payroll.

Quamae drove for thirty minutes before he pulled up in an apartment complex where one of his hitters lived and stepped out of the car. He walked up to the second floor and knocked. It wasn't long before Amp opened the door. They slapped fives and patted each other on the back before going into the living room.

"What it do, fam?" Amp asked as they took a seat on the sofa.

"Stacking this money so I can get prepared to take care of my lil' one on the way."

Amp handed Quamae a book bag full of money. "Nigga, you finally got a baby on the way? Congrats, my nigga, that's what's up."

He unzipped the bag and counted the money. "Thanks, man. It's about that time, you know. A nigga ain't getting no younger."

"Yeah, I feel you on that."

Quamae knew Amp since he was a young boy because he used to hang with his older brother Buck. When Buck got killed, he took Amp up under his wing.

Quamae stood up and threw the bag on his shoulder. "I have to finish doing the pick-ups, so I'll holla atcha later." They slapped hands again and he left just as quickly as he came.

After running around town picking up drops, he had a little over $200k, so he was satisfied even though two people were short. He wasn't worried, though, because he was gon' collect the rest no matter what.

On his way home he swung by Gigi's apartment to drop her off some food and bill money. Five thousand dollars was well over the amount she needed, but nothing was too much when it came to her and their unborn child.

When he finally made it home, he put the money in his safe. He struggled to squeeze it all in and made a mental note to find a new stash spot and start a legit business. Shit was about to hit the fan, and he had to protect his future.

Chapter 22

Two months later

Moving day for Emani was finally coming to an end, and she couldn't be happier. She had to wait until the fifteenth of the month instead of the first, due to the apartment not being ready. The movers had just brought up the last piece of furniture. Quamae tipped them and thanked the guys for their services before they departed.

"Woo, I am so happy this is over with." Emani sat down on her new leather couch and stretched out with her arms across her face.

"I don't know what for, you ain't do shit but complain. I should be the one happy. I had to tip them boys extra because they had to wait on you to finish packing."

She moved her arm to look at him. "I had to pack up all my stuff by myself since Sasha wouldn't help nobody."

Sasha looked at Emani like she was crazy. "You knew you was moving two months ago. You waited until the night before to pack. I only came to watch."

"And eat my snacks."

"We were hungry."

"Oh yeah, speaking of which," she looked in her brother's direction. "You said she wasn't pregnant. See how yawl be lying?"

"I didn't know she was pregnant."

She then turned to her sister. "And you said you wasn't pregnant."

Sasha shrugged her shoulders. "I didn't know, either."

"Well, I can't wait to meet my niece or nephew."

Quamae and Sasha were quiet because she had no idea what they were going through. They were trying to wait until the right time to tell her that they were separated. Emani had a lot of love for Sasha, and they didn't want to burden her with their problems. So, for her sake, they had been the loving couple she had grown to love and respect over the past two months. That meant showing affection toward one another while they were out shopping together for her new place. They knew it would break her heart, and they were not ready to drag her into the mix like that.

Quamae grabbed his keys from the counter. "E, we out, baby. Come give me a hug."

Emani got up from the sofa, walked over to him, and hugged him tight. "Thanks for everything. I love you." She kissed him on the cheek.

"I love you, too."

Sasha walked over and gave her a hug as well. When Emani let her go, she rubbed her stomach. "I'm so happy for yawl. I love you, sis, even though you didn't help me."

"I love you, too. I'll check on you later."

"Okay, drive safe with my baby."

Quamae forced a smile. "I will."

And they walked out the door.

***

Quamae sat in the den, disappointed Gigi had to cancel their plans for the night to go to work. He had already paid for the tickets in advance, arranged a flower delivery to send her one hundred long-stem roses, along with a diamond necklace and bracelet set. He wanted to show her how much he loved her and to right his wrongs for leaving her in the past. He picked up his phone and called the company to let them know there had been a change of plans.

Instead of having them deliver to her apartment, he had it sent to her job. That would surely brighten up her night.

Not wanting the tickets to go to waste he woke up Sasha and decided to take her instead. She was grumpy, irritated, and not in the mood to get up before her body said it was time. She didn't know what was going on, but she knew it better not be for any bullshit.

"Why are you waking me up? I'm tired." Sasha stretched, placed her hand on her stomach to rub her belly. The movement felt like butterflies fluttering their wings.

"Are you okay?" he asked, thinking she was feeling bad.

"The baby is moving, that's all." Sasha grabbed his hand and placed it on her stomach to see if he could feel it.

Quamae was amused by what was happening. He immediately thought about Gigi and his own baby. The baby stopped moving, and he moved his hand. He didn't touch it that much because he was afraid to get attached to a baby that didn't belong to him. On the other hand, he would rub Gigi's belly all day and night, rub the skin off of that motherfucker, and that attached him to her even more.

"Get up and get dressed," he told her politely as possible.

"For what?"

"Because we're going somewhere. Now, can you please get up and get dressed so we can be on time. Thank you."

She slowly dragged herself from the bed and into the hot, steamy shower. After spending thirty minutes of basically standing under the showerhead, Quamae walked in to rush her out.

"Do you have to take this long in the shower?"

"I'm about to get out now."

"I swear, you slow as hell." Then he walked out.

Sasha pulled herself from the shower. She would've stayed in longer if she had time. Standing in front of the full-length mirror, she dropped her towel to see how her body was changing. She rubbed it in a circular motion imagining how she would look in a few more months. She smiled at the idea of becoming a mother, period. When she stepped into the bedroom Quamae was completely dressed. He looked so sexy as if he had just stepped off of the cover of GQ magazine. He was wearing a pair of Robin jeans, with the matching shirt and some Giuseppe sneakers he purchased the other day. For the finishing touches, he splashed on some Gucci Guilty cologne, a gold Rolex watch, and his 30-inch Cuban link. But, of course, he wasn't complete until he had his banger in hand.

Sasha walked into the closet and pulled out the dress she purchased on her mall run. It was a black halo body-dress made by Ally Sheath. She grabbed a pair of colorful red bottoms, the matching clutch and walked back into her room. It took an additional forty minutes to apply her make-up and be fully dressed. She walked back into his room.

"I'm ready."

Quamae helped Sasha into his Infiniti QX80 and closed the door once she was seated. She didn't know where they were going, so she assumed it was a surprise. Lyfe Jennings' song *Brand New* was still playing from earlier that day when Gigi was in that very seat Sasha was sitting in.

Back when Quamae and Gigi were dating, he used to sing that song to her all the time, so when he picked her up, she gave him a CD she made personally for him. He knew she was trying to make him remember what they went through when they were together and how much fun they used to have. That was before he got on the map and started dealing with real weight and a lot of money. The more money he made caused her to become insecure, because now he had groupies checking for him on a daily basis, and Sasha was the main one. It became too much to bear, so they broke up. Not once did he forget about what they shared, and the lyrics seeped into his soul because her tactics were working like a charm.

It was 6:30 p.m. and the sky was bright. As he backed out of the driveway, he took his cell phone from his pocket and placed a call. "I'm on my way right now. I just pulled out of the driveway." He paused, then ended the call.

Sasha crossed her legs and rested her elbow on the console. "Where are we going?" She was curious because he still hadn't mentioned anything to her.

"To the comedy show at the Improv."

"And who was that on the phone?"

Quamae was getting slightly aggravated with the twenty-one questions. All he wanted her to do was sit back, be quiet, and look pretty. "Chauncey."

She tooted her nose up. "Oh." Then she let down the sun visor, applied a little bit more Ruby Woo to her lips, and popped them together. As they entered the gate, he called Chauncey to let him know he was outside. Quamae stopped the truck in front of the entrance. Stepping from the elevator was Chauncey and some broad she didn't recognize. She was dressed in a burgundy two-piece pencil skirt set, exposing her flat tummy and navel piercing, with a pair of nude red-bottom pumps. *Fish was cute.*

Chauncey was wearing a fit with similar colors to match her. He opened the door for her to climb in and sit directly behind Sasha, while he took a seat behind Quamae on the driver's side. He happily introduced his little date as

Monica. She finally had a face to the name of the woman who stole him right from under her nose.

When they finally arrived at the Hard Rock, it was almost eight o'clock. They skipped the line and went inside to where the VIP members waited in the A/C.

Quamae and Chauncey ordered bottle of Grey Goose and Cranberry Juice, while Sasha and Monica ordered Strawberry Daiquiris, but of course hers was virgin. Her first impression of Monica was she was young. Sasha wondered where he found her from. After waiting until nine p.m., the show finally started. The comedian on stage was Corey Holcomb, and the dude was funny as hell. He had the entire crowd laughing so hard, Sasha thought she would pee on herself.

After his performance, she whispered in Quamae's ear and said she was going to the ladies' room. Monica got up and accompanied her. Chauncey had the biggest smile on his face, showing those pearly white teeth. From the looks of things, he seemed to be perfectly happy with her in his presence. She couldn't help but wonder if he was doing all of that to make her jealous.

In the restroom, Sasha took their alone time as a perfect opportunity for her to be nosey. As she stepped from the stall and into the mirror, she washed her hands and removed her make-up from her clutch bag. "So, Monica, how long have you and Chauncey been dating?"

She had a surprised look on her face. Clearly she was not expecting to be questioned, but she answered anyway. At first she hesitated like their relationship was a secret.

"Well, Chauncey and I are not really in a serious relationship with each other. We're just," she held up both index and middle fingers, mimicking quotation marks, "causal friends."

Sasha nodded her head yes. She thought maybe she was a stripper. "So, what do you do?"

"I'm in school for Computer Engineering."

"That's good, and how old are you?"

"Twenty-one. I just want to enjoy my last year in college before I commit to anything. My parents take care of me right now so I can focus on school. So I don't need a man to take care of me. Just someone to be there for me mentally, physically, sexually, and financially when needed."

"Oh, I see." Sasha responded as if she wasn't prepared for that type of response.

Back at the table, the host was up on stage announcing the Comedy Queen Sommore. Everyone in the audience stood and gave her a standing ovation, one she deserved. After the show, the men wanted to end the night off in the casino on the Blackjack table. Sasha and Monica stood by their sides as if they were their good luck charms. After 45 minutes of just watching them play Blackjack, they collected money and went over to the slot machines.

They had an interesting conversation while they went from one slot machine to the next. They were actually having a good time together, laughing and talking.

"I'm thirsty, let's go to the bar." Monica said, as she stood up to adjust her skirt and flip her bundles over her shoulder.

They walked to the bar and waited for the bartender to walk over in their direction. Monica ordered two Pepsi's, one for her and one for Sasha. Now it was her turn for questions.

"So, how long have you and Quamae been together?"

"We've been married for two years," she flashed her two karat princess-cut diamond ring.

"That's pretty," she held her hand and pretended to be interested in in her jewelry. Monica didn't give a damn about her flaunting her ring. She wanted info on Chauncey.

"So, you and Chauncey are like brother and sister?"

"Yeah."

Monica sat her drink down and looked Sasha in her eyes to let her know she was serious. "Okay, I need to ask you something. I need to know if Chauncey fucking other people. I know I said I didn't want anything serious, but that's only semi-true. I'm fucked up about him, but we're not on that level yet. He act like he ain't ready."

Sasha almost choked on her drink.

"I know yawl close and all, and you don't know me, but I need to know what I'm dealing with, and you should understand where I'm coming from."

Sasha couldn't wait to throw salt on Chauncey's game, and it served him right for bringing this young-ass bitch around her. "Well, he has his share of women, and all I'm going to say is be careful with him, because he'll probably break that little heart of yours."

Monica started to smile and blush, but Sasha didn't know why, especially after what she just told her. She turned around to see what she was looking at. It was Chauncey. He walked up and put his arms around Monica, and his hands roamed all over her ass. Sasha was heated.

Quamae grabbed Sasha's hand to help her up. "Come on we're leaving."

The ride back to Monica's place was fairly quiet, except when Chauncey and Quamae were talking to each other. Monica was laughing on the inside about her conversation with Sasha. Apparently they weren't as close as she claimed for her to throw salt on his name like that. Monica didn't believe her at all, so she needed to keep an eye on her. She caught Sasha giving Chauncey the side eye and that's what made her ask those questions in the first place.

Once they made it back to Monica's house, they said their goodbyes, then watched the couple disappear behind closed doors.

Chapter 23

Twelve noon came pretty quickly the next day as Sasha glanced at the digital clock on the nightstand. Not ready to get up and start her day, she rolled over and put the pillow over her head. Quamae was in a deep, deep sleep, and his snoring proved that fact. He was drunk from the night before and drained from the sex they had. Drifting off into part two of her sleep, her cell phone rang. She felt around for it without taking her head from under the pillow. She put the screen close to her face and saw it was India. She didn't want to talk, so she let the voicemail catch it.

Right after that, Quamae started to move around in the bed. He stretched his arm out like he was looking for something. His movement stopped when he felt a warm body next to his. He opened his eyes and was astounded to see Sasha in bed with him. He leaped out of bed quickly and realized he was completely naked. Then he noticed she was naked, too. He rubbed his face with his hand. He couldn't wrap his head around what he was witnessing.

"We had sex last night, didn't we?" He knew it was a dumb question, but he asked anyway.

"Yes, we did."

"Damn!" He shook his head and went in the direction of the bathroom. He looked down at the floor and the scattered clothing was confirmation to what he already knew. He picked up his boxer briefs and put them on.

"What's that supposed to mean?" she asked.

"Nothing," he slammed the door. He immediately felt bad for allowing the alcohol to impair his judgment. He was supposed to be transitioning away from her and not causing mayhem.

He stood in the bathroom, staring at the wall. "Fuck," he screamed. Then he punched the wall, making a hole. "Calm the fuck down, 'cause it's your fault," he gave himself a pep talk. He waited a few minutes before he went back to the room. He needed to nip the situation at hand in the bud quickly.

Sasha was sitting on the side of the bed, doing what she did best, crying. This was exactly what he was trying to avoid, mixed feelings. *See what you did, Gigi? All you had to do was call out and I wouldn't be in this shit,* he thought to himself. Now he had to fix the mess he made. He walked over to her and sat down. She had a sheet wrapped around her.

"Come on, stop crying and listen to me. I'm sorry about last night, it was a mistake, and I take full responsibility. We are in a fucked-up place, and sex will only complicate things, like it's doing now."

"I thought we were trying to fix things. Isn't that why we went out last night?"

He couldn't tell her the real reason why because he couldn't hurt her feelings more than he already had, so he needed a quick, truthful answer. "I thought going out with you would remind me of what we used to have. I tried to convince myself we could fix this, but I can't do it, Sasha. I'm sorry. We have to get a divorce. I can't live like this."

She broke down. "No, please don't leave me. What am I supposed to do without you?"

"You'll figure it out. I'll pay for you to move, and I'll give you fifty bands, but we have to do this now."

"I don't want to lose you," she screamed. "What about the baby?" She rocked back and forth, crying.

Quamae held her and shed his own tears. "If it's mine, I'll take care of it. I promise, but we can't be together anymore. I have to let you go. We're too toxic for each other. And even after I caught you with the nigga, you was still fuckin' him behind my back. That let me know you didn't want to be married anymore."

"I'm sorry."

It hurt him to let her go, but he couldn't forgive her for what she did and what she continued to do behind his back. After he said what he needed to say, he left the room, wiping his tears away. He had to get away from her before anything else transpired.

Quamae went into the den to text Gigi back. She had been trying to reach him since she received the delivery.

My Future: Busy night bae just seeing ur texts

Gee: Yeah... I love the gifts you sent to my job

My Future: I knew u would. After I leave the sports bar I will be there

Gee: What time is that?

My Future: When the game go off

Gee: Okay

Quamae lay on the couch to relax until it was time to meet Chauncey at the sports bar so they could watch game five of the finals between the Cav's and Golden State.

***

Sasha was feeling down about the way things panned out after having sex with Quamae, so she left and went to Carmen's condo to spend the night.

"So, let me get this straight," she held her finger to her temple. "Yawl went out last night, had a good time, and did the whole shebang, and he wakes up acting like nothing happened?"

"Carmen, you have no idea how he made me feel," she dropped her head. "I felt so low. I mean, he offered to pay for my moving expenses and to give me fifty bands to walk away."

Carmen held her hand up. "Wait, and you said no?"

"It's more to us than money. Yes, I love the lifestyle he provides, but I love him more than that. I would still love him without it."

"Yeah, I hear that."

"When he's good, he's the perfect man. But when he's not, things get real bad."

"Yeah, I witnessed that before."

"I love him despite all things."

Sasha and Carmen sat for hours talking until they fell asleep. In the wee hours of the morning, Sasha's phone rang off the hook. She blinked her eyes repeatedly to shake away the sleep. Her vision was blurry as she tried to make out the number on the bright screen.

"Hello," she answered groggily.

"Sasha!" Chauncey shouted, scaring her half to death.

"What?" Her heart was beating so rapidly she was sure he could hear it through the phone. He was the last person she wanted to talk to, and if he was calling with the bullshit, he was getting the dial tone.

"Listen to me, I'm about to tell you something, but I need for you to stay calm, okay?"

Her voice trembled and her hands started to shake. "What's going on?"

"Quamae got shot."

Those words hit her right in the chest, and her heart dropped to the pit of her stomach. She opened her mouth, but nothing came out, like a hit child who refused to cry. Chauncey called out her name again.

"Sasha."

She sat up in the bed, frozen in her thoughts, like time was suddenly at a standstill.

"Sasha, please say something." Chauncey pleaded.

All of a sudden she let out the loudest scream she could muster up from deep down inside her soul, scaring Carmen out of her sleep. "Sasha, what's wrong?" Tears were running down her face, but she didn't say a word. Carmen got up to turn on the light. "Did something happen?"

Sasha nodded her head yes and then passed her the phone.

"Who's on the phone?"

She trembled with fear and rocked back and forth. "Quamae was shot."

Carmen took her phone and clutched it tightly in her hand. "Who is this?" The number was programmed in her phone as *Brother*.

"Chauncey."

"What's going on? What happened?"

"Quamae got shot, and I'm on my way to the hospital."

"Which one?"

"Broward General."

"Okay, we are on our way there."

"A'ight."

She held Sasha tight in her arms and told her everything was going to be okay. The only thing she could do was sob and cry. "Do you want to go to the hospital?"

Sasha nodded her head. "I never wanted anything bad to happen to him, India."

She rubbed her head. "I know you didn't."

Carmen picked up her car keys off the dresser. "Come on, let's go."

Chapter 24

When they arrived at the hospital, Chauncey was sitting in the waiting room. He had his face buried in his hands. When he looked up and saw Sasha, he wiped the tears from his face and stood up to greet her with a hug. His eyes were red and puffy from crying. She held him tight. "He's in surgery right now. I can't lose my nigga like this. I was right there when that shit happened."

"What happened?"

"We were at the sports bar in Dade, and the shit just happened out of nowhere. We didn't see the niggas until it was too late. Q was already on the ground, bleeding out." His sobs grew louder. "I didn't have my banger, so I couldn't do shit. Man, if I lose my nigga, I'ma lose it out here on these niggas."

She knew how much he loved Quamae, and it showed. Hell, they both loved him. Hearing him break down made her do the same. They stood and held each other for dear life. They cried for his pain, their pain, and the treachery among the two.

"We can't lose him like this."

After finally releasing him from her grip, he grabbed her by the hand and escorted her to a seat, then he sat down beside her. Carmen sat in the corner, heavily engaged in her phone. Hours went by, and there was still no word on his condition. She was worried sick about her husband. No matter what was going on between them, she still loved him very much. Chauncey leaned close to her and whispered in her ear. "You have to calm down. If not for me, do it for the baby. You can't stress like this, it's not healthy for yawl."

She nodded. "I didn't think you cared."

She caught him off guard, but he let it slide for now because he was going to address that later. Right now the only thing on his mind was Quamae.

"I'll be right back." Sasha got up and went to go sit next to Carmen.

A few minutes later a tall, light-skinned man wearing a white lab coat walked over to where they were sitting and asked to speak to Chauncey. The two men walked away to talk in private.

"He's in I.C.U. right now, where he will remain so I can watch him closely and make sure his body responds to the medication properly."

"Is he going to be okay?" Chauncey scratched his temple.

"He's going to be just fine."

They shook hands. "Thanks, Doc."

When Chauncey turned around, Sasha was standing behind them. "Can I see him?" She asked.

"Not yet. He needs his rest right now, but you can come back tomorrow."

After they let everyone know Quamae was going to make it, their visit came to an end. They were tired from sitting in those uncomfortable chairs for all that time.

Chauncey pulled Sasha to the side. "Listen, I need to put this stuff up for Quamae at the house. Then after that I'll drop you back off at Carmen's house, okay?"

"Okay."

Sasha told Carmen she would be back after she made a quick stop by her house. They got into Chauncey's 745I and pulled off. She gazed out the window in a fog, regretting the arguments, the cheating, and the fighting. If only she could turn back the hands of time, she would undo all of her wrongs. The pain she was feeling wasn't worth it.

She felt lost and numb. Losing him in death would be far worst than losing him in a divorce.

It wasn't long before they were pulling up into the driveway. He grabbed a bag from the trunk and disappeared into the house.

"What's in the bag?" She asked out of curiosity.

"Nothing."

When they made it into the house, she didn't follow him into the den and she didn't ask any more questions. Instead, she went into the kitchen and took a bottle of water from the fridge. The cold water was exactly what she needed to quench her thirst. Her mouth was extremely dry. He walked into the kitchen, but she walked away and went back upstairs.

Sasha kneeled down on the side of the bed and folded her hands to say a prayer for the love of her life. "God, please don't take him from me. I know I have done a lot of things I'm not proud of, but if you keep him here, I promise to make things right with him." The emotional state she was in was too much to bear, and a painful scream echoed through the room. "Why did this happen to you? I just need one more chance, please! God, please don't take him away."

She heard heavy footsteps running up the stairs, but she never lifted her head from the bed. Chauncey rushed in to be by her side. He lifted her by her arms and helped her onto the bed. "Come on, now, you have to relax."

"How can I relax when he's laying up in I.C.U.?" she screamed.

The sound pierced his ears, but that didn't deter him from comforting her. "I know you upset, but you have to try and relax." He pulled her close and she rested her head on his shoulder. She was an emotional mess, leaving wet stains on his shirt, but he didn't care. He just wanted to hold her again.

"I got you, baby. I promise."

He wiped the tears from her eyes and stroked her cheek with his forefinger. She closed her eyes and let his words comfort her. "Here, lay down and try to get some sleep."

"No, I can't sleep right now."

"I'll lay with you, come on." He removed her shoes, then his, and pulled the blanket back so she could crawl in. They lay face-to-face in silence for a few minutes before he decided to say anything to her. "I'm sorry for blowing up on you the way I did, and I hope you will forgive me."

Sasha was about to respond, but he shoved his tongue down her throat before she could get a word out. She tried to push him off of her, but the resistance left her body and she kissed him back. He placed his hand between her legs and played with her clit until she was nice and wet. His soldier was already at attention and ready to go to war. He rolled on top of her with precaution of her stomach and re-moved her clothes.

"No, we can't do this right now."

"I missed you, and we both need to take our minds off of things for a little while." Ignoring her pleas to stop, he slid inside of her and took deep, long strokes while grip-ping her hips. "Turn over."

Sasha endured the pain and gritted her teeth, fighting the urge to make him stop. "Ooh, it hurts," she moaned. The pressure from the baby and his length made doggy-style a tough position to handle. His hands against her ass sounded off like thunder. She was in pain, but it felt good at the same time. Minutes later, the intense pressure came to an end once he released thousands of his little soldiers into her body.

Chauncey eased out of her and lay on his back. Sasha looked at him, and for the first time she felt bad for all the times she betrayed Quamae. She had just made a promise to God less than an hour ago, and she was messing up already.

"What are we doing?" His actions confused her.

"I don't know," he answered honestly. "It's all so crazy. I love my nigga, I really do, but what we have just seems so right at times."

"Don't play games with me, Chauncey, because I have enough shit going on in my life already, and you know that. I just feel like you playing with me right now." Quamae was already doing it to her, so she couldn't afford to let another man take her down the same road she's trying to get off of.

"I'm not playing with you." He rubbed her thigh and licked her on the neck. She hated when he tried to manipulate her with sex. It was like sex was his weapon, and that's how he controlled the situation.

"Why did you invite us on a date with your girlfriend?"

"I wanted to make you jealous and show you what you missing out on," he kissed her lips. "Did it work?"

Sasha closed her eyes because he was making it difficult to be serious at the moment. "Stop," she pushed his face away from hers. "I'm being serious, Chauncey, what do you want from me?"

He blinked a few times. "I want you."

"You surely picked a hell of a time to tell me this." Her husband was in the hospital from gunshot wounds and she had just finished having sex with his best friend. Now he finally decides he wants to be with her.

"You just said you love him and you can't lose him. So, do you honestly think us being together won't make that happen?"

"It ain't like he wants you, so I don't see what the problem is." Chauncey had a quick slip of the tongue, and now she was about to question his ass to death. He didn't mean to say it, but she was making it seem like their marriage wasn't over when he knew better.

"Are you serious?" She folded her arms over her chest, because she wasn't about to let what he said slide.

He needed to clean that up quickly or she was gon' carry on for real. "Quit acting like I don't know what's going on with yawl situation."

"I'm sure you do." Those were some hurtful words to hear, but she couldn't think about that right now. Her main focus was to nurse Quamae back to health, and if he didn't want to be with her, then she would file for divorce. Sasha held her head in her hands because she didn't know what to think. Chauncey had her confused and curious. "I just need some time to figure things out."

Chauncey cut his eyes her way, looking at Sasha curiously as if to say *bitch, please*. He was the type of man who got what he wanted, and it had to be on his terms or nothing at all. "I'm going to give you two weeks, because I can't keep waiting on you. I think you know what you want though."

"No, I really don't. I'm so torn right now."

"How? When you and him getting a divorce. The choice is simple." He peeped her facial expression. "Stop looking confused. I know everything."

"It's not that."

"Then what is it?"

"I don't know who I'm pregnant from."

240

He was surprised she was so forthcoming with that information. He definitely wasn't expecting her to tell him about it, and he didn't want her to know he knew already. "Out of who?" He placed his hand on his chest. "Me and Q?"

She hesitated. "Yes."

He wanted her to go further and keep it a bill. "You sure 'bout that?"

"Yeah."

Chauncey knew she was lying because Quamae wouldn't lie about something like that, but he let her have that. He decided to stay until morning since he was too tired to drive.

Before the sun set completely on the horizon, Sasha walked Chauncey outside after being laid up all night with him in the house that Quamae paid for. She stood in the door in her bathrobe, looking around to see if the neighbors were out. The coast was clear, so she leaned in and gave Chauncey a goodbye kiss. In the midst of it all, they never noticed the old Toyota Camry that was parked on the side of the road.

Chapter 25

Quamae was finally out of I.C.U. after three days and moved to a regular room. He suffered from three gunshot wounds to the back, and two of the fragments were removed during surgery. Hematoma was present, but it was removed successfully to control the bleeding. And by the grace of God, the third bullet missed his spinal cord by a few inches, keeping his spine intact. The neurosurgeon thought it was too risky to remove it, so he left it in place to prevent causing any additional damage.

Sasha stood by his bedside, rubbing his arm with tears in her eyes. "I thought I was going to lose you. How are you feeling?"

"Grateful to be alive," he slurred. The medication had him feeling woozy. "I thought I was going to die." He reached for her hand and held it. "I thought about you before I passed out."

She was surprised. "You did?"

"Yes," he said just above a whisper. "I owe you an apology for all of the things I did and said to you. You didn't deserve that." He paused for a second to pace his breathing. "And for that, I apologize. We both broke our vows and stepped outside of our marriage." A single tear escaped his eye. "I'm sorry, and I want you to know I forgive you."

She wiped his tear away. "I forgive you, too, and I'm sorry for everything I did to you as well." She wanted him to elaborate on the subject a little more for clarification, but decided now wasn't the time. She would have to wait it out and see if he had a change of heart about them getting a divorce. For now she was going to accept his apology and be by his side until he was well enough to take care of himself.

"Where is Emani?"

"I called her, but she's in Key West with her friends. I didn't tell her since she will be back tomorrow. I didn't want to ruin her trip, since you are okay."

"If she calls you, don't tell her. I want to be the one to do it, I don't need her panicking."

"Okay, I won't say anything."

A knock on the door interrupted their sentimental moment. Sasha looked up as the door creaked open slowly, and in walked Chauncey and Dirty. They locked eyes for a brief moment before he focused his attention on his partner. "Damn, my nigga, you had ya boy crying. I'm so happy to see you right now."

Chauncey walked over to the side of the bed where Sasha was standing. She backed up so he could get through. He leaned down and hugged him gently.

"I'm happy to see you, too, bruh." He paused to catch his breath again. "I thought I would never see you again."

Dirty walked up and stood on the side of the bed. "My G, you had me scared, and you know that ain't no easy task."

Quamae struggled to laugh a little. "You too hard for that."

"Not when it comes to you." He pushed Chauncey to the side. "Slide over, nigga, let me in here." Dirty leaned down and hugged Quamae as well. "I'm glad you straight, but I'm 'bout to make these bullets fly once I get a name on them niggas."

Quamae agreed. "Dat part." He nodded his head toward Sasha, and Chauncey understood the message loud and clear.

Chauncey put his hand on his arm. "You cold?"

"Yeah."

Chauncey turned to Sasha. "Hey, go get him some blankets, please." She walked away to do as she was told.

As soon as she left the room, Quamae addressed his boys. "Have yawl heard anything on the streets?"

Dirty rubbed his hands together. "I slid up on my young zoes, and they told me Dred's squad is wetting shit until they find out who did his ass in."

Chauncey chimed in. "Yeah, word on the street is he hit the supplier, which is us, and they did his ass in. I'm sure the zoes caught wind of that shit. I'm packing heavy and walking light, 'cause I know how they get down."

"Yeah, I was laying here thinking the same thing. I'm sure it was one of his niggas that clapped at me."

Dirty rubbed his hands together. "If them boys want war, I'ma give it to 'em."

"Nigga, *we* gon' give it to 'em," Chauncey added.

Quamae was trying to shift his body a little to the left, "Aw, shit," he squinted up his face in pain.

Dirty reached down to help him. "Be still, my G, whatchu trying to do?"

He closed his eyes tight. "I'm trying to get comfortable."

"Nah, don't do that. I'm standing right here. I gotchu."

Sasha walked in carrying two blankets in her hands. She made it to the bed and tried to cover him up, but Dirty stopped her. "I got my dude. You can take a break for now."

She handed him the blankets. "Knock yourself out. I'm about to go down to the cafeteria. I'll be back."

Quamae glanced at her. "Okay."

For the next hour they sat and discussed business, since he was going to be in the hospital for a few weeks at best. He provided them with the names of the dudes who still owed money, and specific instructions to smoke one in particular that he hadn't heard from since they got back from Atlanta.

Dirty aimed his trigger. "Consider that nigga smoked, 'cause I heard he down bad on that flakka, so I know he ain't got the money."

"What about yo' li'l niggas?" he asked Dirty.

"Oh, my niggas good. They already know how I get down. All that money accounted for, so I'ma hit the nigga up and reload."

Chauncey patted his hand. "We got this shit under control. You just focus on healing, and we'll worry about this bread and the niggas that ran down on you."

"I appreciate yawl boys, for real."

Dirty smiled. "It's all love, my G. You know we ain't going nowhere."

Chauncey leaned down and hugged him again. "I love you, man. Get some rest, and we'll be back tomorrow."

"A'ight."

Dirty walked over to hug him again, and then they left.

***

Sasha had been in the cafeteria for an hour talking to Blue. To say she was confused now more than ever was an understatement. Here she was, praying to make things work out with her husband, and lo and behold he apologizes for everything he did, shedding hope on repairing their marriage. Then there was Chauncey, who wanted to be with her all of a sudden. And last, but certainly not least,

Blue, who wanted to be with her and the baby. Her heart was being tugged into three different directions at the same damn time. She had no clue what she was going to do.

"Sasha!" he shouted, snapping her from her daze.

"Huh?"

"What's on your mind?"

"Nothing."

"Don't lie to me."

"I'm not lying. I'm just tired."

The lady working in the cafeteria waved her hands to get Sasha's attention. When she finally looked up, she was pointing at the clock, indicating they were closing. She grabbed her belongings and got up from the table.

"So, what time are you leaving from up there?" Blue was sitting in the car, doing a stakeout while they talked.

"I'm spending the night up here."

"So, you rather sleep in a hospital bed instead of mine?"

"No, that's not what I'm saying. You know I would rather be down there with you."

"Well, show me, then."

"I want to, but I need to stay up here at least once. We are still married, and I still live in the house."

"Because you want to, and yawl are separated."

"Baby, please don't do this to me right now. I'll come up early tomorrow and stay with you."

"You got that." Then he hung up.

"Blue!" she yelled. When he didn't answer, she realized he hung up. She tried calling him back-to-back, but he sent her to the voicemail.

Sasha took the elevator back up to the room, and when she walked in, Quamae was asleep. She sat down in the chair next to the bed and watched him sleep peacefully. In a way it looked scary because he looked dead with his hands folded across his stomach. She figured the meds knocked him out, so she pulled a book from her purse and started to read.

Two hours passed, and her mind was on Blue. She fought with the urge to go and the urge to stay. In the end she decided to leave. For one, Quamae was still sleeping, and he probably wouldn't get up until morning. For two, she didn't want to risk her relationship with Blue, especially if her and Quamae still didn't stand a chance at reconciling.

Sasha left the hospital and hit the highway to go and make up with her man, because at the end of the day, he was there for her through it all, and she didn't want to disappoint him. For some reason it took her longer than she anticipated to arrive at his house. Traffic was heavy on the I-95, and it was after ten o'clock at night. When she finally made it through, she saw construction was the reason for the delay. She got off on the exit and drove another ten minutes to his house.

She pulled up in the driveway and got out to ring the doorbell. When the door opened, her smile turned into an instant frown. "Where is Blue?"

The girl looked her up and down and smiled, but she didn't respond.

Then she saw Blue walking up. "Who is that?" When he made it to the door, he didn't look too happy. "What are you doing here?"

Sasha went from zero to a hundred. "You know why I'm here. So, this what you do when I don't come down here?"

He grabbed the girl by the arm. "I got it," he said, then she walked away. He faced Sasha. "I thought you were staying at the hospital with dude? What happened?"

"I changed my mind, but fuck that, who is that bitch?"

"Calm down with all that, 'cause that ain't necessary." He tried to keep his composure, but he couldn't. It was funny in his eyes. "Man, you crazy."

"What the fuck is funny?"

"Bring your mad ass in the house."

She stood there with her arms folded. "Not until you tell me who the fuck that is."

"That's my cousin."

"Yeah, right."

"Do you think I would let a bitch answer my door? And if she was my bitch, don't you think she would've said something to you?" He grabbed her arm. "Come on."

Sasha walked into the house and followed Blue to the same bedroom the girl was in. "Tia, who are you?"

She laughed. "I'm his cousin."

Blue laughed with her. "Didn't I tell you she was crazy?"

"Yeah, he did. He knew you was outside."

Sasha slapped his arm. "Why you play so much?"

"Because you tried me earlier. A'ight, T."

They went into Blue's room and closed the door. "Why you changed your mind?" he asked.

"I wanted to be with you."

He walked over to the bed and lay on his back. "Yeah, after I hung up on you. If I didn't do that, you would still be up there."

"It gave me a chance to think about it, so I left and came to you." She walked over to him and climbed on top of him, straddling his lap. I didn't want you to be mad at me."

"You got that right," he sat up on his elbows. "'Cause you would've been the mad one tomorrow."

She leaned forward and kissed him on the mouth. "I doubt that very much. You can't resist me."

"I can, but I don't want to."

"Same difference."

"Yep, and I'll hurt a nigga 'bout you."

"I would like to see that."

"Be careful what you wish for." He lay back and tugged on the bottom of her shirt. "Take that off." She pulled her shirt over her head and threw it on the floor. Blue admired her baby bump, rubbing it in a circular motion. "You think this my baby?"

"I hope so."

"But do you think so?"

"It's a strong possibility. We wasn't really sleeping together like that."

"I'll take that." Blue placed both hands on her breasts and caressed them. "I want you to ride me to sleep. Can you handle that?"

"I got you." She removed the rest of her clothing as well as his and straddled him. Then she eased down onto his rock-hard limb and fulfilled his request. One hour later, they both were snoring in each other's arms.

Chapter 26

Three weeks later

Quamae had just made it home after making a miraculous recovery in the hospital. After his first week in a regular room, they immediately started the rehabilitation process. He had a daily routine of motion exercises and limb movements to keep him active. If it wasn't for the small caliber of the gun he was shot with, he probably would be a paraplegic. It took two weeks for him to get into the swing of things because he felt helpless and dependent.

He wasn't use to that, therefore he couldn't wait to get back on his grind. Although Chauncey and Dirty held it down, he needed to be a part of the action. So, he made that his focus, and he was able to heal a little faster. Therapy wasn't over just yet, so he would have to continue over the next few weeks. There was still pain in his back, and his walking improved drastically.

It had been three long weeks since he last talked to Gigi, and he thought about her a lot. He hadn't spoken to her since the night of the shooting, and he knew he had some explaining to do. He wanted to talk to her while he was in the hospital, but he lost the smartphone he used to call her. He purchased that phone solely for that purpose, since he knew Sasha was nosey. And for the life of him, he couldn't remember her number.

"How are you feeling?" Sasha was sitting on the bed, watching him as he gathered his clothes at a turtle's pace.

"I'm in a little pain."

"Do you need me to help you with anything, your pain pills?"

He made his way toward the bathroom. "Nah, I'm good."

Quamae made the water as hot as his body could stand it before getting in. His back was sore thanks to the remaining fragment lodged in his back. The heat mixed with the water pressure was soothing to his aching body. He wanted to stand in the shower forever. His muscles that were once tensed began to relax. Quamae didn't want to spend too much time in the shower, since he was on a mission. He carefully stepped from the walk-in shower, removed the excess water from his body, and got dressed slowly to keep from causing more pain.

"Where are you going?" Sasha was all up in his business once again, being nosey. "Shouldn't you be resting?"

"Nah, I got somewhere to go. I'll be back."

Quamae clutched his keys in his right hand, held the rail with his left hand, and took baby steps down the stairs. He was halfway to the door when the knocking started. That was strange, because he wasn't expecting anybody, and he never had pop-up visits. *Except from Carol.*

He unlocked the door and swung it open. His jaw hit the concrete when he saw her face. It was Gigi. She was standing at the door, shaking a can of mace. "Where the fuck have you been for three weeks?" she snapped.

"Bae, calm down and let me explain everything." He stepped onto the porch to talk to her. "What are you doing here?"

He could see the water build up in her eyes, and he immediately felt bad for not putting forth the extra effort to reach her.

"I came to find your ass since you forgot about me and your child."

Gigi was loud as fuck, and it wasn't long before Sasha stepped outside to see what the commotion was all about. She couldn't see who he was arguing with because he was standing in front of her, trying to calm her down, but when she finally saw her face, she went berserk.

"What the fuck are you doing here, Gigi?" Sasha was walking up to them, so Gigi stepped to the side to give her a full view of her bulging belly.

"I'm arguing with my baby's father, what the fuck does it look like?"

Sasha stopped in her tracks when she heard that. She looked at Quamae for confirmation. "What the fuck did she just say?"

"Bitch, you heard me, but in case you didn't, I'll repeat it. I'm arguing with my baby's father."

Sasha lost it as she ran up and swung on Quamae. "You got this bitch pregnant?"

He tried grabbing her arms to push her back, but a sharp pain went shooting up his spine and he let her go. "Fuck!" He doubled over in pain. "Sasha, please go in the house."

She stopped trying to fight him when she realized he was hurting. "No! You tell this bitch to leave our house."

He was trying to keep his cool and not hit her. He turned his attention back to the mother of his child. Gigi wasn't paying attention at first, but then she realized Sasha was pregnant, too.

"So, this why you got missing all of a sudden, because you got that bitch pregnant, too?"

Sasha screamed, "Damn right, ho. You mad because you're the sideline ho?"

Quamae didn't like that one bit. He promised he wouldn't disrespect Gigi, and no one else was about to, either. He turned back to face Sasha. "Man, take your ass in the house, because that's probably not my baby, anyway."

"Sideline? Ho, he don't want you. I know all about the divorce, and where the fuck you think he be at when he don't come home? At my house, in my bed, eating this pussy, ho!"

Gigi ran up on Sasha and hit her in the face with a two-piece combo. Everything happened so fast, she didn't know what hit her. Sasha stumbled, but caught her balance and returned blows. They stood toe-to-toe, going blow-for-blow. Their fight was better than Pacquiao and Mayweather.

Quamae rushed over to break them up. "Gigi, stop before you hurt my fuckin' baby." He grabbed her from behind and pushed her toward the car so Sasha could go in the house.

She was crying and shouting out all types of obscenities. "Fuck you, Quamae. Let me go before I kill you."

"Calm your ass down, man." He let her go, and when she turned to face him, she started swinging on him. He managed to duck a few of her blows, but she caught him in the lip. He tried to run from her, but the pain was too much to bear. He stopped and placed both hands on the hood of her car, breathing heavily. "This too much. I'm in muthafuckin' pain, and yawl with the bullshit." Gigi was standing on the driver's side of the car. "Man, you tripping. Can you calm down, please? I told you I was gon' explain everything to you. It's not my fault."

"No, fuck you and that ho. You will never see my baby." Tears streamed down her cheeks and her anger turned into sadness. "You promised me you wouldn't make me do this alone, and I fell for that shit." She pointed her finger in his direction rapidly. "You knew she was pregnant all along, and you lied to me, in my face. I will never forgive you for this." She wiped her tears. "I hate you," she screamed.

It hurt him to his heart to see her suffering behind his actions. If he would've put everything in check a long time ago, he wouldn't be risking his chance at fatherhood. "Just let me explain." He sucked up the pain he was enduring and limped to her side of the car, but Gigi got into her car and sped off without giving him a chance to speak.

After watching Gigi drive up the block, he went back indoors to check on Sasha, who was upstairs throwing her things into a suitcase.

"Are you okay?" He noticed her face was red and she had a bruise up under her eye.

"Get the fuck away from me." The hurt was real. She had been dealing with her pregnancy alone, and he had the nerve to get another bitch pregnant and be there for her. She heard Gigi when she asked him about his whereabouts. That explained why he always had somewhere to go on the nights he didn't come home. She couldn't believe Gigi had the nerve to dot her doorstep with her presence.

"Let me explain." He was happy the cat was finally out of the bag, but not about the way it went down. And he definitely didn't want them to come to blows.

"Don't explain shit to me, go explain that shit to your baby mama." She was grabbing all type of shit and throwing it in a bag. Not once did she give him eye contact.

"I told you I slept with her, but I didn't know she was pregnant."

She looked around for the closest object she could find. Her eyes locked in on the alarm clock, she snatched it out the wall and threw it. Quamae was able to dodge it.

"Stop fucking lying. I heard that bitch ask where you were for the past three weeks. You knew she was pregnant." Her blood was boiling, and she could see red. He had a secret family going on, and she didn't have a clue. "You around here giving me grief about my pregnancy when you know this is your baby. I slept with dude with a condom, and you still don't care. But I tell you what, go be with that ho and your maybe baby. You so fucking stupid, you don't even know if that baby yours or not."

She pushed his last button, and he was ready to get off on her ass, the wrinkles on his forehead were proof of that. He was trying hard not to choke her out, but she was making it hard to resist.

"Stupid?" he repeated. "No, you the stupid one to think I believe you only fucked Blue. I don't trust you, and I'll be damned if I let you kill me slowly." He picked up his IPhone and keys, then slid them into his back pocket. "I tell you what, though, get ready to sign these papers, because this marriage is over. And for the record, I know for a fact she carrying my seed."

Sasha heard enough, and she wasn't leaving without a fight. He disrespected her for the last time. Quamae was walking down the steps when she kicked him in the back. He stumbled off the last two steps, but he didn't fall. When he turned around, Sasha was delivering wild blows to his body. He grabbed her by the shoulders and pushed her against the wall hard, making a small hole. He was fuming with rage, and he could easily kill her with little effort. He forgot about the pain he was in.

"I told you not to put your fucking hands on me. Ho, I'll kill you right now."

Sasha spit in his face. Quamae grabbed her by the throat and banged her against the wall twice and slapped her. He squeezed her neck, stopping her air supply. She clawed at his neck trying to break free. Her eyes rolled to the back of her head, and her breathing was shallow. Then suddenly he let her go, and her body slid to the floor. She hungrily gasped for air. The only reason he let her go was because he thought about Gigi and his baby. If it wasn't for them, he would've sent that ho to meet her maker. He looked down at her like she was the scum of the earth.

"You disrespectful-ass ho, get out my muthafuckin' house right now. Get your shit and leave."

Quamae ran up the stairs to get the things she packed and her keys, then rushed back down. His adrenaline was pumping so hard the physical pain seemed non-existent. She was still sitting on the floor. He opened the door and slung her shit onto the pavement, removed his house key from her key ring, and escorted her out the door.

"Don't bring your ass back here, either. I'll send the rest of that shit to wherever you want me to."

Sasha stood there crying because she knew she fucked up. He got into his truck and left.

Thirty minutes later, he stumbled into Gigi's apartment. The pain had finally kicked in. His back felt extremely tight, and he could feel a burning sensation shooting up and down his spine. When he made it into the room, she was laying in bed crying. He sat down on the bed and took a deep breath. He had no idea where situation number two was going or how it would end.

"Gia, stop crying."

"Get the fuck out my house!" she yelled. "I told you, you will never see my baby, so why are you here? Go back home to your wife, because I don't want you here."

"That shit dead. And you will never be able to keep my child away from me. I thought I told you that already."

Gigi rolled her eyes. She was not in the mood to argue with him about a decision he forced her to make. "And you made that decision when you disappeared for three weeks. You wasn't thinking about your child then, so don't think about her now."

He was calm when he talked to her. His breathing was steady and slow, and his hands were relaxed in his lap as he gazed into her eyes. Quamae was determined to make things right with her. "I just got out of the hospital today." She didn't give him a chance to tell the truth before she started sucking her teeth, huffing and puffing, and making faces.

"Stop being rude and let me finish." He waited for her to get it out of her system so she could listen effectively. "Are you done?"

She just looked at him crazy and didn't bother to open her mouth.

"Now, like I was saying, I just got out of the hospital today. I was in there for three weeks for physical therapy. The night I was supposed to come over here, I got shot three times in a sports bar in Dade."

Her eyes lit up, and she looked frightened as he explained the details of that night. He stood up and removed his shirt slowly so she could see the scars from the bullets, in case she thought he was lying. "In case you don't believe me, just look at my back and you will see the scars. One of the bullets is still there because they thought if they removed it, it would cause more damage."

He turned to face her, reached into his pocket, and pulled out some papers and handed them to her. "In case you still don't believe me, here are my discharge papers. And if you think those are fake, look it up when you go back to work. I was admitted under the name Reginald Grey."

Gigi felt bad for blowing up the way she did, because he could've easily died without her knowing, leaving her alone to raise their baby. But she didn't feel bad for whooping Sasha's ass, because that was a long time coming, and she deserved it. She held her head in shame and tears dripped from her eyes, splashing onto her lap.

Quamae grabbed her by her hands and pulled her off the bed. "Come here. I'm okay, stop crying."

Standing face to chest, she rested her head and allowed her tears to flow freely. "I'm sorry. I didn't know."

"I know you didn't, and it's okay, because I should've figured out a way to contact you."

Quamae kissed her on the forehead, and she looked up to meet his stare. She noticed scratches on his neck and a split on his lip. She knew she busted his lip, but those scratches didn't come from her.

"I'm sorry about your lip."

Quamae smiled, because that didn't faze him one bit. "It's all good."

She rubbed her finger across the scratch. "What happened?"

"That's another story, but fix me a drink and I will tell you all about it, 'cause this pain is kicking my ass."

Quamae sat at the table while Gigi fixed him a cup of Hennessey and sat it on the table in front of him. He wished he had some weed to smoke, but unfortunately he left it at home, trying to hurry up and leave. "We got into a fight because I told her I want a divorce and because I told her I knew your baby is mine."

Gigi definitely wanted the dirt on that, because she caught the comment, but was too mad to address it. "Yeah, what's up with that, anyway? I heard you say the baby might not be yours."

He downed the entire cup of Hennessey. "Fix me another one." She obliged. "I wasn't talking about you, I was talking about her."

She sat his second cup down and joined him at the glass table. That really peaked her interest. "So, the baby not yours?"

"I don't know. She was sleeping with some nigga, and it might be his. I hope it ain't mine. After this divorce is over, I don't want shit else to do with her. Oh yeah, I kicked her out the house, too."

Gigi wasn't convinced she didn't live there anymore, and her facial expression showed it. "Really?"

"Yeah, I almost choked that motherfucker to death for spitting on me. That's how I got the scratches on my neck, she was trying to get loose. After that I slung her shit out the door. That's the nastiest shit you could do to a person. Ain't no coming back from that shit, and that's on my dead daddy."

Gigi was happy as hell on the inside. If she would've known this was going to happen, she would've done it sooner, but everything worked itself out for the better.

"So, where does that leave us?" She held both palms up, asking the questions with her hands. "What are we doing?" Gigi needed confirmation they were officially a couple.

"Whatever you want? Do you want to be with me?"

He already knew what her answer was going to be, but he needed her to say what she wanted. He looked her in the eyes and waited for the answer.

"I want to be with you more than anything in this world."

He leaned forward so she could meet him halfway across the table and kissed her on the lips. "You got it."

She smiled. "So, we're official?"

"Yeah."

"And I don't have to worry about you seeing her again?"

He held her hands in his. "As soon as the ink dries on those papers, it's a wrap."

Chapter 27

One day after the fight, Sasha found herself on Carmen's step. She knocked on the door just in case she had company and waited on her to answer. She needed someone she could vent to, and she was at the right place. Carmen opened the door and caught a glimpse of the bruise underneath her eye. She folded her arms over her breast and shook her head.

"Don't tell me, you and him was fighting again."

Sasha stepped in and walked past her. "Yep, that's the story of my life." She plopped down on the sofa. "But this fight was better than all the rest."

"And why is that?" She walked over and sat down.

"Because I fought Gigi yesterday."

Carmen's eyebrows shifted down. "You mean Quamae's ex?"

"Yep!"

"Damn, bitch, what happened?"

"She had the nerve to come to the house looking for him because she hasn't seen him since he got shot. I mean, she was going off like that's her husband."

Carmen put her feet up to get comfortable. "Damn, he still fuckin' that girl?"

"Apparently so, but here is the kicker!"

"What?"

"She's pregnant, too."

"Hell nah! She told you that?"

"Yeah, but she didn't have to, her stomach spoke for itself."

Carmen slapped the couch. "Bitch, I can't believe this shit. They been fuckin' around all this time and you didn't know. So, why did you and him fight?"

"Because he tried me with that ho, and I spit on him."
Sasha didn't see anything wrong with what she did.

"Really, bitch? You spit on that man?"

"Surely did."

"I'm sorry, I would've beat your ass to sleep. So, it's over between yawl?"

"Yeah, he said he wants a divorce." She looked down at her phone and sent Blue a text.

Sasha: I'm officially out the house now. It's over between us.

"Damn, so they together?"

"Yep."

"Well, maybe that's for the best."

She sat her phone down and waited on his reply. "Yeah, I guess so."

"Are you okay with that?" Carmen felt bad for her because she knew how she depended on him for everything.

"Shit, what other choice do I have at this point?"

"You have several choices."

Her phone alerted her she had a text.

Blue: What happened?

Sasha: I'll tell you about it later

Blue: So whatchu gon do?

Sasha: Idk... I'm trying to figure that out now

Blue: Well let me know cuz my door is open to you

Sasha: Aww bae that's sweet. I'll be over later

Blue: Aight

Despite her situation she managed to smile, because behind every dark cloud was a silver lining. And Blue was hers. She hoped he would be everything she needed and more. However, there was one more person she needed to reach out to, so she texted Chauncey to see how he would react to the news.

"Get out that phone, 'cause I know you hear me talking to you."

She held up one finger, but her eyes stayed on the screen. She was focused. "Hold up, I'm texting."

"Duh, I can see that."

Sis: I'm officially out the house now. It's over between us.

She sat her phone back down. "Okay, what were you saying now?"

"I was saying you should have options. Have you saved any money?"

"I have a li'l something."

Carmen shook her head. "See, that's what India was trying to tell you."

"Oh no," she put her hand up. "Don't mention none of this to her. And stop sounding like her."

"You know she gon' find out, right?"

"She don't need all the details, and you better not tell her, either, with her imperfect-ass," she folded her arms and sucked her teeth. "She makes me sick sometimes, I swear."

"Why, because she always giving you advice?"

"No, because that bitch too judgmental." Her phone beeped again, and the screen lit up with a text message from Chauncey.

Brother: Since when?
Sis: Yesterday
Brother: I haven't heard about that yet. Where r u?
Sis: Carmen house for now
Brother: Then where
Sis: Idk yet
Brother: Let me know what you need and I got you
Sis: K

Sasha received confirmation from the two men that hung in the shadows of her marriage they would be there. And that was all she needed. Things didn't go as planned with Quamae, and now she understood why. That alone gave her the strength to walk away for good. She regretted not taking him up on his fifty thousand dollar offer, because now she knew she would never see that money.

She sat back on the sofa in deep thought to figure out a way to secure her future and her unborn child. If Blue was the father, she knew life would be easier than with Quamae, because they stood a chance at being a family. Every thought she had of reconciling with her husband was out the window the moment she found out Gigi was pregnant.

***

After dropping Gigi off following their lunch date, he went to meet up with one of his runners to drop off some work. He stood at the door with his keys in hand and a backpack over his shoulder when he heard footsteps behind him. He pulled his Tooley from his waistband, spun around, and took aim at his target.

"Don't shoot!" Carol had a devious smirk on her face with her hands up in the air. "You're a hard man to catch up with. I've been trying to catch you for the past few weeks, but you haven't been home. Are you sick of her yet?"

"I was in the hospital." He put the Tooley back in its place.

"For a whole three weeks?" she probed. "That's a long time to be away from home with a wife like Sasha."

He didn't know where she was going with her tactics, but he wasn't in the mood to play around with her. And he wasn't about to tell her why he was in the hospital, either. He had business to conduct, and she was holding him up. He cocked his head to the side. "Is there something important that you need?"

She patted her pocket. "Nope, but I have something you need."

"And what is that?"

"I think you'll be interested to know what and who Sasha was doing while you were away."

Now that caught his attention. "What are you talking about?"

"Like I said, I've been looking for you for three weeks when I stumbled up on Sasha and a man kissing in front of your house. He was there a lot while you were away." She fumbled around in her pockets, but she never pulled anything out of them.

"And I'm supposed to believe you?"

The temperature was hot, and Carol began to sweat. She wiped her face with her shirt. "I see she got to you and now you don't believe me. I knew that would happen, so I have a little insurance in my pocket, and it's yours if you pay me for it. I'm sure this will interest you."

"What do you want for it?"

Carol was always down for a hustle. "The question is, what is it worth to you?"

Quamae unlocked the doors and invited her in. "I'll give you what it's worth when I see it."

They walked into the house and headed to the kitchen in the exact same spot of their first meeting. Quamae sat the bag on the floor and fixed her a drink, as well as himself. He took a deep breath. His heart was racing with anticipation. "Alright, let's see it."

"I need to see the money first."

He held the bag up and showed her what was in it, and then he lifted his shirt revealing his gun to her. "Don't play games with me. This better be some legit shit, or I'm smoking your ass right here, right now."

Carol put all jokes aside when she realized who she was dealing with. "Okay, okay, no need to get all hostile on me." She pulled out her cellphone and fumbled through it before handing it to him.

"Press play."

Quamae watched as he saw Sasha and Chauncey standing on the porch, kissing like it was all good. His face suddenly scrunched up as he bit down on his bottom lip. He was furious, and he was ready to kill somebody. He sent the video to his phone and handed it back to Carol. Then he bent down to retrieve the money from the bag, but not once did he take his eyes off of Carol. If that bitch tried anything, she was going to be swimming with fish.

"Do you recognize the man in the video?" she asked.

"I know him."

Quamae handed her ten grand because she just saved him a hell of a lot more than that. With that type of evidence, there was no way he would have to sell his house and split the money with her or buy her out in order for him to keep it.

"I hope that's enough for you, if not, too bad. And don't come back here, because me and your daughter getting a divorce."

Carol wasn't expecting that much from him, so she was overly excited about what she received.

"I won't, and nice doing business with you."

After Carol left, he called Sasha and told her he wanted to apologize about what happened and give her some money so she could find a place and get situated. He knew

she would take the bait when he mentioned the money, because that's the type of female she was. It took everything
in him to keep from going off on her, but he kept his composure. He was proud of himself for that.

Shortly after, there was a knock on the door. It was
Sasha. They walked into the living room and sat down on
the sofa. He looked at her, and all he could see were vivid
images of her and Chauncey fucking in his home. He put
his elbows on his knees and buried his face in his hands.
He was trying so hard not to go off the deep end because
his emotions were gripping him by the heart. And the baby
didn't make it any easier. True enough, he no longer
wanted her, but what she did was the ultimate betrayal, and
there were consequences for disloyal hos.

Quamae looked up at her through hooded eyes. His top
lip curled down and his face was tight with anger. "No matter what I did for you, it just wasn't enough, huh?"

Sasha looked at him, puzzled. "What are you talking
about?"

"*What am I talking about?*" Quamae stood up and
glared down at her. "I'm talking about how I gave you everything you wanted and more, but you still managed to fuck
it up. Yeah, I made mistakes, but I would've never crossed
you the way you did me."

"Quamae, what are you talking about?" she repeated.
She was truly confused. Her mind started racing over the
transgressions she had kept secret. She prayed he hadn't
uncovered more dirt of hers.

"I'm going to ask you one question, and you better not
lie to me."

"I won't," she promised.

Quamae didn't bullshit around. "Are you fucking
Chauncey?" he asked.

Sasha's mouth flew open, but nothing came out. That classified as a dead giveaway, and she struggled to cover up her guilt. "Um. Uh."

"Yo' ass can't even formulate an answer for me?" He chuckled derisively and stepped right into her space. Now he was hovering over her ominously. "Are you fucking Chauncey?"

"Hell no! Why would you ask me some shit like that!" She tried to hide behind feigned anger, but Quamae wasn't buying her act.

"Sasha, you better tell me the truth before I hurt you." His fists were balled up and his eyes were red like he'd been crying.

"I told you the goddamn truth! You must be delusional! Why would I do something like that?"

"You don't want me to answer that." He smiled maniacally. "I'm giving you one last chance to come clean. Lie about it again and you'll regret it!"

Sasha felt trapped, but she refused to confess. *Deny everything. Don't let him play you into telling on yourself. He don't know shit! If he did, he would be going the fuck off.*

"Baby, there's nothing to admit to, because I haven't fucked that nigga. I don't know where you're getting your information from, but somebody is lying to you." She stood firm.

"Really?" he chuckled again.

"Yes, *really*," she mocked.

"Lying-ass bitch!" Quamae reached into his back pocket, pulled out his cellphone, and located the video. "Here, look at this."

Sasha hands trembled as she took the cell phone. Her heart rate increased rapidly as she tried to guess what damning proof he had. She took a deep breath before pressing the play button.

When the video came on, in high definition, what she saw was enough to make her drop dead twice! The phone slipped from her grasp and clanged down onto the table. She lowered her eyes to the floor, afraid to look at him now that her betrayal was exposed.

"Cat got your muthafuckin' tongue?"

She shook her head no. "I'm—" she started to apologize, but Quamae cut her off.

"So, let me get this straight, because I don't want to be confused. While I was in the hospital recovering, you were in here getting fucked by my best friend? That's how you get down, ho?" His voice roared like a shotgun blast.

Sasha shuddered. When she looked up, she saw something in his eyes that put fear in her heart. She grabbed her bag and stood up to leave before shit turned tragic. Fuck sitting there waiting for an ass-kicking. She wasn't that type of bitch.

"Where do you think you going?" He boomed.

"I'm getting the fuck away from you!"

Quamae's jaw twitched with hot anger. "You fucked my best friend, in my goddam crib, and you have the muthafuckin' audacity to talk slick to me out your mouth?"

He knew she felt safe bumping her gums at a time like this because she was pregnant. *She must think that baby gon' spare her a thrashing? But she got the game twisted!* He reached over and snatched her by the hair. "Bitch, sit yo' ass down!"

Sasha was frightened, but she still snatched away from him. She knew she had crossed the line for the last time, and no words could save her from what was about to happen. Her only chance of survival was to try to get out of that house before it turned into a crime scene.

Sasha walked away slowly. She could hear his footsteps behind her, but she didn't bother to turn around.

Pow!

A sudden gunshot whizzed past her head and struck the door, leaving a small bullet hole. She stopped dead in her tracks and her heart began to pound. Shaking badly, she turned to face Quamae. "I'm leaving," she said on a quivered breath.

"Oh yeah? Walk out that door and I'll put a hole in the back of your head! I promise I won't miss this time." His grip was tight on the handle of his gun. Of course Quamae knew the answer, but he wanted her to say it.

Sasha just couldn't bring herself to admit what the video confirmed. "It's not what it looked like," she muttered.

"If you confess with your mouth all of your sins, then you may be forgiven," he quoted a piece of Romans from the Bible and adlibbed the rest.

Sasha's face was blank, emotionless as fear took control of her body, as the moment of truth settled in on her conscience. She nodded yes to indicate she did what he accused her of.

"Nah, I can't hear you. What was that?"

Tears were pouring from her eyes like a running faucet. "I'm sorry, Quamae, I didn't mean for any of this to happen."

All he could see was red, and before she could finish her sentence, the butt of his Glock was crushing the left side of her skull. Her scream was horrific, but so was her betrayal.

"Ho, you fucked the nigga in my house, where I sleep!"

Sasha was dizzy from the blow. "I didn't mean to. He came in the room on his own," she pleaded. She held her head and stumbled toward the door, but he delivered another painful blow, causing her to hit the floor.

"But you didn't stop him!" he spat. "I'ma kill your ass!"

"Quamae, please!" she begged. "I don't want to die."

Her maternal instincts kicked in, and all she thought about was her baby. She managed to pull herself into the fetal position and cover her head with her arms.

He struck her again. The blood from the laceration splattered onto his face. Quamae had a crazed look in his eyes, as if he was having an out-of-body experience.

"You should've thought about that before you betrayed me!" He struck her across the face two more times, and she lost all consciousness. He lifted his foot to stomp on her head, but then something stopped him, and he realized what he had done.

He sat the gun on the floor and, as he wiped the blood from his face with his hand, he stared down at her motionless body. Instantly his eyes watered and a few tears ran down his face.

Quamae dropped to his knees and choked up. He cradled her bloody head in his hands and wept. "Sasha, why did you make me do this to you? Huh? Why couldn't you just keep it real?" His tears dripped onto her soiled shirt.

He held her like that until his tears dried and his survival instincts kicked in. Thinking quickly, he gently laid her head back on the floor, and then he ran upstairs and changed clothes. After that, he emptied out his safe, removed the security tapes, and fled the scene, leaving Sasha to die all alone.

To Be Continued...
Bride of a Hustla 2
Coming Soon

Coming Soon from Lock Down Publications/Ca$h Presents

TORN BETWEEN TWO
By **Coffee**
LAST OF A DYING BREED
LAY IT DOWN **III**
By **Jamaica**
GANGSTA SHYT **III**
By **CATO**
BLOOD OF A BOSS **IV**
By **Askari**
BRIDE OF A HUSTLA **II**
By **Destiny Skai**
WHEN A GOOD GIRL GOES BAD
By **Adrienne**
LOVE & CHASIN' PAPER
By **Qay Crockett**
I RIDE FOR MY HITTA
By **Misty Holt**
A SAVAGE LOVE
By **Aryanna**
THE HEART OF A GANGSTA
By **Jerry Jackson**

Available Now

RESTRAING ORDER **I & II**
By **CA$H & Coffee**
LOVE KNOWS NO BOUNDARIES **I II & III**
By **Coffee**
LAY IT DOWN **I & II**
By **Jamaica**
PUSH IT TO THE LIMIT

By **Bre' Hayes**
BLOOD OF A BOSS **I II & III**
By **Askari**
THE STREETS BLEED MURDER **I, II & III**
By **Jerry Jackson**
CUM FOR ME
An **LDP Erotica Collaboration**
A GANGSTER'S REVENGE **I II III& IV**
By **Aryanna**
WHAT ABOUT US **I & II**
NEVER LOVE AGAIN
THUG ADDICTION
By **Kim Kaye**
THE KING CARTEL **I, II & III**
By **Frank Gresham**
THESE NIGGAS AIN'T LOYAL **I, II & III**
By **Nikki Tee**
GANGSTA SHYT **I &II**
By **CATO**
THE ULTIMATE BETRAYAL
By **Phoenix**
DON'T FU#K WITH MY HEART **I & II**
By **Linnea**
BOSS'N UP **I & II**
By **Royal Nicole**
I LOVE YOU TO DEATH
By Destiny J

BOOKS BY LDP'S CEO, CA$H
TRUST NO MAN
TRUST NO MAN 2
TRUST NO MAN 3
BONDED BY BLOOD
SHORTY GOT A THUG
A DIRTY SOUTH LOVE
THUGS CRY
THUGS CRY 2
TRUST NO BITCH
TRUST NO BITCH 2
TRUST NO BITCH 3
TIL MY CASKET DROPS
RESTRAINING ORDER
RESTRAINING ORDER 2

Coming Soon

TRUST NO BITCH (KIAM EYEZ' STORY)
THUGS CRY 3
BONDED BY BLOOD 2
IN LOVE WITH HIS GANGSTA